Advance Praise for Street Disciples & Isaiah David Paul

"*Street Disciples* is a tale filled with wonderful characters that are facing demons that have infiltrated their lives.

It's a powerful story of people gaining strength to battle life's trials and tribulations in search of redemption and peace. Isaiah David Paul has chosen an array of colorful characters in this humbling story, and I won't be surprised if you find a bit of yourself within the pages."

--Barbara Grovner
Author of the *COLD* series

"Isaiah David Paul's style is edgy and breathtaking, yet elegant."

--BNTasty 1
Author of *Life of an Ex College Bandsmen IV: Wedding Bells*

"Isaiah David Paul will have you turning pages."

--Mike Sanders
Author of *Thirsty 1 & 2, Hustlin' Backwards* and *Snitch*

STREET
DISCIPLES

Also by Isaiah David Paul

Gritty Faith Fiction
Blessed Not Stressed
King of Kings
Street Disciples
Broken But I'm Healed
Closing My Legs
Try A Little Tenderness (w/Allyson M. Deese)
Ain't Worried About Nothin'
Style & Grayce

Urban/Street Lit/Suspense
I Get Around
KING
Definition of a Bad Girl (writing as MiChaune)

Anthologies
Weary & Will Edited by Sherryle Kiser Jackson
The Triumph of My Soul Edited by Elissa Gabrielle
Soul of a Man Edited by Elissa Gabrielle
Soul of a Man II: Makes Me Wanna Holler by Elissa Gabrielle

Young Adult – Ages 14 & Up
Worth Fighting 4
Boyz 4 Life
U Can't Break Me
R U *That Somebody* (formerly *Age Ain't Nothing But a Number*)
Never Too Much
Man In The Mirror
Still Standing

STREET
DISCIPLES

Isaiah David Paul

10's Lee Phelps

www.writesingwork.com

a literary entertainment company

Winston-Salem ■ Atlanta ■ Denver

10's Lee Phelps & Write Sing Work titles are published by Write Sing Work, LLC, 6255 Towncenter Drive #1669, Clemmons, North Carolina 27012

Book Credits
Author & Cover Designer: Isaiah David Paul for Write Sing Work, LLC
Editor: Tamara A. Grant for Zen Publishing
Associate Editors: Zeniah Latoude, Marlon McCaulsky, K. Roland Williams for OceanBlu Publications, Ben Blaze & Bethany Hamilton Freebird
Photograph: Corbis

16 15 14 13 12 11 10 9 8 7

Street Disciples

Scripture taken from the New King James Version. Copyright © 1982 by Thomas Nelson, Inc. Used by permission. All rights reserved.

Scripture also taken from the Revised Standard Version of the Bible, copyright 1952 [2nd edition, 1971] by the Division of Christian Education of the National Council of the Churches of Christ in the United States of America. Used by permission. All rights reserved.

ISBN 13: 978-1-934195-80-2/ISBN 10: 1-934195-80-4 (print)
ISBN 13: 978-1-934195-75-8/ISBN 10: 1-934195-75-8 (eBook)

The model or models and/or image or images on the cover is a visualization of the story and are not intended to portray any characters or localizations in the book. The photographer and/or models were solicited and compensated for their participation.

Printed in the United States of America & Canada

Dedication

In memory of Phoebe Medlin and Mary Little of Wadesboro, North Carolina's HOLLA organization. I appreciate you giving me a platform to share my works and for the support given over the years.

CHAPTER ONE

DONTE

The flip phone danced, vibrating on the dinner table as the ringtone from the gospel group Mary Mary announced the incoming call.

"Don't you know you, got the victory! Don't you know you, got the victory!" five-year-old Eugene Donte Speaks was singing. He was supposed to be eating his bowl of Cocoa Puffs. His father, also named Donte, watched as his son, who bore strikingly similar features to him at the same age, sang and ate turkey bacon for breakfast. His son loved fruit and had already eaten the chopped up cantaloupe, honeydew, and watermelon. The yellow oversized Gilbert State University t-shirt Eugene wore was completely messy and Donte silently thanked God that he had the sense not to dress Eugene in his church clothes just yet.

"Pick up the phone! You know that's your girlfriend," Eugene teased as he chewed on his turkey bacon.

"Boy, be quiet." Donte tried to sound serious, but could not hide the smirk that snuck on his face as he shook his head.

"What you know about a girlfriend?" Instead of waiting on his son to answer, he pressed the TALK button and flashed a smile as he put the caller on speaker. "Good morning, Elicia."

"Ooh. Daddy's got a girlfriend. Daddy's got a girlfriend." Eugene continued to tease his father as he drank his cranberry juice.

"Boy hush!" Donte commanded as Eugene scrunched his face up and giggled at him. "As you can see, my boy's up and ready to go to church this morning," Donte spoke into the speakerphone as he took his dishes to the sink. He ran hot water and put the stopper in and then squeezed some dishwashing detergent in the pool of water that was developing.

"Well, that's good. I was calling to let you know I won't be able to make it."

"Why?" Donte asked as he turned off the water when the sink finished filling.

"Yeah why?" Eugene asked as he was finishing his breakfast.

"Boy, what did I tell you about getting into grown folks business?" Donte was stern as he finally had drawn the line between playtime and seriousness. Eugene saw the grit in his father's face and understood that he was indeed serious. Donte needed his son to respect his time on the phone. "Go get dressed."

"Sorry Daddy." Eugene got up from the table and brought the empty matching white with blue and yellow striped bowl and saucer with the glass to the sink. Donte watched as Eugene took off the shirt and ran into his room so he could get dressed.

"I pray you aren't being mean to that boy," Elicia teased on the phone.

"Naw, he knows better than to be nosey. I'm raising a young man and not a busy body and a young man needs to know what is and is not appropriate behavior."

"Well anyway, Everette's cancer has returned."

Upon hearing those words fall from Elicia's lips, he remembered the conversation he and Elicia had about her brother's survival rate due to the Glioblastoma multiforme, an aggressive form of brain tumor that was usually fatal within months. The tumor diagnosis was rare for a young, African American male and the doctors could not find out what triggered it.

"They've called for the family to be at Duke."

"Elicia, I'm sorry." Donte fought through the tears. He remembered Everette giving him his blessing to reunite with Elicia a year ago. Everette and Donte had gone to the Smokey Bones restaurant off of High Point Road in Greensboro and over a plate of barbeque chicken nachos sans beef and Smokey Bones' infamous skillet cornbread, they hashed out their differences that existed since high school. Everette confronted Donte several times over Elicia's embarrassment of Donte's infidelity and his decision to became an adult video star. All of that was water under a bridge from that moment forward. Donte had changed his life around and begun working on his ministry and was raising his son solo.

"I just wanted to ask that you update the church on his progress and to put our names on the altar."

"You got it. And as soon as church is over with, we'll be in Durham." Donte responded. As he was coming to terms with his own sadness of Everette's imminent demise, the sound of someone successfully unlocking the door of his third floor apartment caught his attention. Donte was the apartment manager for the complex where he lived and although he had keys to everyone else's apartment, no one else had a spare key to his. "Elicia, let me call you back. I think someone's trying to break into my apartment."

Donte quickly ended the phone conversation before Elicia could say anything else and placed the phone in his pocket. He opened the drawer and grabbed the large butcher knife and quickly walked to the door and also picked up the steel baseball bat that was next to the door.

"Daddy I—" Eugene had entered the living room. He gave his father a confused look. Donte put the knife in his left hand with the baseball bat and dug into his right pocket to get the cell phone, tossing it to Eugene. The phone landed at Eugene's feet.

"Go to your room, lock the door and if you don't hear from me in five minutes, dial 9-1-1!" Donte whispered loudly. He watched as Eugene quickly snatched the phone from the floor and ran to his room. The door opened quickly, hitting Donte on the side of the face. Donte stumbled back and shook his head in an effort to get ready to defend his home. He moved the knife to his right hand, ready to slash upon sight. His adrenaline pumping, he couldn't believe his eyes.

"Eve?"

Donte couldn't believe that the woman managed to pick the lock and was just going to let herself into his home. He remembered the one of the last times he saw her. Six and a half years ago, they both were naked in the bed of his suite after making a video. It also happened to be the night Donte accepted Jesus into his life as his Lord and Savior.

Last time he heard from her was five and a half years ago when she dropped a two month old infant on doorstep of his apartment with a note asking Donte to raise their son. After getting a paternity test verifying that he indeed was the father, she, through her lawyer, had signed away her custodial rights, leaving Donte a single parent. Donte chose not to pursue child support or anything else and for the next five years, played the role of a single father.

"Hi Donte!" She said as she ran up to him giving him a hug as no time had passed and there was no negative history between them. She kissed him on the cheek and when she made a move to kiss Donte on the lips, he quickly turned his head.

"It's been so long since I've seen you."

For five years, he wondered what had happened to Eve and why did she not only hide the pregnancy from him while they were in school, but how she could abandon their beautiful, son in a car seat. He wondered what she could possibly want now.

"It's been a long time since I've seen you too," he replied.

Eve walked in and took a seat on the couch as if she was a fixture in their lives. She was dressed in an impeccably tailored blue blazer and matching skirt that complemented her hazelnut skin tone and brought out her light brown eyes. He recognized that she'd changed her hair color to a mahogany color that was a drastic change from the fiery red she used to wear. Her pressed hair rested right above her shoulders, showing her beautiful silver hoop earrings. Eve was still stunning and for a moment, images of them making love and doing all kinds of things that only married people should be doing flashed through his mind. She had the body of a goddess; well toned but curvy in all of the right places. He quickly rebuked the sexual thoughts running through his mind in the name of Jesus.

"What are you doing here?" Too many questions were running through his mind.

"I came to see you and my baby." She answered matter-of-factly as if she wasn't a woman hadn't seen her son in five years.

"We're getting ready to go to church. You're more than welcome to see *our* son there. But don't you ever pull this stunt again. You understand?"

Eve rolled her eyes as if she was totally ignoring Donte's request. The knock at the door interrupted their exchange.

Two uniformed police officers walked in through the open front door. "Is everything alright ma'am?"

Donte was amazed at how quickly the officers assumed that *he* was guilty.

"I noticed the bobby pins and a credit card on the floor, sir we're gonna have to ask you to put down your weapons."

Donte hadn't even realized that he was still holding the knife and the bat and he dropped everything quickly and lifted his hands up in surrender. He'd seen enough cop shows and heard enough presentations to know that the best course of action was to follow directions and appear defenseless and just maybe the police officers wouldn't shoot him. "May I speak please?" He asked.

"Daddy!" Eugene ran out of the room with the phone in his hand and hugged Donte on the leg. "Who is that lady and why are the police here?"

If Eugene hadn't called the police then who had? In that moment, he knew that Elicia had done the deed.

"Young man, are you okay?" The female police officer asked, turning on her maternal instincts as she lowered herself to meet Eugene at eye level.

"Yeah, why does my daddy have his arms in the air? He didn't do anything wrong." His inquisitive mind asked her as if she were a common stranger in the street instead of the law enforcement agents that were in charge of the situation.

"Well, we were trying to find out what was going on." The police woman leveled with him, trying to make sure he had an understanding.

Eugene innocently began to recount the morning's events. "Daddy's girlfriend called him on the phone telling us she was going to meet us at church. Daddy told me to stay out of grown folks business, but I really like Elicia. So Daddy told me to go and put on my church clothes after I ate my food. Then somebody tried to come in our house and me and my Daddy were scared so Daddy tossed me to the phone and said if he didn't come get me in five minutes to call 9-1-1 and after five minutes so I waited, but I didn't know if it was five minutes so I came out here to ask him if it was five minutes. My daddy had a knife and a bat on the floor next to him, cause we didn't know who was trying to get in our house. That lady there was sitting on the couch and I didn't call 9-1-1. I'm sorry, Daddy." Eugene broke down the scenario the best way he could. He clutched his father's leg as he stared at the strangers standing in their house. Donte relaxed his arms and held his son.

"Thank you," the female officer said as she stood up. "And ma'am, you are?"

"I came to see my son." Eve said as she let the tears fall from her face like a water faucet. Donte shook his head because he couldn't believe how dramatic she was acting.

"Is this your place of residence?" the other officer asked.

"No." Eve continued to cry, wiping her tears away.

"But did you pick the lock?" the male officer asked, trying to get down to the bottom of the matter.

"Yes."

"Sir, is she the young man's mother?" The female officer asked Donte.

Donte exhaled. Now he was going to look like the bad guy even though he clearly was the victim. "She gave birth to him but I'm the custodial parent, she signed her rights away a few months after she gave birth. This is the first time my son has ever been eye to eye with his mother."

"Well ma'am, we're gonna have to place you under arrest for breaking and entering." The male officer walked over and gently placed her arms behind her back.

"Umm…" Donte struggled with what he was about to say. "Look, I don't want to press charges. I just want to know why she didn't knock on the door."

"We'll settle this at the police station." The male officer informed him. "You have a right to remain silent." The officer continued give the Miranda rights and Eve continued whimpering as the officers led her out of the apartment in handcuffs. Donte and Eugene followed her out of the apartment and the female police officer stayed behind.

Donte knew the day would come when he'd have to face Eve again and tell Eugene about her, but he had not anticipated it being this day or in this manner. They watched as the police put Eve in the back of the cruiser and drove off. Donte continued to get himself and his son ready for church. As they walked to the white, 1999 Honda Civic that was in their designated parking space, Donte formulated the words to gently explain to his son that Eve was his mother. It was something he'd have to break slowly to his son, not only for his son's sake, but also to process in his own mind that Eve was back in their lives.

CHAPTER TWO

ABEDNEGO

I knew he wasn't gonna show up," Abednego complained at the end of service. He had periodically looked through all the pews in hopes that his older brother, Meshach Felton Green, would make an appearance. It looked like another Sunday would go by without his brother making his presence known at the church. A part of Abednego wished he didn't have the strong discernment that he had over his brother's spirit and well-being, but every time he wanted to give up on his brother, the Spirit wouldn't let him.

"Who wasn't going to show up?" Abednego looked to see Davon walking behind him with his son, Micah Davon, whom they affectionately called M.D. for short. Abednego was embarrassed when he realized that he was mumbling to himself aloud.

"My brother."

"Don't lose faith man. Next to my own brother, you are one of the most prayin'est brothers I know." Davon put his hand on Abednego's shoulder and peered into his eyes. Abednego acknowledged the only guy in the church who was also five foot six inches tall and could look him in the eyes. He noticed something different about Davon but he couldn't put his finger on it.

"What are y'all talking about?" Shadrach came into their huddle as they moved down the line to greet the pastor.

"Our brother and why he's not here." Abednego said as he faced the pastor and shook her hand. As he moved forward, Abednego didn't see Rahliem, the lay leader and Davon's older brother hanging in the lobby in line as well to greet the pastor. The fact that the young man disappeared so quickly after service confirmed that there wasn't a Street Disciples Ministry meeting. He didn't hear the call during the weekly church announcements. Turning his attention back to Shadrach, Abednego stated, "I have a feeling that if we don't get Felton in here soon, something bad is gonna happen."

Abednego looked at his eldest brother and did not like the look in his eyes. He knew that Shadrach was annoyed with his worrying about Felton and wished he'd give it a rest, but he couldn't.

"Look, your brother will come around." Davon said after he and M.D. shook pastor's hand. "Just don't give up on him. My brother didn't give up on me and look at where I am."

Abednego admitted to himself that the man who had come out as a bisexual while they were in high school was definitely a work in progress. At the last men's prayer meeting, Davon had admitted that it has been a year and a half since he'd been intimate with a man or woman and that with prayer and finding constructive things to do with his time, he avoided hoping in and out of beds he didn't belong in. Yet, as Abednego thought about Davon and his affliction and his fight to please God, he knew in his heart that if Davon could make meaningful steps to turn his life around, Felton could right his wrongs with flying colors. The difference between Davon and Felton was that Davon *wanted* to change and please God and become a better role model for MD, especially when MD's mother died in the war in Iraq a few years ago.

"And you and that temper of yours have come a long way," Shadrach said to Davon. "Keep looking to the Lord and everything will be alright."

Abednego and Davon both shook their heads because they knew that Shadrach's positive word would hold true. As they walked out of the church, they heard Byron Cage's song "The Presence of the Lord Is Here" blasting from one of the cars. Abednego started singing and clapping his hands as he could truly feel the Spirit of the Lord and he wanted to praise Him.

"Your brother is in it again." Davon spoke as he watched Abednego dance and praise God to his car.

"He's alright." Shadrach assured him. "If we could get everyone to act like that, the world would be a better place."

When the song was over, Abednego thanked God and sent praises on high. With a renewed strength and a plan to face Felton, Abednego had faith that's he'd be able to win Felton over once and for all. And he was not afraid to go where he needed to go to get the job done.

CHAPTER THREE

RAHLIEM

Rahliem left church early and abruptly cancelled the Street Disciples Ministry meeting so that he could get some rest and spend some alone time in communion with the Holy Spirit. He'd felt the Spirit moving and prodding him to take his ministry into a whole new direction and though he knew that the Spirit was right in all things, Rahliem needed to work on his doubts about the direction he felt the Spirit calling the ministry to go into.

He spent most of that afternoon and the evening locked in his room and in continuous prayer—reading his Bible and gathering notes for a message he'd been invited to deliver to a young men's youth group at a community center in Charlotte a couple of weeks from now. After giving his spiritual body a work out, he decided to push his flesh to the limit as he did a round of crunches, pushups, sit ups and pull ups.

Rahliem slept for a couple of hours but felt his body being forced to come alive thanks to the loud noises coming from Davon's room. MD had been sent to his grandmother's for the night and he had trusted that Davon was keeping with his vow of celibacy—he wanted to believe that, but as the noises brought disappoint and appeared to confirm a deception, Rahliem could feel his mind slipping in a manner he had not intended. The disappointment of his brother's backsliding caused him to perspire more; the sweat drenched his body as he felt the sheets sticking to his upper torso in the bed.

Rahliem got out of bed and walked to Davon's room and it seemed that the noise had subsided. Rahliem thought back to the agreement Davon and he had when he first moved in that neither one of them would have pre-marital sex while the other was home—the agreement was particularly important to Rahliem because he knew that Davon had a taste for men and women and he definitely didn't want to see the former walking around naked or moaning in pleasure in their home. Rahliem put his ear to the door, hoping not to hear something he didn't want to hear. Satisfied that his brother was sleep—or at least quiet, Rahliem took a trip to the bathroom to wash the funk off his flesh.

Rahliem wiped the moisture from the fogged-filled mirror and faced himself. The multiple tattoos that covered the upper torso of his six foot maple sap colored canvas framed his neck, chest and arms stared back at him. Some of the secular designs were mistakes he made while serving the first two years of a five year prison term for assault with a deadly weapon. Rahliem remembered the day like it was yesterday—his arch-rival, Quentin Coleman had pursued Davon because he'd learned that Davon had cheated on his female cousin with another man. Quentin had him on the ground in the parking lot of the newly built Chick-Fil-A and was beating him with a bat. Rahliem couldn't stand by and watch and finally obtaining the reason he needed to whip Quentin's butt, he jumped in the fight with a bat of his own and went to work protecting his brother.

Truth be told, back then Rahliem enjoyed a good fight that involved one-on-one fisticuff action. The high endurance for pain —getting hit as well as throwing punches—threw Rahliem head first into underground MMA-style matches, boxing, cutting himself on the arm and obtaining the first set of illegal tattoos. He loved the way the needles pieced his skin and the little pricks, especially the ones near his veins, sent him on a high. As he looked down on his frame, he had to admit that some of the designs he was ashamed to show God—but he also knew that it was what he was doing with his body now—not what he done in the past, that mattered most.

The tight cornrows ended right above his shoulders gave him the demeanors of any other harden brother in the hood. The herbal, Shea butter-based shampoo and conditioner that he'd used to clean his hair matched the scent exuding from his body's pores. His sharp facial features that were set off by his rounded-tip, spear-shape nose. His eyes were piercing, often mistaken for being menacing, even when he was smiling. He shook his head and water jumped like a child stomping in a mud puddle as it fled from his face and hair. Some of the water drops still managed to cover his eyes though. His broad body frame testified to the years of pumping iron and focus on physical fitness.

He was supposed to be celebrating the seven year anniversary of his release from the custody of the North Carolina Department of Corrections system. He served an adult term of attempted murder and aggravated assault protecting the very man who was about to drive him crazy enough to go back to prison. The anniversary also reflected nine years of serving the Lord and Savior Jesus Christ as a disciple who studied and encouraged others to follow the master. Rahliem had been introduced to Jesus by an older prisoner who'd taken great interest in him and wanted to steer the younger Rahliem on the right path before he'd terminal cancer would send him to his maker. The older man spoke of going to Heaven and being reunited with believers—even those who'd gotten saved after doing the most horrendous acts—and living the rest of their lives serving God. Rahliem had been granted the privilege of watching the man die in peace and he decided right then and there that he wanted to go out the same way.

Rahliem had every right to be proud of the fact that he managed not to compromise his salvation. In the middle of his reflection, he heard those sinful voices again, indicating that his younger brother was entertaining a male guest in a way that went against scripture. As the voices seemed to grow louder, Rahliem could feel the heat from his anger returning.

Even though he could smell the crisp scent of mint—and other flowery scents coming from the air fresheners that were plugged into the wall, he still felt like he was in prison. His spirit struggled with the command to leave the house to read scripture in the park and the fleshly desire to physically escort the sinner from his brother's bedroom. The inability to relax his nerves was conjuring up another bad habit, yet a soothing desire—to smoke a joint. It had been two years since he had confided in the new pastor of Grace United Methodist Church of his herbal addiction and she helped him find ways to kick the habit. But at that moment in time, he needed something strong to soothe and calm him of his anger at his brother's blatant disrespect of the agreement they had made only the night before.

"Satan, leave me alone!" he commanded as images flashed through his mind of the bloodbath that sent him to prison in the first place. His fist pummeling his victim after he tried to terrorize his younger brother over his sexuality almost led him to commit murder.

Rahliem quickly dried off his body, and put on the matching crimson and grey basketball jersey outfit that he was going to wear for his morning jog before he went to church in the next ninety minutes. After getting dressed, he put on the ankle socks and the New Balance tennis shoes that he had just purchased the week before. Once he opened the door to the bathroom, the sounds got louder.

Images of himself getting violent again flashed through his mind—the image of the victim had been replaced by the image of his brother, and his balled fist rained down on the face as if it has been set on auto-pilot.

"I've had enough of this." Rahliem declared as he did an about-face and marched to his brother's bedroom. He exhaled heavily with each step to the room.

Our father, who art thou in heaven, Rahliem thought and mumbled as the sounds got louder.

Hallowed be thy name. His heart beating in anticipation of what he was about to do.

Thy kingdom come, thy will be done, Rahliem ignored pleas to go to his room, or better yet, exit the house and start that jog so he could clear his mind and "relax."

On Earth as it is in Heaven. The moaning was far from angelic and the music was more suitable for a late night creep as opposed to the early morning service Rahliem should've been thinking about.

Give us this day, our daily bread. Other than the Lord's prayer, Rahliem had struggled to remember or repeat a scripture that would calm him, soothe him; perhaps talk him out of this inevitable confrontation.

And forgive us of our debts, as we forgive our debtors. Rahliem was gonna forgive Davon, *after* he put his foot in his butt.

And lead us not into temptation, but deliver us from evil, easier said than done as Rahliem walked to the door.

For thine is the kingdom, his hand reached the door knob and twisted.

And the power and the glory, Rahliem walked as if he were the corrections officer doing an unannounced search. He looked at the television and closed his eyes, shielding his soul and his spirit from the images that flashed before it. He turned his head slowly and his eyes rolled up like a manual garage door being lifted up by a mechanic.

Forever. The light snores coming from the middle of the king-size bed only belonged to the young man whom was raised in the same house as he. No other bodies were found in the bed or on the floors as Rahliem quickly, but thoroughly inspected the room. Rahliem exhaled, thankful that he didn't find his brother engaging in his favorite fetish; one which Rahliem adamantly and forcefully preached against as the guest speaker at the neighboring King Martin United Methodist Church the week before. A sermon which was the cause of their latest flare up that almost brought the two men who shared the same mother and father to fisticuffs because while their love for one another grew deeper and stronger as the days went on; their views on the issue of sexuality and sex before marriage almost always was the cause of World War III and Armageddon in the Victor household.

His brother turned in the bed gently. His eyes flashed open and closed just that fast. Rahliem shook his head and he reached over the television and pushed the button turning the DVD off. Naked bodies were replaced with a blue screen and he pressed a button on the DVD, and after the third try and *still* not being able to turn the blue screen off, he pressed the OFF button on the television. He backed out of the room quietly and closed the door silently. Rahliem exhaled again, thankful that he didn't see what he was sure he wasn't prepared to see. Thankful that the Satan in his mind had been defeated and that Jesus had found a way to make everything all right.

Rahliem walked down the stairs and a smile that reflected that he was a man of God returned upon his face. He had won another battle, he thought. Grabbing his eyes from the key holder inside of the closet, he locked the door, enjoying the fresh smell of a brand new day and felt the dampness of grass under his feet. Instead of jogging, he'd be walking this morning, but at least he'd be getting out of the house. He could tell that only Davon's car was in the parking lot and that all the cars he could see belonged to their neighbors as there were no garages in the condominiums he and his brother lived in. After getting around the block, he looked back at his building and smiled.

Be slow to anger—that was the verse he was looking for—though Rahliem had made great progress, anger seemed to be the thorn in his flesh that would not leave him.

He'd go easy on his brother and that annoying video, he'd decided…he was just happy that his younger brother was not sinning and was lying alone in his bedroom.

Amen.

CHAPTER FOUR

FELTON

Felton had finished following all the directions in the chorus of the hit making song that the rapper Mystical made famous in the late '90's. He was shaking it fast, watching himself and showing all the women and men in the audience what he was working with. As his set ended, Felton grabbed the money that had fallen on the stage and a towel that was handed to him as he headed toward the locker room and the sink. He didn't need to count the money to know that he had at least two hundred dollars in fives and tens crumpled in his hand. Surely enough money to replace the fifth pair of black fishnet see-through swim trunks thrown to his audience and that would now be going home to some patron in the club. He had seen three twenties mingle in with the bills as he danced on the stage and entertained the ladies sitting in the crowd who were some of his regular customers.

As he splashed the water on his face, he thought about the fact that he wished that they cleaned the shower more frequently so he could do a thorough wash up so he wouldn't get in his car sweat funky. He looked at the showers and saw two other dancers trying to cleanse their bodies amongst the grime and shook his head. For him dancing, gyrating and getting naked in front of hundreds at Hunks and Honies was part of the job and being comfortable didn't pay the bills. As he made his way to his locker, he saw another naked stripper also making his way to the locker room. Felton turned his head and worked quickly to put his clothes on. He didn't want to give the other stripper any wrong ideas about what side of the fence he stood on. He knew that most of the dancers were bisexual—some were even gay and yet he didn't judge any of them because they all worked at Hunks and Honies for a different reason.

Some of the men and women who danced at Hunks and Honies were local college students with little family and friend supports. Others really didn't want to go to school and get an education and being an adult exotic dancer was a close to fulfilling their fantasy of being a professional singer or a dancer as they were going to get. Besides, with one of the local banks being bought out and the closing of several local plants, men who were able to maintain a good shape went against their spiritual and moral beliefs and turned to stripping and performing sexual favors just so their children wouldn't have to worry about having anything to eat. Some of the women—as well a few of the men— had pimps and almost every dollar that came into their hands went to support the pimp who was too lazy to get off their butts and find a job themselves.

Felton's pleasure at Hunks and Honies was to rebel against everything his parents had ever taught him about Jesus and the church. While he didn't have a love or a fondness or even a hatred for Jesus, he hated the church that his parents raised him in. He hated the deaconess that put her lips on his chest, his stomach and on both sets of his private parts. He hated getting on his knees before her and sometimes her friends every Monday in the youth choir room at six o'clock at night when he should have been at home with his family eating dinner. He hated that when his parents found out what was going on with him in the church, how they blamed the demon in *him* for making him act out. His parents were church going Christians who said prayers when they woke up, prayers while at work, prayers when there was a joy... said more prayers to God than "I love you" to any of their children. He hated how he felt that God, as well as his parents had turned their backs on him, taking the word of the deaconess who was molesting him rather than their innocent child, who had not been at fault or under the influence of any demon.

Once Felton was dressed and ready to go, he walked out into the cool brisk air and couldn't decide which was worse; being sweat funky and in need of a bath or if he would have showered in the locker room. Either way, his pores would have been open and he would have been at risk of becoming sick and that would've messed up his money. He wasn't having that. Locating his car toward the end of the lot, he was astonished to find someone sitting on the hood of his cream colored 2001 Ford Focus. He could feel his anger rising at the thought of the disrespect whoever it was on his car was showing him.

I'm about to whoop somebody's butt, he thought as he quickened his paced. The stranger on his car didn't appear to be intimidated at all. It was as if he were waiting on Felton to arrive. As he got closer to his car, he still couldn't make out the face of the man in a black sweat jacket and cargo sweat pants sitting on the hood of his car.

It was when the man looked up and their eyes locked that Felton realized it was his younger brother, Abednego. He shook his head. That gave him the courage to yell out at the loiterer.

"What are you doing sitting on the hood of my car?" He slowed down his walking. He decided he'd save his energy in case he had to physically move his brother off his car. "You almost got your butt kicked man."

Abednego looked at him and held up his Bible and began reading passages from the Book of Proverbs aloud, hoping that the wisdom from the great book would seep into his brother's pores and take root deep in his soul before it was too late and he was banished into hell. Felton almost went ballistic—Abednego was always popping up unannounced trying to get him to repent of his ways and to return to the church of God. *God don't know, his church is so full of heathens and hypocrites...I'll never go back there,* he swore as he tried to ignore the Word.

He had so many words and thoughts he could say about the church but he'd decided two confrontations ago that he was through having this conversation with Abednego. And to think that Abednego used to be his favorite brother—the one he could depend on when he wanted some ecstasy pills or some weed so he could get high and stay high above earth and away from all his troubles.

"Meshach…" Abednego started but was interrupted by Felton.

"Felton!" He screamed at the top of his lungs. "My name is Felton! Chocolate Thunder when I'm in Hunks and Honies. And I'm sick of telling you that!"

"Mom named us after the…"

Abednego didn't even get a chance to finish before Felton snapped and pushed Abednego off the hood of his car. He knew it would come to this sooner or later. He and Abednego had not physically gotten into an altercation since the time Abednego was a sinner, moving small amounts of ecstasy, crack and dime bags of weed. Then there was a confrontation over one of the finest ladies in Winston-Salem when Abednego had pulled out a .9mm with a silencer and shot Felton in the arm. Felton still looked at his right bicep and the scar was still there even though the incident took place four years ago, it was payback time. Felton rushed to the side of the car and was surprised that Abednego hadn't jumped up and ran to attack him, swinging and trying to estimate his next move like he normally done. Instead, he found Abednego's hunched over on the side of the car, cowering and concealing himself in a human ball as he'd hoped Felton would show him mercy.

Abednego had picked the wrong day to practice peace and self control. As soon as he saw Abednego peak to find where his brother was at, Felton delivered a sonic blow to Abednego's cheek and when the other side opened up, he smite him on that side, too. Then he kicked his brother in the behind. "You, Mom, Dad and the rest of you church going bastards can go to hell!" Felton harked up some phlegm and spit on Abednego as he kicked him.

He could've sworn he'd heard Abednego weeping and crying like a baby.

"You're pathetic." Felton gave his brother one last kick and then walked to the driver's side.

"Yo man, that's foul you'd do your own brother like that," someone said. Felton looked around to see the stripper from the locker room, fully cloth and trying to help Abednego up. Felton rolled his eyes and forcefully threw a middle finger up in the direction of the stripper and mumbled some choice curse words that would've made his parents blush if they had heard them.

"I just want to save my brother before he goes to hell," Abednego exclaimed. Felton had heard enough. He remembered his baseball bat in his trunk. He was tempted to reach in, grab it and then beat the crap out of Abednego and whatever that stripper dude's name was. Deciding that money was more important than being jail, he threw them the bird again as he jumped in the car, slammed the door and took off to his destination.

CHAPTER FIVE

ABEDNEGO

Abednego looked up at the man who was nice enough to help him get up from the ground. He was embarrassed that tears were falling from his face after being beat up by his sibling. He felt the anger growing within him as he'd wished he'd fought back instead of doing what the Spirit told him to do.

"Your brother is pure evil," he heard the man say once he got on his feet. He saw some of the spectators crowd around him like they were watching a fight at high school.

"Well just pray for him." Abednego said humbly. He looked at the man's hazel eyes and knew they were contacts.

"I will man. I have to add him to my prayer list."

Abednego's eyes got wide as he didn't think the man knew who Jesus was, much less anything about prayer. He didn't mean to offend the man that looked him in the eyes, but he knew that most of the people who were dancers and strippers and escorts at the club didn't believe in the same Lord and Savior he worshiped. Upon closer look, he saw the man was about his age and height, except he was lighter complexion. His waves were tight from wearing skull caps day in and day out. Something about the man was familiar but Abednego couldn't bring himself to remember.

"C?" Abednego questioned as he continued to look at the man. He had thought he'd recognize him from one of the social media sites he used but he wasn't sure.

"Abednego...I didn't think I'd meet anyone from the chat line here."

"Yeah man, I'm on a quest to try to save my brother's soul, what brings you here?"

Abednego knew the answer before the question had left his mouth. The Irish Spring blended in with the Egyptian musk body oil and made for an interesting odor. He knew that C had just got done dancing or stripping or whatever it was he was doing at Hunks & Honies. He thought back to the conversation where the man had told him he was a night worker...now he knew what he had meant.

"This is one way I pay the bills," C answered as he looked away.

"Well, I can't judge you for that. I know the economy is rough out here and we're all doing what we must."

Abednego surprised himself as the words left his lips. It was almost as if he were co-signing on the path the man took.

"But stay grounded in the Word and don't give up. Pretty soon, your job or a vision for a new business will come to you and you won't have to dance anymore."

C smiled, appreciative of the fact that Abednego hadn't judged him. "Yeah man, I have faith that once we get this sorry president out of office that things are going to get better. They can't get worse right?"

Abednego's nodded his head. He'd almost wished he hadn't walked up here but he didn't have a car and the city transit system had returned to its hub after dropping off its last customer hours ago.

"You weren't sitting in the car waiting on your brother were you?" C inquired.

"Naw man. I don't live too far from here." Abednego exaggerated. He lived about four miles from the club but he liked to walk because he never knew who he was going to reach or what exciting task the Lord would have him do next.

"Well, I'll tell you what. My wife and I have been struggling to have a Bible study with some friends and you seem like a good person and I think it'd be a good idea if you joined us."

"I'd like that."

C and Abednego shook hands. Abednego headed off in the direction of the projects he lived him. He hadn't taken a few steps before he felt his phone vibrate in his pants. He pulled out the black Samsung and flipped it open.

"Shadrach," Abednego spoke before the caller could identify himself. He knew that was the only person who could be calling him at this time of night. Abednego liked to do some of his ministry work at night with the people so his eldest brother often called on him to make sure he was okay.

"Where are you?"

Abednego looked at the bright neon orange and blue lights that showed a man and woman in a suggestive embraced with its logo in eloquently written cursive script. Abednego knew that he wasn't near the homeless shelter or on the corner where he normally passed out daily devotions…and he knew that if Shadrach or his wife had questions about where he was doing his nightly ministry they would come out to meet him within a few minutes. A part of him wished lying wasn't a sin, but since it was, he was truthful as he read the name from the sign.

"No!" Shadrach shouted. Abednego shook his head. He already knew Shadrach was thinking before he asked. "Where's Felton?"

Another lie Abednego wished he could tell. "He's on his way home…I think."

"Look, Deborah and I will be there in about ten minutes. Please promise me that you aren't going to get into any strange vehicles or try to exchange one of your miniature Bibles for some time with a prostitute in hopes of getting her saved."

Abednego laughed at himself as Shadrach brought up the incident last month where he and one of the young ladies who was walking the streets of Patterson Avenue were sitting in front of the Churches fast food joint sharing a three piece meal as

Abednego recounted the story of Mary Magdalene and how she went from street worker to disciple. By the time Shadrach had gotten there, the woman's pimp had had Abednego hemmed up against the restaurant as he threatened to slice his throat as the woman Abednego was ministering to began rebuking Satan, praising God and speaking in tongues.

"I promise," Abednego said as he flipped his phone shut.

Abednego turned to the front of the building and he felt light headed as the blood flowed from his head to his midsection, betraying him as he was tempted to give into the desires of his flesh. It has been a while since he had lain with a woman and the thick sistah who was top heavy and had a voluptuous shape had his mind pre-occupied with sinful thoughts. The stiffness created a tent that he had hoped no one could decipher in the brightly lit parking lot.

He walked to the front of the building and stood on the sidewalk, waiting on his brother and wife to come.

CHAPTER SIX

CHASE

Chase watched as Abednego got in the car and pulled off. As soon as the car turned the corner, Chase pulled out his Samsung flip phone and looked at the time. It was past time for him to go home and he knew that his wife wouldn't be home either.

"I oughta find Felton and mess him up," Chase said to no one in particular. It had been a minute since Chase had been in a good fight and he desired nothing more than to inflict the same amount of harm on Felton that he had on Abednego. One thing he couldn't stand was for one person to bully or pick on someone else, especially if the bully was taller than the person they were picking on. He thought about his schedule and realized that it would be four more days before they had the same schedule and he had decided that he was going to handle Felton then.

As Chase stepped forward, his foot almost slipped on one of the pamphlets that was on the floor. Chase picked up the small, pocket-sized magazine and saw the words, *The Upper Room* on the top in bright bold white letters. He couldn't see the picture on the magazine so he walked back toward Hunks & Honies so he could get a better look.

Abednego must have left this by mistake, Chase thought to himself as he flipped open the book and saw a sticker that had Grace United Methodist Church's address, phone number and website on the inside. He thought about the man he was talking to on the internet on MySpace and realized that Abednego was the man he'd been talking to about God and Grace was the church he attended. He flipped through more pages and found the description of the picture he was looking at. He was amazed to find that the artist was able to bring a passage of the Bible to life.

Chase quickly flipped to the devotion for the day and the passage that stuck out to him was:

> *Keep your lives free from the love of money, and be content with what you have; for he has said, 'I will never leave you or forsake you'*

Chase felt a form of conviction as he thought about his motivation for taking off his clothes and showing off his natural body. He loved the dollar bills, especially those that had two digits that were thrown his way. As he read the verse in Hebrews 13:5 and found the testimony of the author about how he had learned to let the love of money go, Chase felt that he needed to let his job go—but if he did that, where was he going to work? Chase had been stripping and whoring since he dropped out of high school in the tenth grade. He used to do it to take care of his younger siblings, but now, he did it to gain worldly possessions.

Chase flipped to the next devotion and found it as enlightening as the first one and the next thing he knew, the light was turned out and he saw a few of the employees leaving the building along with the last of the customers. Chase put the devotion in his pocket and headed toward his car and once he was inside, he turned on the ignition and decided that he'd read the rest of the book when he got home.

CHAPTER SEVEN

FELTON & SHADRACH

He needs to hurry up and come home."

Natalie was pacing her living room as Shadrach and Deborah tried to reason with their sister-in-law. She had applied a thin coat of petroleum jelly on her cinnamon colored face. She was a feisty, athletic sistah at five foot five and a half, one hundred and twenty pounds and she wasn't scared to do a push up or a sit up to keep her figure either.

Natalie had gone with Shadrach and Deborah to Hunks and Honies to pick up Abednego and to find out why he was there in the first place. Natalie hadn't seen her husband in three days and she knew he was staying in some cheap motel either to avoid her because of what he had done to Abednego or to avoid her just because. Felton had been doing that a lot lately because in the past year since Natalie finally broken down and gave her life to God after Abednego kept talking to her about the visions he was having about her soul burning in the fiery furnace.

"I'm sure he's on his way. He told me as much…" Shadrach's voice had trailed off. Turned out that Felton had let him know that he was on his way home and that he'd talk to him later, all in the fifteen seconds Shadrach had managed to get him on the phone. It was right after Abednego broke down and told them about the confrontation and Natalie expressed a few choice words for what she wanted to do as soon as she saw him again. When they dropped Abednego off at his apartment complex, he made them promise that they would not seek revenge on Felton.

All three of them had heard Felton put his key in the door from the other side and Natalie rushed to the door to let him in. Shadrach and Deborah jumped up after her to keep her from jumping on him before he could step in the house good.

"You spat on Abednego!" Natalie shouted as soon as he stepped into the living room. Felton looked at Natalie, Shadrach and Deborah and then back at his wife. He laughed to himself as he pictured all three of them thumping their Bibles at him and screaming for him to repent, repent, repent just like all of the cardboard signs on telephone poles all over the city also known as the Tre-4.

I'm a grown man, I'll do what I want to do, Felton thought to himself as he was confident that all three of them would be harmless and do nothing but scream and shout at him for about an hour or so and then it'd all be over. He felt a little guilty about his behavior but not guilty enough to apologize to Abednego. He looked at the three of them who were still waiting on him for an answer. He'd look at the wedding band that he managed to slip on his finger moments before walking through the door and then he looked at his wife, who was still enraged at the stunt he'd pulled.

Traitor.

"You need to answer me," she demanded as she got in his face. Felton looked down at the woman whom he stood five inches taller than, rolled his eyes, and walked around her to the kitchen to get himself a snack.

"Woman, this is my house and you need to honor me in my house—ain't that what your God said?" he snapped as he opened the cupboard and pulled down a bowl in hopes of getting some cereal.

"You will not mock Jesus in this house." She had was pulling at the long-sleeved button up Felton had on when the thought crossed her mind that she had no idea where he'd gotten the shirt.

And had no idea why he was wearing it if he has just come home from being at Hunks & Honies. She knew he couldn't have done a private show and come back home that fast. Dismissing the thought as Satan trying to deter her from her goal, she pressed on.

"My God, Abednego is such as snitch!" He really wanted to call him the word that rhymed with that—then he realized it was his house so he paraphrased what he had just said with a few bold epithets to get his point across.

"Well I hope you're proud of yourself!" Natalie said as she stormed off and Deborah rushed behind her. That left Shadrach and Felton to face off. Felton looked at him and rolled his eyes. This wasn't twenty years ago when Shadrach used to take the guilty pleasure of disciplining both Felton and Abednego as he was the eldest and in charge. If Shadrach struck him, Felton decided he would fight back.

"Go chase after your wife," Felton challenged him. Shadrach didn't even dignify that comment with an answer. He stood his ground facing Felton as he knew his mischievous younger brother was capable of anything. Truthfully, he didn't come to fight the man in his own house, even though he was confident that he could take on the slightly taller brute. But unlike Abednego, he'd use force if it came down to it and Shadrach prayed it wouldn't come to that.

Felton took a seat on the couch and grabbed the remote and turned on the television. He really wanted to watch ESPN to catch whatever competition they had on the screen.

"I'd never thought I'd see the day when you wouldn't care about Abednego—or me." Shadrach sat down, frustrated that he wasn't able to get through to his little brother. "I know that sometimes Abednego takes preaching the gospel a little too far but he's only trying to love on you the only way he knows how."

Felton looked at him, scrunched his face and got up to go into the linen closet to grab the extra sheets and pillows because he knew he was sleeping on the couch tonight—no question about that. Shadrach decided that Felton was a lost cause as he headed to Natalie's bedroom to get Deborah and to inform Natalie they were leaving. Once he did that, they were out of the door and there was peace in the room.

CHAPTER EIGHT

ABEDNEGO & SHADRACH

Abednego looked himself in the mirror. He was proud at how fast his skin healed yet, disappointed in the visions he had of his older brother pummeling him like he was some common street dude two weeks ago. What was done was done and Abednego had forgiven his wayward brother and hoped and prayed everyday that Felton would not only embrace his birth name, Meshach but that he would become saved and that he'd be able to see him on that glorious day when they all got to the other side and got to see and be around Jesus.

"So what are you going to do about Felton?" Shadrach yelled from the dinner table.

Abednego looked at himself in the bathroom one more time. He washed his hands, dried them off and then he left the room.

"He'll come around," Abednego replied as he sat at the table and opened the packages of *The Upper Room* that had arrived to his apartment when he and Shadrach had come in. *The Upper Room* was a nondenominational devotion guide that was distributed bi-monthly filled with daily Bible verses and personal testimonies of each of the writers. There were also tips for worship and some history about the church on any given season. The covers usually featured contemporary inspirational based paintings inspired by stories in the Bible.

"Come around or not, you shoulda fought back man!" Shadrach released his frustration as he looked Abednego in the eyes. His fists were clinching, wishing to do bodily harm. "You have no idea dude. I was *this* close to spazzing out on him when I seen him a few nights ago."

Abednego listened to Shadrach vent as he sorted the books out into seven piles for each member of The Street Disciples Ministry Group to collect and distribute when they went on their route on Saturday night to go out into the world and make disciples as Jesus had commanded.

The Street Disciples Ministry Group was started by Rahliem Victor, an ex-convict whom returned to the church shortly after his stint in prison. Now a lay leader, the ministry consisted of all male members whom have unusual or undesirable pasts a chance to show the world that they have come a long way from their sins and are actively working to build a ministry with God. The members of the group commonly meet in various areas of the community and distribute the literature on the street corners. Abednego joined the group after his own short prison stint for distribution of controlled substances with intent to sell. Once he had rededicated his life to the Lord while in prison, he had been trying his hardest to live on the straight and narrow ever since.

"And what good would striking our brother have done to *you*? It was me whom he assaulted," Abednego finally responded as he'd put the stacks of books into the maroon mesh backpacks that had been lying on the table.

"I'm just saying. I love Jesus and all that and I understand that if a man strikes you on the right cheek you are supposed to turn your left one for him to strike as well—let's just say I'm not *that far* on my journey. And I've been saved longer than you."

Abednego smiled. "Patience, my brother. Patience."

Shadrach shook his head. "I thought I was gonna have to restrain Natalie, too."

"See, you all were up there handling it your own way instead of stepping aside and letting God do his thing. That's why you had all the commotion." Abednego had tied the last bag and placed it to the side of the table. "I asked you all and y'all promised me you all wouldn't seek revenge. I'm just glad that things didn't get much worse."

Shadrach looked at him and closed his lips tight. He really wanted to say the first thing on his mind, but he knew that Abednego was right. They could've tried to handle this any other way but the group confrontation against a man whom only thinks about self and not others wasn't the best idea. Shadrach exhaled and just shook his head. "I'm just saying, you can't continue to let Felton use you like a punching bag at will. Don't you get tired of that sh—"

"No." Abednego cut him off sharply. He wasn't about to let his brother use profane language in his personal space. Before he could say what was on his mind, they heard a key jiggling and a lock being unturned. Their younger cousin, Oscar Street had come in from his shift at the local call center. He looked weary and his eyes were hazed from staring at the computer screen all day. Oscar had a bag of food from Q'Doba, their favorite Mexican restaurant, and pretty soon, the smell of grilled food filled the air.

"Aww man, Shadrach, I didn't know you were going to be here." Oscar apologized as he set the food on the table.

"Naw man, I was just getting ready to leave." Shadrach stood up. Upset that he couldn't get through to Abednego, he headed toward the door. "I'll have to catch up with you another day."

Shadrach looked at his brother and shook his head. He just didn't understand how Abednego was able to keep it going and not think to strike back. But when he crossed the threshold of the door that separated his home from the rest of the projects, he had to respect the man for standing on his convictions.

CHAPTER NINE

DONTE

Donte looked at Eve sitting across the table at Olive Garden as she enjoyed her never-ending pasta and salad. Eugene looked from him to his mother and wondered with amazement about the woman and what role she was going to play in his life. Up until two weeks before that time, his concept of a mother was Donte's mother, who'd come around every now and then to cook, clean, hang out with Eugene. Surprisingly, Eugene never asked too many questions about his mother, he'd accepted Donte's original answer that she was where God wanted her to be. For his part, Donte couldn't believe that not only did he tell the police officers that he did not want to press charges, but that he bailed her out and agreed to revisit the idea of him and Eve coming to some kind of visitation agreement.

Donte would've preferred that they'd eaten at a neutral place, not a restaurant that happened to have many of Eugene's favorite foods. Donte made the mistake of taking Eugene with him on one of his dates with Elicia and the boy discovered that the bread sticks tasted better than cake and the pastas came in many shapes and sizes that fascinated him. Though he would've objected the idea, Donte thought about how he could keep Eugene's face stuffed, to avoid him asking so many unnecessary and uneasy-to-answer questions.

Donte observed the interaction between Eve and Eugene and they both acted like nervous kindergarteners getting ready to go to school for the first time. Well, Eugene was sure to have that moment at the beginning of the next school year; but there was no reason Eve was feeling that way at that moment. After all, she'd broken into their home to see their son.

Donte looked around the restaurant and prayed that he didn't see anyone from the church come in for Sunday afternoon dinner. This was the second Sunday they'd missed in a row and not only was that unusual for Donte, but he barely said two words to Rahliem about what was going on with him and Eve when Rahliem asked about it. Donte had promised to meet with Rahliem and explain things with him another time but two separate opportunities had come and gone and Donte had yet to say a word. But looking at them, one would've thought they were the perfect family who had just left Sunday service like the other professionally dressed patrons in the restaurant.

"Mom, what's your name?" Eugene asked as he brought Donte's attention to their table. Donte looked on as Eugene chewed the rolled that he'd stuffed in his mouth. Donte made a mental note to work with him about his table manners.

"Mom." Eve responded as if there were no other answer.

"No—I mean your first name. I know my daddy's name is Donte Eugene Speaks and my granny's name is Alice Mae Speaks and my papa's name is Eugene Miguel Speaks and my uncle's name is Edris Tyler Speaks—I want to know your name."

Donte didn't know how to respond to that. Normally, he'd chastise Eugene for being so forward, but on the other hand, Eve wanted to be a parent—at least for the day, Donte didn't see any reason why he'd deny her the opportunity to see the good and the bad traits in their son. And in his eyes, the question was harmless, innocent even. Eugene had the right to know who his mother was. Even he had a hard time remembering Eve's name and when Eugene asked him a week ago about it, Donte was struggling to put to words how he barely knew his mother at the time he was conceived in a manner in which a five-year-old would understand it. Donte noticed the way that Eve looked at Eugene with an attitude—the audacity she had to suck her teeth in and roll her eyes at their son irritated him. How he wished he weren't at the restaurant so he could rip her a new one. Yet before he could dig into her grill about that, the waitress who'd been serving their food walked past them. Donte silently thanked God for this intervention because he knew he was going to say some words that were un-Christ-like. "Can we get three to-go plates and the ticket please?"

"Sure," the waitress was surprisingly chippy and upbeat—a stark contrast to the mood that was developing at their table.

Eugene kept eating while he waited on Eve to answer and she ignored his question, giving her response by stuffing her face with the third helping of the chicken Alfredo. Donte saw the pout beginning to form on Eugene's lips. Before he could address his son's disposition, the waitress came back with the doggy bag and the ticket. Donte originally wanted to pay for the meal with his Visa card but found that he had two twenty dollar bills in his billfold and stuffed them in the black leather ticket case she'd handed them and instructed her to keep the change. Donte grabbed Eugene's plate and dumped his food in the Styrofoam container and did his plate the same. He grabbed a few of the bread rolls and two spoonfuls of salad and added that to their containers so they could leave. He looked toward Eve, who appeared to be appalled that they were leaving. Donte offered Eve a container and she looked him up and down like he was the crazy one.

"Where are y'all going?" Eve got loud, drawing attention from the other patrons as they looked on as if they were in the middle of watching a Tyler Perry play.

"I'm taking my son, and we're leaving." Donte spewed, struggling to control his anger. He was trying to remember the Psalm or the Proverb that said something about being slow to anger but the verse left his mind. At that moment, he was boiling hot and needed to escape before he truly forgot he was a Christian and cursed the rude un-virtuous woman out that he'd wasted forty-five minutes with at table. While his inner spirit encouraged him to leave, he did an about face and swiftly returned to his seat. He leaned forward as close as he could stand it and twisted his face in a way that would make even the Grinch blush.

"Let me explain something to you. *My son*, is not a damn toy, so if you don't have an interest in being part of his life, you need to leave him alone and let him grow up to be around people who do."

His words were stern and sharp as Eve dropped for fork full of pasta that bounced from her chest to her plate, making a *ding* to announce its perfect landing.

"And I'm not going to tolerate you treating him any kind of way. You need to be thankful that I chose allowing him to visit with you as opposed to go to church this morning. But I'll tell you this, if you think you are going see him again after you couldn't give him your freakin' name, you can go to hell."

On that note, Donte stood up, forcefully grabbed Eugene's hand and stormed out of the restaurant. He could hear Eve cursing and he could've swore he saw some noodles and a piece of bread fly by him but he chose to ignore it because turning around could possibly put him in jail. He reached in his pocket and pulled out his keys, wishing he had the remote to unlock his car. Something wet landed on the back of Donte's head as if a bird had flown over him and done its business. Once he unlocked Eugene's door, Donte shoved him in and closed the door quickly. He felt Eve grabbing at his arm and he shoved her off as she continued to say every word of degradation and profanity that was in the English language, even having the nerve to call him an unfit parent.

"You need to be glad I didn't abort your little bastard!" Eve yelled when Donte looked her in the eyes.

Donte opened the door and was about to say something foul when he shook his head and held his finger up. He refused to give her the satisfaction of seeing him ticked off.

"I'm glad you didn't. But you don't have to worry about me and my son, because you'll never see us again." Donte took his seat as he slammed the door. He forced the key in the ignition and without looking in his rearview mirror, he backed out of the parking space.

At that moment, it ran across his mind that he'd picked Eve up at the Mi Pablo restaurant on Stratford Road. He looked in the passenger seat and was surprised that Eve had left her mesh handbag in her seat. Donte quickly rolled down the window and threw the handbag out and he didn't wait for the bag to make a *thud* on the pavement before he sped off.

***

"I don't even know why I bothered entertaining Eve's request for her to get to know Eugene," Donte said as Rahliem had taken a seat on his plush couch. Donte sat on the love seat while Elicia was in the kitchen getting everyone cranberry juice and Sprite to drink. Donte wished that he had something stronger, but the non-alcoholic mixed drink would do. "I wonder what she really wants from him…and from us."

"I understand your frustration," Rahliem graciously took the drink from Elicia and took a sip after Donte did the same. "But you were wrong for going off on her like you did. Proverbs 15:18 says '*A wrathful man stirs up strife, but he who is slow to anger allays contention.*', yet you went from nice to nasty in two seconds flat."

"I was provoked." Donte defended himself calmly as he caught a side view of Elicia's profile as she took her seat next to him.

"That's true." Elicia pointed out. "But think about the example you set for Eugene. He's seen you snap at and go off on the woman who gave birth to him and now he will think it's okay for him to snap and go off on her."

"Eugene knows better," Donte responded more sharply. "He's knows better to pull that stunt with me."

"That may be true, but just because she's acting childish doesn't mean you have to," Rahliem looked from Donte to Elicia.

"Now before the pot calls the kettle black—trust me—I have my moments. But please understand that everything you and Eve do from here on out will be scrutinized more carefully by your son. Eugene may have known Elicia better and have a fondness for her, but he understands what the word "mother" means and he also understands that he is supposed to feel a certain way for Eve that he may not feel for Elicia or your mother. I'm not saying that you can't get anger and that you can't get upset. What I am saying is that we are encouraged in the word to be wise and to use the wisdom He's given us to good use at all times. It's hard and challenging when people do and say things we don't like, but we show the true spirit of Christ when we rise about that and make do, despite of that."

Donte nodded his head, agreeing that Rahliem was right and that perhaps he'd let his anger get the best of him. He thought about the scene they made and how he was going to have to make an extra trip to the cleaners behind some decisions that could've been avoided if he'd kept his cool. As Donte rose up to collect the glasses from their drinks, he saw Eugene looking at him and Donte realized that everything Rahliem and Elicia said began to take root in his child's mind. The last thing he wanted was to set the wrong example for Eugene because he knew that God would hold him accountable for the lessons that he'd taught his son. At that moment, he knew that he'd need to reach out to Eve and set some things straight—the question was where they would go from there.

CHAPTER TEN

RAHLIEM

Seven young black men wearing black baseball caps that said 'Jesus Saves' long black T-Shirts, baggy but not sagging jeans and various brands of sneakers stepped out of the white, silver and maroon van. From a distance, they could have easily been mistaken for a reincarnation of the Wu-Tang Clan. By the way they attracted attention from the crowd, people at the nearby shopping center flocked to them expecting them to put on an impromptu rap concert in the middle of the street. After the last man stepped out and pulled the door shut, the driver of the van drove off cautiously trying to find a parking space near the barbershop at the top of the hill. The young men made their stop on this popular hill that was on the corner of Martin Luther King, Jr. Boulevard and New Walkertown Road of Winston-Salem.

On this Saturday after payday, people were at this busy shopping center trying to catch fish dinners being sold by a local chapter of the Winston-Salem State University Alumni Association raising money for a Mr. Alumni contestant. Next to the fish vendor was a man who had faithfully sold hip hop inspired gear and African American Art, and next to them, the sweet smelling soap from the make shift car shop greeted customers as they made their way up the hill to the shopping center. Well, some people never made it up the hill. In the intersection, members of the Nation of Islam were competing with a carrier to spread the news. Customers seemed to equally stop to support *The Winston Salem Journal* and *The Final Call.* It was there where Rahliem sent half of the Street Disciples Ministry.

Rahliem knew that his group was just a little over a mile from Winston-Salem State University and their home, Grace United Methodist Church. At the church, Rahliem was the lay leader and also vice committee chair for the outreach committee which Street Disciples Ministry Group spun out from. He made sure that each member had their maroon backpack filled with copies of *The Upper Room*, and a couple of books in their hands ready to pass out. Each of the young men who followed Rahliem out of the van, had come from various backgrounds and each had their own mission and method to spread the word of God in the hood.

Rahliem watched as Donte led some of the young men who traveled with him to the busy intersection, he couldn't help but notice his nemesis, Minister Vincent X. Muhammad glaring at him. The two young men, who once were best friends, were known to get into public spats in the past. Vincent was always preaching about Elijah Muhammad and the Nation of Islam teachings as well as Mohammed, the great prophet of Islam. Rahliem would quote scripture and point out passages in the Bible that proved that Jesus Christ was the Son of God and the Messiah that the Jews were waiting on, but ultimately rejected. Rahliem looked away mainly to avoid the confrontation and argument over whose faith reigned supreme. Besides, Rahliem had to be a role model for the two new recruits he was left to train. And he wasn't trying to go back to prison as an inmate and he knew that engaging with the man from the Nation of Islam would take him there.

As Rahliem was passing out copies of *The Upper Room*, he noticed that Donte still was drawing a larger crowd of ladies who were more interested in him autographing their bootleg versions of his old videos from his former life. To these women as well as some of the men, Donte wasn't a man of God, but Donte

Longstocking, a man who knew how to, well, he doesn't talk about that aspect of his life anymore. Donte didn't make it any easier by forever being forgetful about wearing the sun glasses that they had *just* stopped at the mall to pick up to avoid this incident. Rahliem knew that Donte would have it the hardest in spite of the fact that he was one of the first members of Street Disciples and the most experienced. But Donte knew that with this ministry, issues of his past as a local and famous adult video star would always come to play. Rahliem was just hoping that Donte wouldn't be asked to leave the corner as he had one time before. But being the true business man that Donte was, he had the ladies lining up along the sidewalk of New Walkertown Road just before the Wachovia bank.

Rahliem watched as woman after woman walked up to him and wanted hugs and pictures and sometimes reluctantly took the devotion that Donte sometimes had to force into their hands. Some of the women were bold as they let their hands wonder for sneak feels in front and in back of his midsection or lifting up his torso, hoping to get their hands on his most famous appendage. That would be when one of the guys with Donte would kindly escort her away so Donte could do the ministry work he had came to do and to be about God's business.

Abednego didn't have an easier time. Faithful fans inquired about his latest incident with his brother and he appeared to be brushing it off. He was a hustler at heart and great with words and he used those words to convince anyone within the sound of his voice to try the product he was most passionate about—salvation. Rahliem enjoyed watching Abednego work the most because Abednego reached out to some of the junkies and prostitutes he used to make money off of and used his gift with words to preach to them the Word of Christ. Rahliem respected that Abednego was good for reciting a quick Proverb or singing a verse of Psalms and that he was not afraid to stop passing out copies of the daily devotion to offer a quick word of prayer or to lead everyone in a soul stirring rendition of a Kirk Franklin or a Kiki Sheppard tune. The healing bruises on his face had garnered him more attention than was warranted as the faithful were concerned and some were angry that a man of God would be attacked. However, Abednego was obedient unto God and stayed jolly in the midst of those seeking justice against this transgression. Abednego probably would have done better to wear glasses but he'd never been the one to hide who he was or his love for God.

On the next intersection, Rahliem realized that Celtius remembered to bring his glasses. Unlike the other famous member of the Street Disciples, Celtius only wanted to be revealed by God. Celtius was often mistaken for a certain male model that had appeared in numerous gospel plays that won audiences over with his incredible singing voice. It had been over two years since Celtius chased after any man who told him he was beautiful—including his brother. Many of the men who had sex with men lusted after him and missed the way Celtius entertained them in parked cars next to vacant buildings, fitness center bathrooms or any other place where they could sneak and get their freak on. At first, Rahliem didn't think he could look past Celtius' indiscretions—he despised the fact that for a couple of months, he and Davon knew each other better than any man should and the fact that they were together for a number of years in high school and their early twenties, through Rahliem's incarceration made the fact that he now was part of the ministry ironic. When Rahliem was first questioned about Celtius' purpose in the ministry—former lovers, rivals and admirers testified that the number of bed partners he had, both male and female, rivaled the boisterous claims of Wilt Chamberlin. But the Spirit would reveal to Rahliem not only how serious Celtius was about loving the Lord, but how bad he wanted to please God. When Celtius got saved, the first thing he wanted to do was cut it off so he could be eunuch. He feared his member that much and called various members of the church leadership everyday for a quick five minute prayer session. Rahliem admitted that at first, Celtius got on his nerves about wanting to pray all the time; eventually, Rahliem and Pastor Phelps had become concerned when Celtius didn't call. Celtius led a class on celibacy and taught abstinence classes to the youth. Of course, his sexual orientation always came to question, and at times, Celtius fell weak to the flesh but for the most part after a few minutes of talking to Celtius, there was no doubt where he stood in his relationship with God.

And at least Rahliem didn't have to keep Celtius and rival Street Disciples' member Mya from fighting anymore. Under no circumstances did Mya like homosexuals, even reformed ones like Celtius as he would say. When Celtius left the ministry for a time to keep from having a physical altercation with Mya, Rahliem would learn how troubling Mya's spirit was and was motivated to push the current choir directed from the team. Like Rahliem, Mya had to learn how to calm down and not be so quick to react or come to a quick judgment so that he could be the leader of the ministry God had placed on his heart. Since Mya agreed to go to a support group for his anger management issues, he's learned to let the Holy Spirit guide his steps and keep his attitude in check. True, Mya still sported a perm that made him look more like a girl than a boy. Save for the mustache, if one had looked at his side profile, they wouldn't have been able to tell the difference. Mya still had a very dangerous tongue that was lethal and no matter how many Bible verses you pointed out to the boy, he still had a hard time taming it. Rahliem hoped that this wasn't the thorn in his side that God wasn't removing, like that thorn he didn't remove from Paul. Mya couldn't spit game like Abednego could, but Mya could hold his own on the piano or with a guitar.

Standing next to Rahliem were Oscar and Calvin, active alumni of Winston-Salem State who were part of the campus ministry organized there. Oscar, just like his brother Orenthal, was a hustler and a true business man at heart and felt that the ministry would have been better served selling the devotions as opposed to giving them away for free. Oscar would have much rather stood on the corner with a bucket and a sign asking people to support the ministry. Sometimes, when various churches around the city needed to raise money, they'd call on Oscar to do just that. But Oscar also needed a lesson in humility and what better way to give it to him by having him serve other people, no charge of course. However, when you compare Oscar to Calvin, Oscar's issues were somewhat harmless. Calvin was older and arguably the most dangerous of them all. Rahliem often kept a close eye on Calvin because he knew the man had a nasty penchant for violence and it didn't take much to tempt him. Calvin was a murderer. He killed the teenage boy who murdered his older sister and terrorized him and his friends in middle school when he was twelve. Some folks say he's been a little off ever since. It wasn't that Calvin was off—he grew tired of folks asking him what it was like to kill somebody every fifteen minutes —testing and tempting him to lift up his weapon and kill again. Rahliem knew that when Calvin twisted his wedding band, he thought about it or was thinking about it. Part of the problem was that Calvin resented that fact that his older brother was *still* doing the time for his crime, even after he confessed it. Even though Carlton was getting out in the next few weeks, he still felt raw about his brother doing the time in the first place. Another issue was that he and his wife were having issues at home and dealing with the recent death of their three-year-old boy whom lost his battle with cancer. Rahliem knew something else was bothering Calvin, but he couldn't put his finger on it. Calvin was never an open person and it would take more than a simple inquiry to pry it out of him.

"I'm glad your little video star can keep his clothes on," Vincent stood next to him. Rahliem had been so busy passing out devotions and watching the members of his ministry that he didn't even noticed that Vincent had gotten next to him. He knew he was slipping on his prison instincts and that Vincent in his own way was testing his gangster. And truthfully, Rahliem should've been able to smell him coming because the sandalwood body oil Vincent wore reek so strong, he was confident he was going to smell like Vincent for the next couple of minutes.

"I'm glad he is, too," Rahliem responded, "one should be fully clothed when doing the work of God."

"Whatever," Vincent responded to Rahliem's dismissal. "I don't see how you got all these crazy people and weirdoes supporting your ministry. Come on, Rahliem, you got a man for almost every deadly sin."

"Yet you are perfect?" Rahliem questioned.

Before Vincent could make a comeback, Rahliem replied, "I don't judge people on their past. That is not what Street Disciples is about. Street Disciples is about meeting people where they are, showing them the love that Christ has for them and bringing people together to make them useful contributors to the Body of Christ."

"Yeah, yeah, yeah, all that together as one bull crap sounds nice, but are they really together as one?"

Rahliem pointed out each member of his ministry, "You see the books they are handing out this time?" He gave Vincent a chance to look and observe. "Regardless of whatever our personal issues may be, we come out here and give the people what they want, what they need in their lives. We come in peace. Just as you have, I presume?"

"I see you trying to save face in front of your friends," Vincent replied. Rahliem noticed him eyeing Oscar and Calvin and them returning grit. "You should have more love, joy, gentleness, goodness and all those other things you believe in. As-Salamu Alaykum."

"Wa Alaykum As-Salam."

Rahliem watched Vincent walk away and then stand at his post. Donte, Abednego, Celtius and Mya were making their way back across the street. They converged to the white tent that was the closest to the corner and interacted with the pastor of the Baptist church across the street. The smell of fried fish had wafted in the air long enough and after spending almost two hours ministering to the souls of the interested and in despair; they simultaneously desired it was time to feed their flesh and their spirits. Going to the table meant more than getting meat and bread—they knew that somebody would have a Word and that the ministering would encourage them to continue in their journey. As Rahliem, Oscar and Calvin made their way to the table and getting their money ready for their own fish dinners, they enjoyed the comfort of fellowship in the name of the Christ that seemed to be taking place. The other motivation they had to come across the street and to return to their table was so that they could be ready to break apart a potential physical altercation between Rahliem and Vincent.

"Why did you greet him back?" Calvin asked once he was seated at the table.

"There is nothing wrong with responding back with the traditional Arab greeting. Yes, Muslims have adopted that as theirs, but the greeting has common and traditional meanings outside of Islam. Besides, he was wishing me peace and I wish him the same."

Upon noticing an objection to his definition from Oscar, Rahliem continued. "I treat all people with the love of Christ. That is my outward sign of being a Christian. I can't profess to be a child of the one who loves if I'm hating on everybody."

When the other young men got to their table, they found that their meals were already paid for—a nice gesture on behalf of the candidate for Mr. Alumni, who happened to be a member of the church across the street. The men smiled and said thank you and bestowed him with gifts of copies of *The Upper Room* and other trinkets that they usually gave out to new converts whom they were notorious for saving on those same street corners.

"Elijah Phelps," he introduced himself to the group. "Your pastor is my little sister. I'm proud to be supporting a ministry that is about uplifting people in the name of God and I'm even prouder to see my younger brothers in the midst. Lauren used to say all the time that a child shall lead them."

Rahliem laughed as he reflected on her promise that a child was leading them during last week's service. Pastor Phelps had let a young man who was interested in preaching get into the pulpit with the sermon he had read and the child had done a good job being used by God to give them the Word.

"I still got a lot to learn," Calvin confessed. "Back when I was younger, I never believed that people could get into the situations they found themselves in. I never understood how we could be so far away from Christ."

"It's not about the situations that people find themselves in, it's about the way that they carry themselves and ask God to work out their problems. And it doesn't hurt if they can follow directions either."

Elijah continued to speak about Jesus and reminded them how at times, even the disciples of Christ failed at following his directions—highlighting Peter taking his eyes off Him, James' and John's desire to sit at the left and right of Jesus and Judas' ultimate betrayal. As the men continued eating, a young, scantly-clad lady came up and hugged Donte from behind. She must have spotted them from the street and observed where he was sitting. Donte turned around and in kind asked her how he knew her.

"Oh my gosh Donte, I'm like your number one fan!" she rambled, trying to sit in his lap. The young lady reached into his personal space and massaged Donte's well-developed chest. Her hands reached around his head in an effort to cuddle him and grinded her seat into his lap, attempting to arouse him into seduction. She didn't care that she was sitting amongst a group of men who looked at her not with lust, but with contempt that she would disrespect her temple and their presence. Donte was a little heated because he dropped some of the fish he was eating the ground. As she realized her mistake, she jumped up from his lap seat and apologized profusely for her actions. "I'm sorry, baby, I didn't see you eating! I hope you didn't swallow on a bone."

Donte quickly chewed on a piece of bread and swallowed the soft drink he was drinking. He wiped his face and the fish grease on his fingertips on the napkin and placed it gently beside his plate. "Not at all. What can I do for you?"

Rahliem knew Donte well enough to know that the man was putting on a show, masking his emotions so that he wouldn't say something or do something that he would regret.

"I just want your autograph. I can't wait to tell my girls that I met Donte Longstocking in person!" She danced and giddied as if she were cheering for Michael Jackson at one of his concerts. As she moved, Rahliem saw that in her hands was a DVD of one of Donte Longstocking's most infamous movies. The name that made Donte millions has become the name that he knew Donte had came to abhor.

Nevertheless, Donte pulled out a copy of *The Upper Room* devotion from the maroon backpack that he had placed on the floor, signed it and handed it to her.

"I want to you to read today's devotion with your girls. If you agree with the message that God is bringing, come to Grace United Methodist Church on Sunday."

"Oooh, you gon' be there!" Rahliem knew that the girl didn't hear a word of what Donte said about being at church or reading the message. What Rahliem was sure the girl heard was "*I will be at Grace United on Sunday, bring your girls.*" Plus, it was obvious that all she cared about was getting next to the man who was still more famous for his videos that sold thousands of copies and generated just as many illegal downloads from various websites. And she showed Rahliem and everyone else at the table that she didn't care what she had to do get next to him. As far as she was concerned, Donte was a rock star.

"Yes, I'll be there." Donte said as the young lady cooed, never taking her eyes off of him. "And I hope to see you there too."

"Oh, I'm going to be there." She took the book and kissed him on the cheek. "Thank you so much and I can't wait to tell my girls to come and see you on Sunday."

The girl hastily ran across the street. Rahliem watched as the young lady turned around to see if Donte was watching her and the look of disappointment when she saw Donte pick up the piece of fish that fell from his mouth off the ground, wrapped it up and placed it beside his nearly empty plate. Donte addressed the group with a smile and said, "It's too late for the five second rule."

"You handled that situation very well young man," Elijah commented, "I don't know too many people who would not have taken the opportunity to sit in the seat of judgment and talk about that woman."

"Well, I had to learn that with any mistake I have made that there is always a way to fix things. What I learned to do with my situation is to take each and every opportunity given to me when I meet a fan of the old me is to give them a chance to meet the new me. Sure, I get people that call me all kinds of names and say derogatory things about me, but for the few who take me up on my offer and come to church, have seen a change in their lives."

"Amen," Celtius added.

"It may not feel good, but it works out for my good."

"You always take an opportunity to share Christ with anyone young man, you never know whose listening."

After the young men finished eating, they cleaned up and got ready to go to their spots. They knew that everyone would stay on or near the intersection for a few more hours. Fortunately, their rep was strong enough to have a lot of repeat customers who came to find then so they could get their little leaflets or the large print versions of the books. Often times, some of the volunteers at the nearby Baptist church would allow them to operate from within their youth ministry room when the weather got too bad. The young men ran into community leaders, old friends and even a few celebrities and were often asked to speak everywhere. Rahliem, Donte, and Mya were even involved in starting a second Street Disciples Ministry group in Greensboro to support the numerous colleges they had in the area.

Rahliem, Oscar, and Calvin took their turn and joined Donte in operating from the intersection. Mya, Celtius, and Abednego went on the hill. Upon seeing Rahliem on the Dr. Martin Luther King stretch, Vincent rushed over and switched places with the young man selling *The Final Call* on the street. Rahliem expected as much as they both were expected to be leaders of their respective groups. Rahliem disliked viewing their rivalry as part of some Christianity versus Islam war but sometimes, he felt like he couldn't help but play into the feelings folks had about their run ins. A car came up bumping "And I" by Mary Mary featuring

Kirk Franklin. Rahliem felt reassured that God was pleased with the work he was doing so he kept pressing on.

It was as surprise that Rahliem and Vincent avoided an altercation while working the same strip. Usually, the two just entered into a light disagreement about Jesus, Mohammed, and whoever else there was to talk about. Rahliem continued to work hard to get the people to receive a copy of *The Upper Room*. He was somewhat fortunate as the cover depicted African inspired characters and it was appealing to the eye of all beholders. The usually uplifting set of devotionals focused on forgiveness and healing in this particular issue and that was what a lot of people needed.

When it was time to pack up and leave the street, Rahliem and the other young men headed straight to the van. They were surprised to see Elijah and their pastor having fun and laughing like they were little kids. They almost didn't see them coming.

"So how did the Street Disciples do today?" she asked. Pastor Phelps was excited and already anticipating good news. Each of the young men took off their backpacks and looked at how many copies they had left.

"I only have twenty copies left," Donte proclaimed.

"And he signed half of them," Abednego added.

"I take it we'll have some young ladies joining the church this Sunday. That can be a good thing." Pastor Phelps responded light-heartedly. Despite its faults, Donte was one of the main reasons women joined the church.

"I only have twenty, too," Rahliem said.

"I only have the large prints," Mya added. Truthfully, he forgot about the large prints in his bag. It was a blessing because the pastor knew she would need copies for Sunday Service.

"I got thirty five," Calvin added. His cell phone rang and he quickly excused himself as he picked up the phone to talk, presumably to talk to his wife. Rahliem looked on when with concern as he could hear him raising his voice and being very stern with whomever he was speaking to. Ever since Calvin's wife had that affair with a church leader of another church, their relationship continued to stand on rocky ground.

"I got thirty," Celtius added, bringing the focus back to the subject at hand.

"I got thirty, too," Oscar finished counting. "People don't want free books like they used to."

"Well," the pastor interjected, "this wasn't a contest to see who could get rid of the most books. Our goal is to get the books into the people's hands and to let them know that the devotions exist. I remember the first time we did this each of you had about seventy books left so we are improving with each issue."

"I got forty left," Abednego added. "I did spend some time praying with this older man at the church though."

"I knew you would be praying and singing with someone," she smiled. Abednego usually had the most books left. "This is the plan for next week when we go to Greensboro to meet with the young men interested in the ministry. We have enough books to show them how this works. Did we decide which street we were going to try and set up at?"

"Dudley and Market Street would be good," Donte answered. "That's right there where A&T is at, plus Bennett and Gilbert are down the street. The shopping center down south is black owned and a few of the shops have agreed to carry copies of the book."

"And we get to meet with the brothers on Friday night," Rahliem added. "We'll probably get some pizza or something and fellowship—may turn it into a Bible Study. I'm still working on my message for next Sunday too."

"You ready to give the Word, Rahliem?"

"I'll be ready with whatever the Spirit puts in front of me," Rahliem had gotten over being nervous about speaking the Word. Evidence of that was that Rahliem no longer stutters as much in his sermons.

"Well, don't feel like you have to rush the Spirit and come up with something right now. Let the message come to you."

Rahliem thought of the pastor's words as he rode home. The van dropped everyone off at the church and he watched as each individual member got in their own cars and left the church.

CHAPTER ELEVEN

ABEDNEGO

Abednego didn't take five steps out of his apartment before he coughed up some phlegm that was troubling his throat and expelled it in the nearby bushes that greeted his doorstep.

Man, he said to himself. *Now I got to go back in here brush my teeth again.*

Abednego was already ten minutes late out the door trying to meet with C. He had promised the young man he would come to their prayer meeting at his house. Abednego didn't mind because the meeting was in the afternoon before he went to the college for a sociology class and for his night job as a clerk at a gas station on 14th and King Street. Abednego started to turn around and do just that when he noticed a young driving down the block with the Wild Berry Skittles logo on a 1967 Chevy Impala. He shook his head at the waste of resources that could've went to further a ministry. He wanted to take a second look because at first glance, the dude looked like the light skinned version of the popular secular rapper, Plies. And the woman in his car didn't look too bad either in with red and black barrettes hanging at the tips of her twisted braids, looking like Da Brat.

"Aye yo!" C shouted from the car but Abednego went inside. The accent threw him off as well as he frowned at the idea of being addressed in such a manner. He ran up the stairs, hoping he didn't upset the elderly couple that lived next door that always complained about all the noise their neighbors were making and rushed into the bathroom so he could handle his business. Once inside, he lifted up the extra long tee shirt and made sure he was right. Abednego had a thing for hygiene and he always made sure that he was fresh and clean cause whenever he went out to minister, he never knew what would happen. And the last thing he wanted was to embarrass himself or misrepresent the Spirit. He checked his breath and under his arm and as he was feeling confident that his freshness was still intact, he walked down the stairs and headed out the door.

"Yo man—that was rude how you ran into the crib after I know you heard me calling you." C had pulled his car right in front of Abednego's doorstep and was leaning on the driver's side of the car. Abednego got a good look at the dude and though he didn't want to show it, he was a little shook because C was showing a side of himself that was different from the image he presented himself on Facebook or at Hunks and Honies a few weeks ago.

How did he know where I rested my head? Abednego thought. The street senses that he usually had weren't as sharp after he was saved.

"Abednego right?"

"Yeah man, what's good with you?"

This is not the way he presented himself to me online, Abednego thought as he shook the man's hand. He tried to keep from refraining from making judgments because he didn't want to be judged on his indiscretions so he kept it moving.

"I came to do what we said we was gonna do—but first, I want you to meet my girl NuTameka."

What kind of name is NuTameka? Abednego thought to himself as he nodded to the girl. Her oversized Carolina Hurricanes hockey jersey and her baggy jeans on further solidified her ability to pull off a job as Da Brat's stunt double.

"What man? You not gonna give a chick a hug?"

Abednego walked over to meet and obliged with her request. He smelled the coconut and papaya fragrance that could have only come from the use of some Nubian Heritage products. As he felt her soft body brush up against his, he was almost jealous of this man whose full name he still had to acquire. Thoughts of his past came to mind and the things he wished he could do with her every night and as the blood rushed below his waist, he pulled back so that he wouldn't so easily fall into temptation. He watched the rock on her noise rise up as she strongly sniffed the air around him.

"Indian Hemp and Haitian Vetiver right?" she asked smiling.

"How did you know?"

"Chase, he's good. He wearing the same kind of fragrance you got on. We don't do that fake mess they sell at Wal-Mart— only the best goes onto and into our bodies. If I can't pronounce it or trace it back to a plant or a tree, it doesn't go anywhere near me."

So his name is Chase, Abednego thought to himself again, it matches what he said so far when he said his name started with a C. Even though Abednego was cool on meeting different people on various websites for prayer meetings and bible study, he always was willing to give someone a chance. He knew that on various social media websites, peopled lied on their profiles. Chase had originally told him that he was twenty-five, but so far, he didn't act like it. He reminded him of some of the guys who just walked on the corner with their shirts off, smoking some trees or drinking a forty or both just talking, yelling and grabbing their crotches.

"That's what's up," Abednego responded. "I believe in the same thing. I like natural products."

"Aye yo Abe, get in the backseat man. I'm a let my girl drive to the store for a minute while we discuss business."

Abednego clutched his Bible tight as he was used to conducting a different type of business in the back seat. Yet, he didn't argue with the request and he did what he was told. Chase got in on the other side and once the seatbelts were secure, NuTameka took off as if she were an ambulance driver.

Abednego appreciated the fact that she wasn't scared to flex behind the wheel.

"You think my girl nice huh?" Chase asked and licked his lips when he saw Abednego look his direction. He took his seatbelt off once she got on the busy city street.

"Yeah man—where'd you find her?"

"MySpace. Man, how come you don't have a girl?"

"I've been focusing on being a better servant for the Lord. Doing his work and ministry keeps me busy so I haven't found the time for a girl."

"Awe come on." Chase put his hands on Abednego's shoulder. Abednego wanted to brush his hand off but he remembered he wasn't in his car. "You don't have a chick on the side to do your thing with."

"No."

"Well we need to find you one. You know, NuTameka got a sister named Africa if you want to holler at her."

"I think I'll be alright for now." Abednego said as he cracked his bible open. "Where are we having this Bible Study at?"

"My house. I'm gonna have one of my homies there who don't think God is real. I'm not a preacher man or anything like that, that's why I reached out to you. I seen you handing out those Jesus papers and I figured that you would be the best person to make sure my boy met God."

Abednego nodded and shook he head.

"And check this, a good chick is hard to find." Chase nodded his head. "After we hang for a minute, maybe I can introduce you to one of her friends."

The more Abednego looked at Chase, the more he reminisced about his past. Back in the day, Chase would've made the perfect running buddy. Abednego used to use the language Chase did. He took note of the black and white bandana on his forehead and the light brown contacts in his eyes. The navy blue Dickies outfit reminded him of what some of the peoples from the left coast wore but he didn't sweat it.

"You leave your account on don't you?" Chase said, breaking Abednego from his dream.

"What you mean?"

"You stay logged into Facebook all the time don't you?"

"Yeah it's aight. I check in from my Palm every now and then."

"You missed my note telling you I was close by and that I'd come and get you."

"Oh word? How you know where I live?"

"Yo, I do my thing in these streets. It's my job to know everything about you."

Abednego nodded his head. He knew that Chase knew him from his past life somewhere. He tried to remember whether or not he'd wronged him somewhere down the line but the moment that fear crept in, he decided that whatever happened didn't matter. He wasn't gonna become a victim to his past and he wasn't gonna let his past rule his present.

"And what you know?"

"I know that your parents are proud of the changes you've made in your life, your brother owns Shadrach's and your other brother is a stripper/escort at Hunks and Honies. When I'm not performing, me and my girl stop by from time to time to check him out cause it keeps the spice going in our relationship. Anyway, you've been holding down that apartment for a minute and looking out for your little cousin—I get my gas at the WilcoHess station you work at every now and then. I know that even though you stay in the hood, you go to some kind of school cause I see those books you be bringing in. And that you love Jesus and can't keep your mouth shut talking about him."

"What are you? A spy?" Abednego was getting uncomfortable sitting next to Chase. He wondered if one of his former enemies had come for him but decided he was being paranoid and that he had nothing to worry about.

"I told him about the Street Disciples," NuTameka jumped into the conversation as she parked her car and got ready to go into the Food Lion. "Y'all keep it hood when you trying to reach the people. I like that." NuTameka took the keys out of the ignition and was about to step out of the car. "You want me to get you something?"

"Naw, I'm straight. But thanks." Abednego responded.

"Aight." She laughed to herself and jumped out of the car.

"You carry that Bible around with you all the time?" Chase asked, watching NuTameka's backside as she walked into the store. Abednego could see the lust in his eyes as he licked his lips and squeezed as his crouch. "Aye my bad. Nu be playing games with me. Teasing me talking about how she wants to celibate one minute and be trying to do sneaky stuff to turn me on the next."

"I remember when girls used to tease like that all the time." Abednego let loose and allowed himself to be comfortable with Chase. "And I used to enjoy the chase too. Once they found out who I *really* was I had them chasing me. It was fun while it lasted…but in the end, I'm trying to get closer to God and I know that when I reached that point where I'm supposed to be with him, he'll show me my wife. Could be looking at her and not recognizing her to be such."

"Man—" Chase looked at him at disbelief. "The way you be acting now, I'd swear you were a virgin. Probably hadn't had none since—"

Abednego didn't give him room to speculate. "Long enough to say I'm a born again virgin."

Even though he let loose, Abednego was uncomfortable thinking about the last time he had sex. It had been almost six months ago. His flesh had gotten the best of him and he and his ex-girlfriend sweated up the backseat of her car at a drive in car wash for old time's sake. He had felt so guilty afterward, he almost decided to quit the Street Disciples Ministry, but after a private talk with Pastor Phelps, she assured him that he couldn't give up the fight. Thinking about her again almost made him wanted to dial her digits.

"What's your favorite book in the Bible?"

"I like the Proverbs, full of affirmations and wise words."

"I like Song of Solomon and Acts."

Abednego shook his head. Maybe Chase wasn't so bad after all. Abednego opened his Bible and read from the highlighted passage. "One of my favorite verses starts with the second verse in the first chapter of Proverbs that goes:

"For attaining wisdom and discipline; for understanding words of insight; for acquiring a disciplined and prudent life, doing what is right and just and fair; for giving prudence to the simple, knowledge and discretion to the young-let the wise listen and add to their learning, and let the discerning get guidance- for understanding proverbs and parables, the sayings and riddles of the wise. The fear of the LORD is the beginning of knowledge, but fools despise wisdom and discipline."

"That's a true statement." Chase said as he looked away from Abednego, distracted by a beautiful woman coming out of the credit union next to the grocery story. "There are a lot of fools out here."

"And you're one of them!" NuTameka shouted as she opened the door. "You like what you see Chase! I'm in the store buying all of the stuff for Bible study and you're over here looking at some girl's breast!"

"I wasn't looking at her breast," Chase struggled to get the lie out of his mouth. "I was listening to Abednego speak the word."

"Forget you Chase!" NuTameka shouted as she opened the door and pulled Chase out of the car. "Drive us home so we can study the Word and try to save some souls."

"You always catch an attitude," Chase whined as NuTameka shoved the keys into his bare chest.

"And now it's my turn. Drive!"

"Always poppin' off at the mouth, you get on my nerves with that." Chase was carrying on a conversation with himself as Abednego continued looking at them go back and forth. He couldn't believe that Chase and NuTameka were carrying on the way that they were. NuTameka got into the back seat and put the seatbelt on. She threw a package and some other stuff up to the front passenger seat of the car, further infuriating Chase.

"Throw something else up here!" He shouted.

"I'm gonna throw you out this car!"

"I ain't going nowhere." Without warning, Chase sped out of the parking lot and ran the red light getting onto the street, causing the car in the right of way to swerve and everyone else to honk their horns. Fortunately, everyone else was okay. Chase acted as if the other drivers were at fault and started spewing some derogatory words and hand gestures at them.

NuTameka rolled her eyes. "This ain't NASCAR."

"Shut up," Chase yelled and proceeded to say some profane things to her. Before NuTameka could finish her thought, she heard a rapper spitting some freaky verses over the radio. NuTameka shook her head and balled her fist. Abednego was starting to wish that he didn't agree to meet up with Chase and NuTameka cause this was more drama than he wanted to be bothered with.   He was down for doing ministry with other people, praying for them, visiting the sick and that type of thing, but he normally avoided drama at all costs.

NuTameka took the Bible from Abednego's lap and began reading some passages on her own. Abednego looked out of the window, partially in hopes that they wouldn't get pulled over by the police.

When the car came to a complete stop, NuTameka was deep into the Word and Abednego noticed that they didn't live in the hood liked they acted like they did; Chase and NuTameka actually lived in a community full of adjacent town homes. They appeared small as four of them lined side by side in the building. The buildings were off white, each home having a black door for the entry. Smaller bushes were at the right of each step that led into the door.

"Some of the people are already here so just make yourself at home." Chase said after he turned down the radio and put the car in park. Once everybody was out of the car, they headed into the town home.

"Everybody take your shoes off," NuTameka turned around and put her hands on Abednego chest. She looked him in his eyes and smiled. "I just cleaned these floors the other day and I don't want them getting messed up."

The town home had a new house smell mixed with the vanilla incense that had to have been burning before Chase and NuTameka left. Abednego was impressed with the mahogany and sandalwood furniture and the Dominican art that was hanging all over the house. Chase turned on the HDTV and had a seat on the couch. Scenes from the latest gospel play were blaring from the screen and the subtle conversations had come to a halt as the play grabbed everyone's attention. Abednego saw two other young men and three females sitting around the television in the living room.

"You have to forgive my husband, he is so rude," NuTameka said as she waltzed in front of the television. Abednego did a double take because this was the first time she heard him refer to him as her husband. Abednego tried to discretely look back and forth to see if either of them had been wearing their wedding bands. "You want something to drink? We got cranberry juice, some fruit juice smoothies and some red Kool-Aid."

"Nah, I'm good, but thanks." Abednego replied as she walked away and then focused on the play. Abednego looked at the group and knew that working with Chase and NuTameka was going to be challenge. Once NuTameka arrived with the drinks for everyone else, Chase turned off the television and Abednego introduced himself to everyone, after a short prayer, he led the group in Bible study, remember to keep his judgments of others at bay and to step aside so that the Lord and Savior could work towards a bigger goal.

CHAPTER TWELVE

CHASE

I want you to meet me on 10th and Patterson," Abednego told Chase a few days after the Bible study.

Chase looked at the phone like it was crazy. He knew that 10th and Patterson was notorious for being a spot where many homeless shelters were and the last thing he wanted was to be around some beggars. "Do we gotta meet there?"

"Yes, we do." Chase was surprised at how firm Abednego was with him. He decided not to argue with him. Chase hung up the phone and decided that he would walk to the corner as opposed to drive. He didn't live that far in retrospect and he felt that the walk would do him good.

"You getting ready to go?" NuTameka asked as Chase grabbed the keys from the table and put them in his pocket.

Chase started to say something smart, but he thought better of it and shook his head. "Yes, I'm going to meet Abednego by a homeless shelter."

"Oh," Chase noticed the look of disbelief on NuTameka's face.

I'm not in the mood to start arguing with her again. Chase thought to himself. "He just called me a minute ago and asked me to meet him up there. Maybe he's going to hand out some daily devotions or something—you know he does that."

"Well if he's handing out anymore, make sure you get me a copy too."

Chase was surprised to hear NuTameka say that. Just last night, after he decided to pray, he found NuTameka repulsed to see him on his knees with his hands clasps before him and him whispering the words on his heart to the savior. In the background, Dr. Charles Stanley was giving a message and reading the scripture. Chase had wanted to address what he felt were nasty looks that he was receiving from NuTameka, but he felt compelled to read the Word with Dr. Stanley and that's what he had done.

After reflecting on the change in his wife's behavior, Chase walked out the door and made his way down Patterson Avenue to head toward 10th Street. He walked past the sign that warned not to solicit for prostitution, drugs or commit other crimes and he shook his head. Chase thought the whole sign was a joke because it appeared that nothing but prostitution, drugs and other crimes ran rampant on the street he lived on. He was determined that his neighborhood would return the way his grandparents had bragged about it's heyday in the sixties or seventies.

Chase smiled when he saw the word "repent" on one of the telephone poles.

Where would I start? He asked inwardly, halfway expecting the Spirit to pop out of nowhere and answer his question. If it weren't the sex and the adultery that he knew he and NuTameka would need to atone for, it was the lies, the stealing, the fighting—too many sins that he felt were necessary for survival—too much for him to give up and truly live for God. Even though his heart pegged for him to leave Hunks & Honies, he felt stuck. He'd applied for several jobs at many of the fast food restaurants and at the grocery stores and the only call back he got was from a lady at a small hot dog stand downtown, but even she commented on his "thug-like" appearance. Chase couldn't change who he was and what he was attracted to. And since he made in a week between the club and the private events he scheduled what some people couldn't make in a month, he found it hard to just walk away.

"Yo man, I'm over here." He heard Abednego call for him. He looked at Abednego's attire and to him, he looked just like any other brother on the street—except his pants didn't fall past his waist, they were just baggy. The Carolina blue NY hat Abednego wore was fitted and tilted downward to conceal his eyes and the Carolina blue and white stripped Polo was long enough to be mistaken for a dress if Abednego hadn't worn jeans under them. Even his Air Force Ones gave him more of a thug appeal. The only difference between what Abednego wore and what Chase had on were the grills in Chase's mouth. He'd had them since he was eighteen and the ladies and the dudes who paid for him to dance loved them. Two of the gold teeth were actually caps and he had the other mouth piece built around it.

"You must've scared away all the homeless people." Chase was sarcastic as he walked up the steps of the building. Abednego looked at him and laughed and Chase caught an attitude. He could feel himself getting mad and even tempted to punch Abednego in his grill.

"You thought this was a homeless shelter?" Abednego asked. Chase just nodded his head. "Naw, man, my bad. That was rude for me to laugh at you like that. This isn't a homeless shelter. This is a place called The Prayer Room. A lot of people mistake it for the homeless shelter because they still have some of the former shelter's insignia still on it, but come inside, I'll show you what I mean."

Chase followed Abednego in the building and was nothing short of amazed at what he saw. Richard Smallwood and his choir could be heard singing a hymn on the inside. He saw a young man who looked to be close to his age sitting on an old, green-gold vintage couch reading a paperback-bound Bible with tears streaming from his eyes.

"Celtius," Abednego called to the man. Chase watched as the man stood up a few inches above him and reached out and shook his hand. "This is Chase, the young man whom I told you called the church when he found one of *The Upper Room's* I'd left on the floor."

"Nice to meet you," a baritone voice and firm grip greeted Chase.

"Like I was saying, this is The Prayer Room. The building is actually owed by a cooperation of Methodist, Baptist, COGIC, Presbyterian, AME, Moravian and Non-Denominational churches. People come here to pray, to hear the Word when they can't make it to church on Sunday and to get out of trouble. You'll find some of the homeless men here that can't get shelter in some of the other shelters in town. You'll also find youth whose parent's can't afford daycare or after school programs. Some of the money we get from the sales of *The Upper Room* are used to keep this place going. I saw this place in Charlotte called 24/7 and I, along with a few other Christians decided to create an affiliate place here."

Chase was impressed. The lobby was well lit and white Christmas lights were strung about everywhere. There were many small booths that were created so that individuals could go inside and read the Bible or pray in peace. He looked at the Prayer wall and saw that many people asked for healing from smoking weed, sex, gluttony, being lazy—Chase couldn't believe how people felt free enough to bare their souls and to openly confess to their sins. As Chase followed Abednego and Celtius around, he saw a young man listening to one of the local Christian rapper's CD's and surprisingly, saw a recording booth where another man was doing Christian spoken word. He walked into another room where he saw a taping of Joyce Meyer in the background and a few people were listening and taking notes.

The Prayer Room was nothing short of amazing. Chase felt his Spirit being at ease and knew that he too could give up his sins and repent if he worked hard enough. Being able to come to The Prayer Room was enough motivation for him to start on the right path. At the end of the hallway was a room with a red door on it. Abednego took out a key and unlocked the door. As they stepped inside, Chase found white walls and a huge picture of a gold cross hanging from the wall.

"This is our home away from home," Abednego pointed out. "Sometimes, when one of the members of the Street Disciple Ministry meets someone who doesn't want to join Grace but wants to meet with other believers or new believers, we bring them here. We don't do it to go against the church, rather, we know that many people come from a variety of backgrounds and for some, the people in a particular church may have harmed them. So sometimes, we offer this room to those coming to know Christ and we help them find a local church home here."

"Wow," Chase let out with amazement.

"I brought you here because I wanted you to see that ministry is so much more than the four walls inside of a church. True, you have to go to a Bible-based church to get the Word and to fellowship with other believers, but I also wanted you to see the Word at work. Everyone here has come from a variety of backgrounds and they all contribute something to this ministry."

"Can the ministry help me get a job?" Chase let it slip. He hadn't mean to voice his concern so soon—he trusted Abednego and believed that the young man wouldn't do him any harm, but he'd never realized what the Lord had done and blessed him with already.

"We don't guarantee a job, but we work with the Goodwill Industries to do job trainings and we help those who dropped out of school enroll in a GED program so they can get their lives together."

Chase shook his head. He'd never thought about going back to get his GED. But at this rate the idea didn't seem too bad. "I'm interested in the GED program."

"Go ahead and have a seat, I'll get the paperwork for you."

Chase sat down and he looked at the cross. He pictured all of his burdens that he carried about abandoning his younger siblings and being unfaithful to his wife—thinking about NuTameka made him feel guilty for marrying her in the first place. They both had agreed to having an open marriage when they first met and the two of them often sought pleasure in other people but themselves, but as Chase stared at that cross, he found that he could no longer allow for his wife to sleep with any man she chose —nor could he hop in and out of any bed as he please.

A tear streamed from his eye as he realized that The Prayer Room was the perfect place that he needed to be. Chase got on his knees and repented for as many sins as he could think of and when he was finished, he graciously accepted the forms from Abednego and filled out all the information so that he could start a new life—one that would require him to keep his clothes on.

CHAPTER THIRTEEN

DONTE

verette had held on as long as he could, but the inoperable brain tumor became too much and he went on to eternal glory while Donte and the other members of the Street Disciples Ministry were passing out copies of *The Upper Room*. They said no man knew the time or the hour of Jesus coming, or when He'd come for them and just shy of his thirtieth birthday, Everette would know what that meant.

Elicia and Mrs. Edmonds had anticipated the day of his departure and had decided not to waste time laying their beloved to rest. They had surprised everyone with their decision to cremate Everette and to bury his ashes within his favorite garden park a few days after his demise and in lieu of a funeral, they requested a homegoing celebration where the pastor would preach a special sermon about taking care of God's kingdom and sing some of Everette's favorite gospel songs. They also wanted to use the time to give souls who may not have known Jesus a chance to get to know Him before their time came.

"I'm glad we did things this way." Elicia mumbled into Donte's ear as they sat on the front pew. Eugene looked on as he the well-wishers walked up to Mrs. Edmonds and Elicia and offered condolences. Mrs. Edmonds, Elicia, Donte and Eugene shook countless hands as they looked on at a big blow-up picture of Everette smiling in front of the camera. He had worn a dark gray suite with a tan button up color with a dark maroon and silver tie. Even in death, his smile lit up the room.

"I understand," Donte agreed, "this way, it's not so sad."

Eugene leaned closer to Donte and when everyone else had paid their respects, Elicia stood up and commanded everyone's attention. "I want to thank all of you for coming." She struggled to hold back the tears and Donte almost got up to help her but he saw a look in her he hadn't seen before and let her be. "We've known for a while that this time was coming and one of the blessings we've had in all of this, was that we were able to make peace with Everette—not that we had many disagreements." A smile beamed from her face when she spoke. Even beyond the lace and spotted veil, like her brother, Elicia knew how to light up a room. "My mother and I appreciate the fact that we got to honor his wishes to be buried in one of his favorite gardens and that we've used his memory to offer others a chance to renew their relationship with the Lord and to seek salvation from the one and only Jesus Christ. While I can't make anybody come to know him, I'd be happy if you did."

Elicia returned to her seat and leaned into Donte's arms for support. As Pastor Phelps began her sermon, he looked around and was surprised to see that Eve had managed to be seated in the front on the opposite aisle. He'd slowly exhaled but he trusted that Eve would not try to start no mess at someone else's funeral. A few glances here and there and Donte knew when Eugene noticed her when he started tapping his arm and waving at her. Donte saw Eve wave back and smile but once their eyes met, she immediately began to face the front.

When Pastor Phelps offered everyone an opportunity to join the church and enter into a personal relationship with Jesus, no one stood up—except the ushers who were already standing.

The service moved forward as the family was led to a reception. Mrs. Edmonds and Elicia were fixing their plates when Donte sensed Eve's presence. The smell of the jasmine and lily perfume was overpowering. Before Donte could open his lips to speak, Pastor Phelps had called for everyone to bow their heads in prayer so that the food could be blessed.

"Ms. Eve, I didn't know you knew Mr. Everette." Eugene eased in barely a second after Pastor Phelps said 'Amen', yet excited to be in her presence again. Donte looked to Eve for an answer and knew that either he wouldn't like what she had to say or that like last time, she'd avoid answering the question altogether.

"I'm glad you could come." Ms. Edmonds spoke, surprisingly calm and subdue given the circumstance. Donte was sure that Elicia had spoken to her at some point and filled her in on what was going on between he and Eve. "You're welcome to stay and spend some time with Eugene."

"No ma'am." Eve choked up. "I am sorry for your loss Ms. Edmonds and Elicia," Eve said as she looked to Elicia. "I just wanted to come and pay my respects, being that I know how important Everette and Elicia are to Eugene."

Eve gave both Ms. Edmonds and Elicia a hug before she departed, leaving the four of them flabbergasted.

"I still don't know her last name Dad." Eugene interrupted, taking Donte out of his gaze and slight frustration.

"We'll find out son, I promise." Donte spoke as he grabbed a plate and filled it with foods he knew his son would not waste. Upon sitting at the table, he grabbed a Buffalo wing, some grapes and a Monterey Jack cheese cube because that was all he could stand to eat. He watched as Ms. Edmonds and Elicia ate solemnly and quietly, barely speaking a word to each other. He bit into his piece of chicken and closed his eyes, remembering the haunting dreams he used to have about Eve being pregnant and wished he could make them go away. When he opened them, he saw Eugene picking at his food, barely nibbling on the carrot that was in his hand. Donte had decided that he wasn't going to make his son eat, but he'd take the plate home for consumption later on. He could still smell the flowery fragrance long after Eve had left, and that was enough to spoil the appetite in him too.

CHAPTER FOURTEEN

RAHLIEM

We need to talk," Rahliem heard Davon say upon entering the kitchen. Rahliem had bent down to take out the vegetarian pizza he had just baked in the oven and was getting ready to enjoy with the fruit salad. Rahliem looked at Davon unzipping his barber jacket, revealing a new navy, gray and white Sean John polo shirt and matching, navy blue baggy pants.

"Have a seat," Rahliem encouraged as he took the pizza cutter that was lying on the counter and divided the pie into eight equal slices. "How many pieces you want?"

"Two." Davon had grabbed the plates and some glasses and placed them on the table. Davon walked to the refrigerator and grabbed a bottle of store brand ginger ale and cranberry juice and mixed the two together in the glasses.

"I don't want any fruit," Davon declined when he seen Rahliem getting ready to pour him a bowl.

Rahliem brought his plate and bowl to the table. "Let's bow our head." Upon seeing Davon's head bowed he continued. "Lord, thank you for allowing Davon and I to commune as we partake in this light feast for the nourishment of our bodies and for strengthen. In all things we give thanks, Amen."

After Davon said 'Amen', Rahliem bit into his slice of pizza. He hadn't eaten anything since having a cup of dry oatmeal and some strawberry banana yogurt that he'd grabbed on the way out of the door for his community service project. Rahliem had spent time mentoring some ex-convicts who had recently completed their sentences and trying to readjust to civilian life. His return home was intended to be brief before he went to out to volunteer at the homeless shelter. Employment for Rahliem was sketchy at best because even after seven years, he'd still had a hard time holding down a steady job. In the spring, summer and fall he divided his time between doing yard work and doing light construction work he could obtain at a temp agency. During the Christmas season, he usually found work at one of the gift shops who'd benefit from the extra help during the season. When he wasn't working, he'd volunteer at different homeless shelters or food kitchens or expand his outreach ministry. Even after becoming a certified layman, all the congregations weren't so crazy about having a man who used to be in prison in front of the congregation, much less the pulpit.

"I just want to let you know I'm trying." Davon had barely touched his food and appeared to be irritated at how fast Rahliem had devoured his slice of pizza and a healthy portion of his fruit bowl. "But being who I am and fighting my urges aren't easy man." Davon exhaled. "I'm not making excuses, I'm just saying that fighting this thing isn't easy for me alright. It's not a disease, it's a thorn like Paul had."

"I know." Rahliem had finally addressed what he saw a few weeks ago upon entering Davon's room. The two of them had avoided each other except for a few run-ins at the church and the occasional moment when the two of them were together in front of MD.

"All I can ask you to do is to pray for me and trust that I'm doing my best to beat this—and to not get angry with me when my flesh gets weak."

"I wasn't angry."

"Bro, you've barely spoken to me in a few weeks—sometimes, I feel like you can handle and deal with it when it's Celtius but because it's me, you hold me to a whole other standard."

"I'm sorry you feel that way," Rahliem said as he took a sip of his drink. "I didn't realize I was treating you and him any different. You're still my brother and I love you. What you are and what you and he did, I'm moving beyond that. I have my own demons to fight and I'm definitely not in any position to stand and judge you. But at the same time, I am called to speak on what's right and what's wrong according to scripture. You know I'm the first one to point the finger at myself before I turn my hand to point at someone else."

Davon rose up from the table. He'd barely eaten any of the slices of pizza he'd placed on his plate. "I know you mean that and that in your heart that is true for you. But I always feel like you got a finger pointed at me all the time."

Davon had left before Rahliem could respond. Rahliem thought back to that late night where the animated video had woke him up and he'd struggled to get through the morning routine as the video's playback had become unbearable to him. He had wanted to call out to Davon but decided to leave his brother at peace. They'd talk again and he had faith his brother would come around.

Rahliem was finishing up washing the dishes from the vegetarian pizza and fruit salad he had for dinner when he heard a faint knock on the door. He assumed that either Celtius needed to hide out from one of his former boyfriends that was looking for him or that Calvin got put out of the house again. He was surprised at who he did see at the door.

"What's up, Vincent?"

"I'm good."

Gone was the black suit and bowtie. Vincent looked like Kanye West in his oversize sweater over a button up shirt and some baggy jeans. The oils he was wearing were strong and began to infiltrate the living room before Vincent stepped foot in the door. Vincent took a seat on the couch and Rahliem sat across from him in the love seat. In spite being a minister of a Nation of Islam mosque in the city, Vincent actually came from a family of Baptist ministers. He converted to Islam when he was incarcerated while Rahliem focused more on building his relationship with Jesus.

"I swore when we got out of prison that I wasn't going back but Craig is going to send me there real quick."

Rahliem knew he was up for a long night when Vincent mentioned Craig. His plans to work with the homeless were definitely on the back burner as he'd be doing the whole community a favor babysitting Vincent. Craig Johnson was Vincent's sister's baby daddy and boyfriend depending on what day of the week it was and how much she had been drinking. Not that she'd had an alcohol problem but a few drinks made the panties loose and Craig knew he could take advantage of that. Craig and Vincent couldn't stand each other and have had numerous fights over everything from religion to how Craig abuses and mistreats his sister. Neither one of them were strangers to county jail either, doing bids at a time, usually over something one had done to the other.

"Let me get my keys and my shoes and I'll be ready in a minute."

Rahliem knew what Vincent's request was before he uttered the words out of his mouth. Truth was Vincent couldn't afford to be making too many more trips to jail or he risked losing his mosque. And as much as Rahliem wished Vincent would come back to his Christian roots and re-join a church, any church that was about the business of Christ, he wasn't going to let Craig be the reason Vincent went back to jail either.

In no time, they were riding in Rahliem's 2004 Nissan Sentra, making their way to Patterson Avenue. Rahliem rarely drove the car as he'd preferred to walk or take the bus—Davon drove it more than he did half the time just so it wouldn't sit around. The car had been a gift from Pastor Franklin, the preceding leader of Grace United. As they rode in the car, it was getting dark outside and various people walked up and down the street. Some were looking for a temporary home and others searching for night work. Vincent touched the beaded cross that was hanging from Rahliem's rear view mirror. "When did you get this?"

"I've had it for about three months now. This lady down the street was making them and I figured I'd give her some support."

"They remind me of these rosary beads that Caryn used to have on her dresser." Caryn was Vincent's ex-fiancé before he got locked up. She stayed with him until he converted to Islam. She left him and started dating a deacon of a church in High Point.

"Yeah, they kind of do, but they looked more African to me when I first got them."

Rahliem pulled up to the house that Craig and Vanessa were sharing. Craig was just leaving and he bumped into Vincent on the way out. Whether or not it was intentional or not, Vincent was two steps from making a decision that was going to put him back in county jail. Rahliem grabbed his arm and escorted him inside the house. A little five year old boy who just finished eating cake ran up to Vincent and gave him a big hug on his leg.

"Uncle Vinnie!" Vincent's nephew yelled in excitement. The little boy looked like a miniature version of Craig. Vincent put the boy down and he noticed his sister coming out of the kitchen.

"I see you brought reinforcement," Vanessa smiled at Rahliem. He looked around her house and admired her collection of black angels and church figurines that lined the mantle. Some of which must have been recently disfigured in Vanessa and Craig's latest fiasco.

"I needed to bring someone who I knew would keep me out of trouble and keep me grounded. Besides, I have to speak at the mosque next week and I can't put them through another incident leading me behind bars. I think they've been through enough."

"I do thank you and Rahliem for coming," Vanessa said, focusing on getting her shoes on and bringing some bags from a bedroom. "I need to get Junior and get out of here."

"You want to go back to Mom's?"

Rahliem was shocked that Vincent would make that suggestion. Vincent and his parents hadn't seen eye to eye since he announced he couldn't eat pork over the slab of ribs he had been offered for dinner.

"Yeah, but call first. You know they still think they are in their twenties and expect folks to warn them of emergencies this late at night."

"You didn't call them?" Vincent responded with a little hint of frustration in his voice.

"I want to call granny and papa," Junior was making an already tense situation worse. Vanessa reluctantly left to make the call to their parents.

"I'm glad I didn't swing on that fool."

Rahliem cracked a smile. "You didn't look like you came to fight."

Vincent shook his head. "You always try to doubt my skills in the ring, playa."

"But you remembered mine, though."

Both Vincent and Rahliem cracked a smile and grinned for a minute. The last time Vincent saw Rahliem get into a fight, they both went to jail for disturbing the peace among other things.

Vanessa rushed past them and got her bags. Vincent picked up Junior and they got up and got ready to go. Rahliem took Vanessa's bag and put them in the trunk of his car. Vincent rode with Junior in the back seat, leaving on the light in the back seat so he could read to him from the book *Micky, Ticky Boo! Says Hello!* by Sabra Robinson. Listening to the two of them interact and discuss each of the characters, made the ride to Vincent and Vanessa's parents' house easier. They noticed the light on in the middle of the street and their father waiting outside of the door. Rahliem popped the trunk and Vincent got his sister's bags out. Rahliem got cut off the engine and followed the family to their house. It had been almost ten years since he had been inside the Harper household, he almost felt like a little kid again waiting on Mrs. Harper to bring out freshly made cookies and a cup of water. The Harpers were a little tired, but they were happy that their daughter and grandson were safe from harm for the night.

After making sure that Vanessa and Junior were situated, Vincent cut the trip short and he and Rahliem went back to Rahliem's place.

"Good looking out for taking me to my sister's house."

"Anytime, man, anytime. I'm going to have to go back to get Mrs. Harper to bake me a batch of cookies."

"Yeah, Mom hasn't baked any cookies in a long time."

The rest of the ride to Rahliem's house was silent. It was hard to believe that these two friends could be on two different paths spiritually. Rahliem was just happy that he got to spend another day spreading the Word of God and he hoped that God was pleased with his actions as he dealt with the new members of Street Disciples and Vincent. Before Vincent pulled out of the driveway, he said a quick prayer hoping that the young man made it home safely and he even prayed that Craig was safe and out of trouble wherever he was at. In a few hours, it would be Sunday and he knew he had to get some rest. He opened up *The Upper Room* and began to re-read the day's scripture from Matthew 7:3-4:

"And why do you look at the speck in your brother's eye, but do not consider the plank in your own eye? Or how can you say to your brother, 'Let me remove the speck from your eye'; and look, a plank is in your own eye?"

He thought of the day's lessons and quickly came up with a devotion that he may use for his sermon next week.

CHAPTER FIFTEEN

ABEDNEGO

Loud firecracker-like noises could be heard as rocks the size of golf balls burst through the cracked window of Abednego's apartment had brought the young tenant out of his slumber. He struggled to see the numbers on his digital clock, but he didn't need that to know that it was too early in the morning or too late at night depending on how you want to look at it for the street dudes to be causing all of the ruckus in the projects. After the fourth rock burst through the window and barely missed him, he instinctively ducked down. He reached under the bed for the piece he used to have in his former life but found a copy of *The Upper Room* instead. He started to curse himself for still staying in the hood after he got out of the drug game and left the hood to begin with but he remembered this was the game he needed to save young souls from and that was the whole reason he was still here. He quickly put on the khaki-colored slacks he had on just hours before and the black T-shirt that was laying on the back of the chair at the desk next to his bed.

"You aight man?" Oscar asked as they met in the hallway. Oscar stood five foot ten and a solid one hundred and seventy-six pounds with very little body fat. The way his athletic sleepwear fit on him left little to the imagination at how well defined he was. Gone were the days when the molasses-colored brother was a few pounds chubby and wanted to hang around his older brother and hustle CD's and DVD's from his backpack. After his elder brother, Orenthal, went to jail twice where he lost his life on the last trip getting into a fight, Oscar knew he needed Jesus. He knew that Orenthal had gotten saved and given his life to the Lord before everything went down and he wanted to make sure he could go to heaven to rejoin his brother someday.

Abednego let his younger cousin stay in the apartment with him to atone for not being the responsible role model his family expected him to be. Not that Orenthal was bad, but he had two years on Orenthal and a handful more on Oscar and all they ever saw him do was sling dope or talk about the money he was getting or the women he was sleeping with.

"I'm good. I'm going to see what the ruckus is about."

"Why you going to go outside with them crazy fools? They could kill you." Oscar tried his best to stop Abednego from doing what he knew he was crazy enough to do. Once Abednego grabbed his Bible and put it in his pants in front of his abs, Oscar knew arguing with him was going to be useless. For starters, Oscar never could figure out when Abednego was acting in the Spirit or when Abednego was trying to be Rambo. Secondly, this wasn't the first time Abednego woke up in the middle of the night to settle a dispute in the Carver Heights projects on Cleveland Avenue. Part of the reason he got free rent was because he could be depended on to keep the peace in this section of the hood and to decrease the number of police visits and negative publicity hitting the news or print. Abednego, for his part, liked the idea of cleaning up the hood and undoing the damage he'd helped inflict years before. Oscar went to his spot by the window and observed the two young brothers that were closer to his age fighting and throwing each other around. A small crowd had gathered to watch the affray and to get their cheap entertainment for the night. It took Abednego less than sixty seconds to get in the middle of it and force the fighters to opposite sides.

"Young brothers, why are you out in the middle of the streets fighting like you don't have no sense?"

"Man forget that…" were the only nice words one of the boys got out before a string of harsh but eloquent use of expletives and insults came out of the heart and into the ears of anyone who would listen. The other young man began proclaiming expletives on his own and pretty soon, Abednego found himself pushed and shoved amongst the young men again.

"Help me break it up." Abednego pleaded to anyone in the crowd.

"Man let them fight. You always trying to be a goody two shoes." One of the neighbors' complained and pretty soon, the whole neighborhood was in on the ruckus. Oscar knew he could no longer stay in the apartment and watch Abednego get manhandled. Even though they both were saved and brothers in Christ, the old adage held true—blood was thicker than water. He called the authorities and he went outside to try to get help for his family.

As Oscar reached the crowd, the fight had intensified. A beer bottle had been cracked against the curb and the man wielding it anxiously jumped into the crowd swinging the bottle every which way but up. Oscar decided to attend to this man first. It seemed that every time the man with the bottle moved closer to the crowd, they in turn pushed him farther away. But a determined Oscar caught up with the man and pretty soon, he and the man with the bottle were fighting too. Upon closer look Oscar realize the young man swinging the bottle could not have older than twenty-one, or even old enough to have the bottle in his hand. The French vanilla brotha wasted no time charging and swinging the bottle at Oscar, slashing his left cheek. Oscar responded by grabbing his arm and elbowing him in the face, causing him to drop the bottle where it shattered to a thousand of pieces in the streets. Oscar felt bad because he knew that Jesus would have preferred that he turn the other cheek and get it slashed too. He asked the Lord for forgiveness and said a small prayer for the young man's soul as he continued to beat the breaks off of him.

Oscar thought to look for Abednego once he was convinced that his attacker would stay put. He could not see Abednego but he could hear the three shots that were ringing through the crowd. Men jumped up and ran away like a stampede of elephants as more shots continued to be fired. Oscar looked for Abednego but failed to locate him. He did see a body on the floor and a puddle of blood near its head, but he was not close enough to see who it could be. As the crowd dispersed, the police came and Oscar still looked around for Abednego but could not find any sight of the man.

The police went to check on the victim and urged others to stay away as onlookers came to see who finally got killed in their side of the hood. Carver Heights hadn't had a dead body in almost three years and that would largely be due to Abednego moving his old crew out and instilling his own version of Martial Law—The Holy Spirit was the commander-in-chief and he being the obedient and loyal private in The Master's army. The police who had come to maintain order were armed and ready to deal with the assailant the moment they had the chance. Oscar scanned the area to see whether or not Abednego had shown up. He looked in the direction of their apartment and did not see the light on so he knew that Abednego had not made it back into the apartment. The ambulance arrived and the paramedics began to prepare the body to be picked up and placed on the gurney. As Oscar looked closer he though he seen Abednego's gold trimmed Bible laying on the floor. He walked to pick up the familiar book but was stopped by the police. He got close enough to see Abednego's face with his eyes being closed before the white sheet was placed over his head.

"Oh my God!" Oscar yelled as he ran over to where the paramedics were placing Abednego in the back of the ambulance. "That's my cousin. Can I ride with him?"

The paramedics declined his request but one of the police officers offered him a ride to the hospital after he showed identification matching what Abednego had in his wallet. Oscar hated being the one to call Shadrach and Felton with the news about their brother. Oscar took out his cell phone and scrolled down the list to find Felton's name. He pressed the "talk" button and was surprised that his call was immediately sent to voice mail. His call to Shadrach yielded the same response. Oscar called Rahliem because he knew that Rahliem would know what to do.

CHAPTER SIXTEEN

RAHLIEM & SHADRACH

Rahliem looked at the waiting room at the five members of his Street Disciples Ministry team. It was praying time for God's will to be done and Rahliem thought the prayer warriors would be ready but found them disturbed and distraught instead. Eugene kept Donte busy, crying about how he did not get any sleep and that he didn't want to go to school in the morning. The father looked beat and drained himself. Carlton on the other hand was relatively calm.

Like Rahliem, he was a former inmate and had just gotten out of prison for murder and aggravated assault and had spend most of his time adjusting to his new life and living with his younger brother, Calvin. Both were nearly identical in red and gray button up shirts and stone black jeans save for Carlton's out of style high top fade hair cut that was a throwback to Kid N Play. Calvin sat at the table playing with the wedding band on his necklace that he received from his soon to be ex-wife, Maria, who left him to be with Deacon Bilal Kodjoe of Cleveland Missionary Baptist Church across town. Neal looked like one of the hood boys Fantasia was singing and rapping about in her video. And Oscar looked the worst of all. His six fresh stitches looked as they were going to struggle to mend the gash he got from being hit with a broken Smirnoff bottle.

"I got here as soon as I could." Pastor Phelps rushed in with her husband in tow. It was unusual to see the Pastor in some jersey sweats and her hair in big yellow and blue rollers. The silky scarf she used to keep them in place glimmered and shined as she searched her purse for her medical pass. After attempting to help his wife find her medical pass in her purse, Mr. Joseph Phelps took a seat next to the group. Rahliem was surprised that he wasn't on the streets searching for who shot Abednego.

Just as Pastor had put her purse down good and made her way to the emergency room, the doctor was working his way out.

"Anyone from the Green family present?"

"I'm here," Shadrach and Deborah walked in. He commanded attention despite being a short, stocky brother at five eight, one hundred and sixty four pounds of muscle. Aside from his oak wood skin complexion, he was a dead ringer for his shorter sibling. Deborah didn't do so bad herself, with the right ambitions and a little work, she could give Alex Wek a run for her money. Her shaved, curvy head was offset by the silver earrings she wore that matched her harem of bracelets. "So what's going on Doc? How is my baby brother?"

"What is your name?" the doctor inquired.

"Shadrach Donald Green, Jr."

"Where is Felton?"

"I'd like to find out myself." Something did not sit right with Shadrach knowing that Felton was not present. Oscar had told him about the failed attempts to get in contact with him. Normally Felton would be the first on at the hospital making phone calls.

"We did everything we could to save Abednego, but he's with Jesus."

"Oh no!" The pastor gasped. She reached for Shadrach's other shoulder to provide comfort while trying to hold back her tears.

A tear streamed down Shadrach's eye as both anger and sadness rose up in him. Shadrach looked around and still no sign of Felton. He held onto to Deborah as she grieved for her brother-in-law. Oscar fell out of the chair and Rahliem and Carlton rushed to pick him up.

"What's going on?" Eugene asked Donte. He struggled with the words to educate his son and comfort Shadrach but could find none.

"My baby brother is with Jesus." Shadrach answered him instead. This was not the way he saw it, but he didn't want to do irreversible damage to such a young and impressionable mind.

"If Abed Go is with Jesus," Eugene had always struggled with pronouncing Abednego's name so he settled on Abed Go for short, "then why is everyone so sad? It's a good thing to be with Jesus."

"It is," Donte answered and wiped his tears away. "We just didn't expect him to go now."

"Oh okay," Donte picked up Eugene and decided that it would best if he took the little one home. He was beginning to ask a lot of questions and Donte did not want to burden anyone else.

"Let me get this one to bed. Shadrach, call me if you need anything."

"No problem," Shadrach hugged Donte and Eugene as they went off.

"I want to go see him." Shadrach told the doctor. Deborah tightened her grip as they followed the doctor into the room where Abednego's body was resting.

"Rahliem, you gonna be alright to speak tomorrow?" Pastor asked. "I'll be ready if you need me to."

"I gotta speak tomorrow. Abednego would have wanted that."

"Yeah."

"We still have to go into the world and make disciples. Jesus commandment doesn't stop with the death of his own."

"Amen brother," Carlton chimed in. "I know the city well enough to get around without too much help. So we have to continue to press forward."

"It's gonna be hard doing our ministry without him." Calvin said.

"I'm just glad my cousin got saved and gave his life to the Lord before someone took it away." Oscar muttered.

"Me too," Rahliem said, "me too."

Shadrach walked out of the room and there was silence. He pressed a button on his cell phone and waited on Felton to answer the other line. When he didn't get a reply, he responded, "Felton, you gotta give me a call little bro. Abednego's in trouble and we need you."

Unlike Shadrach and Abednego, Meshach Felton Green hated his Biblical name with a passion and preferred to be called by his middle name. Shadrach had wondered whether or not Felton was at Hunks and Honies, making that money to support him and his wife. Felton had done the unthinkable, he managed to turn a ho into a housewife. It would be unfair to call her that. She had been forced to sell her body by her stepfather and mother to support their crack habit and once they died off, she never found a reason to stop. But people can change and Natalie was living proof of that.

When Natalie walked into Grace United Methodist Church last year, many of the churches patrons could not see past the mocha colored Halle Berry look a like. Natalie did not let that deter her, she was there for one thing and one thing only, to meet with Jesus and to get her life right with God. Pastor Phelps recognized the sincerity in her eyes and in her heart and was the first to embrace her with open arms.

Ever since then, she's worked tirelessly to prove to the congregation and everyone else that she wasn't going to sell her goodies no more. She'd drag Felton to church some Sundays hoping she could bring him back to the Christian roots his parents had instilled in their children before they left the nest. Felton would come to Grace most Sundays more so to appease his wife or to keep Abednego from nagging at him than to try to receive a blessing from God. He didn't believe in all of that. He'd go along with it all for appearances sake so that his wife wouldn't be embarrassed and so that she could look good, but as soon as the church doors opened at the end of service, Felton was fielding phone calls from the men and women who got great pleasure touching and teasing his body. And they'd pay top dollar for that privilege too. As far as Felton was concerned, if the price were right and if he knew that Natalie wouldn't find out, the vows could be "put aside" as well.

Shadrach called the group together so that he could lead them in prayer before they separated one from another.

"Dear Lord. I pray for strength, courage, wisdom and the ability to accept that Abednego is no longer with us. I know my baby brother, as is our mother and father are being properly cared for in your loving arms. Watch over Felton and Natalie for I do not know where they are and please keep them out of harm's way. I ask that you grant my friends and prayer partners traveling mercy as they make their way home. Father, I ask for continued strength as these Street Disciples go out into the field and work to bring our wayward sheep back home. But most importantly Lord, I forgive whoever may be responsible for Abednego's murder and have mercy upon them, for they know not what they have done. In all these and other blessings, I pray in your son Jesus' name, Amen."

"Amen." The chorus followed by hugs as the group promised to meet up and help with plans for Abednego's home going services. And with a straight face Shadrach called out silently to Felton asking where he could be.

CHAPTER SEVENTEEN

FELTON

anging three feet off the ground and bound by a thick rope that was used to raise and lower his body off the ground, Felton was wheezing and coughing through the duct tape that sealed his mouth shut. The fire in his body had him feeling like he was in Hell and this torture was just the beginning of his atoning for his earthly sins. His feet were bound by another rope and his near naked body, save for some shear boxer briefs that he put on for the performance he was now three hours late to, continued to absorb the numerous and infrequent body blows by two muscular men using his abs and ribs as a punching bag. His breathing pattern was irregular and troubled, and the forced wheezing sounding more in tune with an unapologetic and haunting late nineties rap melody than a human being breathing.

Felton had wanted to take a leak, but there was no way he was going to give his captors the satisfaction of seeing him loose control of his bodily functions. His eyes were sore and badly abused from the fight he put up when he was abducted in his dressing room minutes before he was to go on stage. His fake army fatigues had been stripped off his body on the orders of their boss, who wanted to enjoy him and all of his splendor upon her return. Through the sheer stockings he could barely identify his wife sitting in the chair approximately twenty feet to his right.

He wanted to twist and look her so that he could get at least one last look at her if his final night on earth had to be tonight.

Natalie wasn't doing too badly, all things considered. While the goons were lusting at her exposed breast; touching and feeling on her and getting their rocks off, Natalie was just thankful that their boss had enough decency to allow her to keep her black shear Victoria's Secret panties on. She repeatedly sang The Lord's Prayer just as members of the congregation at Grace United Methodist Church had taught her. As she continued to concentrate on the Word and the Lord, it seemed the goons were going to have their way with her body. She had struggled to learn Psalms Twenty-three by heart but she continued to say it in her mind as it sounded right to her. She believed her attempt would count and God would forgive her for the error as she continued to hone her effort to honor and praise her Lord in this degrading and humiliating circumstance. Her hands were behind her back and each of her legs was attached to a leg on the chair. She looked at her husband and didn't know whether she envied him or not for being blind folded. She felt love and disdained for Felton at the same time and she never thought that could be possible.

Natalie looked down and saw this sexually charged young man who barely had any meat on his bones kneeling between her and inhaling her feminine scent. His smooth caramel pretty boy looks that she normally would have found handsome quickly began to turn ugly as he started doing magic tricks and unmentionables with his tongue as if he were applying for the male lead for Lil' Kim's "How Many Licks" video. The man began to gyrate and twerk his body on the body on the floor, mocking her husband's dance routines as his hands began work his way up her legs with his hands. She wanted to exhale, but couldn't blow out the breathe from her mouth so she settled on relieving her frustrations through her nose, involuntarily raising her breast higher and drawing six pairs of eyes greedily hungering and desiring for a taste of her C cups.

"Fall back Paris—let the ho breathe!" This big ape looking buffoon grabbed the young man by waist of his pants and flung him back. Paris quickly jumped back and straightened himself out. Natalie turned to the left and looked past the goon on that side to see copies of popular contemporary and classic street lit books that were stacked on the table. She questioned when her captor found time to read the books that kept the streets buzzing and wondered which of the prominent street lit authors concocted this scene her and her husband were going through or if it was a twisted version of all of their imaginations. At either rate, she wanted to die already and for this all to be over with. She turned to her right and could smell some crazy brew being cooked in the background and wondered how all of them survived on taking its foul and atrocious smell that reminded her of chitterlings and fish.

Another goon decided to take his turn practicing his blows on Felton's human punching back. This goon had bad aim as he hit Felton's knees and a blow landed on his precious jewels between his legs. Natalie flinched and jerked back as Felton tried, but was unable to wince in pain. She could hear him groan as loud as he could and any resentment she had towards him and Abednego for being in this situation went away.

A thick, hardback version of a newly released street novel flew in the air and landed square in the goon's back, causing him to fall back and writher in pain.

"What are y'all doing?" the woman whose voice was came from the direction in which the book flown had begun come into the light. Her voice bared a striking resemblance to Foxy Brown as she yelled as she made her presence felt in the room. The goons straighten up immediately. "And I better not have lost my page because I was just getting to the good part!"

The red haired, French mocha sister whose body resembled singer Janet Jackson's in the video "If" was prettier than Natalie had ever imagined. Her face didn't reveal her age, although it had been rumored through most of her life that the woman was at least in her seventies or eighties because she was rumored to be a witch who had sex with young men to keep her vitality. Even Natalie couldn't deny that the chick was fine and her face matched the timeless beautify of actress Vivica A. Fox.

The woman walked over to Felton's body.

"Lower it some," she commanded and one could see Felton's feet continue to point downward as if he were trying to either meet the ground or guess how high he was up. Once he was about two feet from the ground, she reached out and tore his underwear off his body. She grabbed his manhood and inspected his machinery to make sure there were no bruises and to admire its respectable splendor. She fondled it to see if it would come alive and once she saw for herself what the hype was all about, she smiled inwardly to herself before facing her foot soldiers.

"I told you punks to scare them, not hurt them!" she yelled to the group of men who stood in front of her with their hands down, scared to face their leader. They were lined up side by side in height order and eagerly awaited her next command. The woman walked up to Paris, who was in the middle of the line and smacked the taste out of his mouth. Paris flinched, winced and quickly jumped back for fear of being attached again. Don't let the woman fool you, she's notorious for hitting like a man and could swing with the best of them. "I saw what you did you little pervert and the next time I see that again I'm gonna cut your jewels off, understand me?!"

"Yes Madame Mulah," Paris whimpered, looked away and flinched for fear that he was going to get struck again.

Madame Mulah got in the young man's face, "Did I tell you speak dip stick?"

Paris started to open his lips to say no but quickly thought better of it and shook his head to indicate a negative response. She inspected each of her goons and Felton watched her backside move like a perfect tidal wave as she went to snatch off the tape from Natalie's lips and quickly backhanded her across the face. Just think, when he was younger, Madame Mulah was one of the women he spent lonely nights and hard mornings fantasizing and to think that she was just as beautiful now than she was fifteen years ago.

Natalie quickly brought her face to Madame Mulah's attention. "Well thank you for not allowing them to rape me."

"No need to thank me yet." Madame Mulah was quick with her response. She snapped her fingers twice and a wheel cart with a TV/VCR combo was brought in. Madame Mulah pressed play and a video showing Felton erotically dancing in a mixed crowd of men and women in a private house party broadcast on the screen. The birthday boy who was dancing in front of him was obviously enjoying the birthday surprise his coworkers and friends had given to him a few days ago. Felton turned his head away from the screen while Natalie grilled him. "Funny isn't it?"

Natalie's failure to respond only served to tick Madame Mulah off as she got in her face. "Sorry I had to do this to you, but I felt you needed to know how your man *really* makes his money. We got to watch out for those freaks."

"The only one who is a freak is you!" Natalie spat as she rolled her eyes and put on her game face and to give off the appearance that she wasn't scared or Madame Mulah or her other captors. Madame Mulah smiled as she moved closer to her.

"Tsk. Tsk. Tsk. Look missy!" Madame Mulah grabbed Natalie's chin so they could meet face to face. The smell of cannabis reeked from her lips as Madame Mulah could tell the last of her high was leaving her. "I may be a freak to you but your husband doesn't seem to know what side he's on, does he?"

They both turned to look at Felton whose head was down and did not want to address either of the ladies at this point. "It's not like he's sleeping with him, it's just a dance." Natalie's attempt at a defense was weakened because she was still disgusted at what she saw on the video.

Madame Mulah wanted to slap Natalie again for being so silly but decided against it. "How noble of you to stand by your man. Next time, don't take Dolly Parton's advice go by what you see. If the dance is what you really want to believe Natalie it was go ahead. What are those vows? Oh yes, 'for better or worse, for richer or poorer.' I'm glad you believe that."

"What do you want from us?"

"Where do these questions come from, a Lifetime movie or something?" Madame Mulah quizzed but quickly responded before Natalie could give an answer. "I want my money and you and your "man" there, are going to work off Abednego's debt for me. I fronted that bastard one million dollars so he could be the King of the Tre-4 but instead of paying me back, he thought he could toss me aside and forget about me and thought that because I was a woman, he could discard me and use me."

"Abednego got saved and gave his life to God. He doesn't live that lifestyle anymore."

"You're right, he doesn't live."

The goon near the television turned the volume up so they could hear Abednego trying to break up the confrontation being staged by the goons earlier that night. Another goon lowered Felton to the ground and snatched off the stockings from his eyes and gets a cheap shot in the head as they watch the melee that ends with Abednego getting shot and falling on the ground, taking his last breath.

Felton yelled and fell to his knees and the two goons quickly picked him up and raised him from the ground.

"Abednego!" Natalie yelled in horror after seeing her brother-in-law murdered in cold blood.

"Uh—Abednego can't hear you!" Madame Mulah sneered and as she shouted at Natalie. "The dead can't hear you so he can't help you come up with the money. But this is what you are going to do. You are going to go on Patterson Avenue, Cleveland Avenue, Northwest Boulevard and any other street that you think you can shake that tail at and you are going to get my million dollars.

"And that sorry bastard that you call a husband," Madame turned Natalie's head so they both look at Felton, still trying to avoid facing them, "he's gonna dance at every party, strip club and if necessary, give up that booty and he's gonna give me a million dollars too."

"Two million dollars?" Natalie was astonished. She quickly tried to calculate in her head how they could come up with two million dollars and how Abednego borrowed that much money and not mentioned a word about owing it, or paying it back.

"See, I knew letting you live wasn't a bad decision on my part. His million plus your million equals two million for me. For all the years I let that punk backslide and duck and dodge me, I should ask for four. But I pride myself on being a generous woman. I figure I could make more money selling y'alls assets than I could if y'all were six feet under. I know you got property and that Abednego's invested wisely and with no parents or children involved, half of whatever Abednego got go to Felton anyway. That should be a down payment." Madame Mulah slapped her again just because she felt like it and added.

"And you skeezers got thirty days to come up with the rest of money. And y'all not getting no grace period. And whatever you do, don't run out of town, call the police, ask for offerings at that sorry ass church of yours either or else you not going to like what I'm going to do in Jesus name. Got that?"

Natalie shook her head yes because she did not want to sass the lady and make her more mad then she already was.

"Put them in the van and take them to their church," Madame Mulah ordered her goons around, "they ought to be able to feed and clothe the homeless there. And Paris," she turned her attention to her freakiest goon. "Go pick up my book and my book mark better be in the page I left it at. If it's not, I'm going to put on a freak show for you—but I'm the kind of dominatrix that doesn't play nice—if you know what I mean."

While Paris followed his boss's instruction, the goons let Felton and Natalie loose and they willingly followed them out into the sunlight and prepared for the embarrassment they were soon to face.

CHAPTER EIGHTEEN

RAHLIEM

"Jesus is love—" Rahliem wanted to go on but found himself getting choked up as he glanced at the various members of the congregation when it finally hit him that Abednego was missing. They had just got done weeping and sending prayers for Abednego's family, traveling mercy for Felton and Natalie, wherever they were. They also asked for mercy and forgiveness for Abednego's murderers and for peace and understanding at Carver Heights, which just experienced another murder within twenty four hours after Abednego's death. Jesus was love and regardless of the death of Abednego or the sudden disappearance of Felton and Natalie, everyone in the church needed love.

Rahliem looked out into the crowd and was happy to see Shadrach and Deborah in their usual spot in the middle of the congregation and he smiled. Deborah was leaning on Shadrach's shoulder, while he fought hard to hold back the tears he was bound to shed when he memorialized his brother in this very church. Rahliem also searched the crowds for Felton and Natalie, hoping and praying that somehow, they would make their way to church this morning.

When Rahliem finished, he gave the congregation a few minutes to continue to give thanks and praises to the Lord and Savior and then he began his sermon. It hit him that Abednego would never see him become a pastor, get married or even grow old in ministry together. "Jesus is love," Rahliem started again, "and I love Jesus."

"Amen." The congregation shouted and he gave the people more time to profess their love for Jesus. He needed the time to get himself together so he could move forward with the word he knew that the congregation needed to hear.

"Everyone take out your swords and turn to the Book of John, chapter twenty-one, verses fifteen to seventeen. When you've found it in your Bibles say Amen; if you don't have it say wait a minute."

A mixture of responses prompted Rahliem to give the congregation time to find the scriptures that inspired his sermon on love. He looked into the crowd again and seen a nice-looking young lady with bob length hair. Her cinnamon-colored skin highlighting her babyface features were sure to light up the room: they sure knew how to light up his world. Unbeknownst to most of the congregation and even those in his Street Disciples Ministry, Rahliem and the lady known to the world as Faith Petree had been dating for a few months. She had graduated from Gilbert State University near A&T a few years ago and now she was a tax analyst for one of the financial firms in Winston-Salem. She gave him a wink as he confidently stepped aside and let the God in him do his thing.

"And the verse reads, 'When they had finished breakfast, Jesus said to Simon Peter, 'Simon son of John, do you love me more than these?' He said to him, "Yes, Lord; you know that I love you." Jesus said to him, 'Feed my lambs.' A second time he said to him, 'Simon son of John, do you love me?' He said to him, "Yes, Lord; you know that I love you." Jesus said to him, 'Tend my sheep.' He said to him the third time, 'Simon son of John, do you love me?' Peter felt hurt because he said to him the third time, 'Do you love me?' And he said to him, "Lord, you know everything; you know that I love you." Jesus said to him, 'Feed my sheep.'

And these words bring to mind the commandment Jesus has called for us in Matthew 28:19-20 in which he said 'Go therefore and make disciples of all nations, baptizing them in the name of the Father and of the Son and of the Holy Spirit, [20]and teaching them to obey everything that I have commanded you. And remember, I am with you always, to the end of the age.'

And in Luke he says 'Go into all the world and proclaim the good news to the whole creation. The one who believes and is baptized will be saved; but the one who does not believe will be condemned. And these signs will accompany those who believe: by using my name they will cast out demons; they will speak in new tongues; they will pick up snakes in their hands,[*] and if they drink any deadly thing, it will not hurt them; they will lay their hands on the sick, and they will recover.' So then the Lord Jesus, after he had spoken to them, was taken up into heaven and sat down at the right hand of God. And they went out and proclaimed the good news everywhere, while the Lord worked with them and confirmed the message by the signs that accompanied it.' Are you with me?"

The congregation confirms with approval and praise, having been familiar the passages.

"In two days church family, if it's the Lord's will, we will be back here for a homegoing celebration, in honor of God's faithful servant who lived the last days of his life, doing what the Lord called for him to do. A service he did out of love.

"In two days we, Grace United Methodist Church, will have the opportunity to welcome some of Abednego's former customers and former enemies he left behind when he left behind the occupation of slinging dope and picked up a Bible and went back into the very communities he almost destroyed and began to repair them. Those who refused Abednego's call to join the Body of Christ when Abednego's was alive have some of the best news in the world and they don't know about it. They have another chance to get their lives together and get right with God. A chance for us to show them, not just tell them the meaning of God's love.

"In two days we are not going to cry, we are celebrate this thing called life—we only get one so why spend it in mourning?

Yes, He told us through Job that because we who are born of woman that our days would be short and full of trouble. But in the morning, whenever the sunrises, we are not supposed worry and fret over our lives, our finances, our spouses, our children. We are supposed to wake up each and every morning and do what the Lord would have us do. I bet if more of us were on our jobs we wouldn't be concerned with what's going on in the world now.

"Now I know it's easier said than done, but I'm only going to repeat what I heard another pastor said, what I've only read Paul say and what Jesus has said in many ways. We have our talents, our gifts we are supposed to using to edify this kingdom of God. All of us have assignments and regardless of our talents, we all have a common assignment, which is to go out into the world and gather all of his lost sheep and bring them back home. Go out into the world and show the people who are on that wide and confusing path that keeps turning them around in circles, what the straight and narrow path looks and how simple and fulfilling it can be.

"When Jesus asked Peter if he loved him, he didn't just mean the love we all are supposed to have for one another. He was asking Peter if he loved him enough to continue the work that he was going to be leaving behind. I'm sure when Jesus asked him, he looked past the fact that he knew that this same Peter would deny him three times and showed him in his mercy that he knew he could forgive him with because Peter's whole heart to love and serve him was not shattered by what would become only a brief moment of betrayal in the grand scheme of things."

This was not the sermon that Rahliem had written for this occasion. Rahliem was being obedient to a bigger calling. It's been said that God has a way of getting the message He wants out for the people whom are meant to hear it. For Rahliem, it was a relief because he could do what the Lord would have him to do and not be in mourning of the fact that this was the first Sunday and the first sermon without his fallen friend.

"Jesus!" Rahliem called out as he was beginning to continue with the message he was sent to deliver. Before the next words could come out of his mouth, a crash was heard in the fellowship hall. For a brief second Rahliem had wondered if the Man Himself was making his appearance but knew immediately to shake the devil's thoughts off. The ushers had already dispatched into the fellowship hall and soon, members of the congregation had followed suite.

Rahliem and Pastor Phelps were able to move toward the gathering of two people who appeared to be nude who were lying in pain in the center of the floor. Rahliem took off his choir robe and handed it to the lady, who quickly put it on in an attempt to be presentable while another member of the choir quickly did the same for the young man. Rahliem recognized Felton and Natalie even though their faces were bruised and scuffed up.

"Welcome to Grace United Methodist Church." Rahliem welcomed the two people who crashed his sermon. He reached his hand for Natalie to help her up and then to help Felton. "And this, my church family, is how we appropriately welcome people into the church. We clothe them, we feed them, and without judgment we share the good news of God. Amen."

"Amen."

Pastor Phelps stood in between Felton and Natalie and called for the congregation to bow their heads in prayers. She thanked God for Felton and Natalie's safe return and that they were returned to church, no less. She prayed for healing in their bodies and that the Lord would return their strength in due time. She also prayed for their families and the families of those who may have chosen to take their vengeance out on these two.

By time Pastor Phelps finished her prayer, the police began working their way to the center of the congregation, so they all could find out what had just happened.

CHAPTER NINETEEN

FELTON

Most people who heard Kirk Franklin's "Looking for You" blasting out of the speakers, be it in a youth group get together or with a thumping bass line from a car passing by, the listener was greeted with instant happiness. Instead, the men of the Street Disciples Ministry were looking for a "Hero." The usually upbeat group of men who competed with the Nation of Islam to spread the news were stoic at best. Baby blue caps were tilted low, mainly to conceal the tears than to provide shelter from the sun. Baby blue button up shirts with dark blue ties and cream colored slacks were not the usual dress attire for the ministry who were inspired to "keep it street."

By now everyone had heard of or had read how Abednego lost his life a few days ago and in addition to picking up their copies of *The Upper Room* they were offering their condolences. Even the Nation were paying their respects and helping collect money for his burial and a scholarship that would be given in his honor.

Felton and Natalie had survived Madame Mulah, being publicly humiliated at their church and hours of questioning of how they got into the predicament they were in by the Winston-Salem Police Department. They were posted up under a white tent, glasses covering their facial bruising with fish, fries and carbonated fruit drinks filling up their bellies. Shadrach and Deborah were at the opposite end of the table trying to enjoy their meal. Today was the first day the siblings had seen each other since being dropped off at church.

"What happened to your face?" Deborah questioned Natalie as she noticed the blackberry ring around her sister-in-law's eye. She knew that under the right circumstances that Felton could be a dangerous man, but she never thought he'd lift a finger to touch his wife. Felton didn't look any better with his normally luscious lips looking more deformed like a liposuction injection gone wrong.

"I don't want to talk about that—" Shadrach kicked Felton under the table before Felton had a chance to finish.

"You got to watch your language around here young blood." Elijah looked away from his grill to address Felton. He was taking fish off of the grill to be prepared for sandwiches and dinners. Elijah wasn't about to allow Felton or anyone else use foul language in his presence no matter what the circumstance.

"My bad." Felton half way rolled his eyes and looked away. Shadrach chose to ignore his young brother's behavior. "We got into a little altercation a few days ago and things didn't end so well for us."

"Do you know who did this to you?"

Felton and Natalie continued to eat as if they were on mute. Natalie had seen one of Madame Mulah's goons and had subtly hipped her husband to him. Natalie knew that in a few hours, she would have to leave her safe and humble surroundings and return to her night life on the streets. A million was a lot to come up with on such a short amount of time and hearing Lil' Wayne rap about it over and over again sounded like torture. Felton must have felt the same way because he got up and packaged his food and she followed suit.

"We'll handle it bro," he finally responded so he wouldn't leave his brother hanging.

"If you need anything."

"Bruh, don't worry about us. We'll see you tomorrow."

Shadrach and Deborah watched with wonder at how fast Felton and Natalie got up and bounced. Shadrach looked around and did not see anyone or anything that may have spooked them.

"These bastards aren't gonna let us eat in peace." Felton let his anger penetrate his voice as a green Toyota Camry drove past them blasting Lil' Wayne's hit song.

"Why don't you play it cool with Shadrach?"

"Cause I don't want him snooping and following us around. I'm not a child and just like we got ourselves into this mess, we can get ourselves out of it."

"*We?*" Natalie was beyond hot. "Abednego got us into this mess from the grave and he won't even be around to help get us out."

"Why you rocking on my brother like that?" Felton grabbed Natalie by the arm. She gasped and looked at her husband surprisingly because he had never manhandled her before. "He didn't know that old witch was gonna come for him."

"But how do you explain the fact that he owes her a mil?"

"She probably lying," Felton said with conviction and faced her to emphasize his point. "Let's think about it for a minute. Who do you know let someone ride on a million dollar debt for two years?" Felton referred to the amount of time Abednego's been saved and living his life as a changed man.

"He's probably *cost* her a million in two years but he probably never borrowed money from her. I don't buy that just like I don't believe she's really a witch. I think she's just a mean and hateful old broad that needs to find a man that wants to screw her."

"Felton!" shocked but not surprised as Felton's use of vulgarity. "Her goons are probably around here somewhere."

"Don't *Felton* me. I wish she were here without her goons, I'd tell her to go eat a big fatty."

Natalie started to protest and then a thought crossed her mind. "I wonder how much of our debt she'd be willing to knock off if you gave her some?"

"What?" If Felton had been swallowing drink, he'd probably choke. Just the thought of what Natalie just said made him wish for the kind of drink they don't serve on Sundays, even though he did consider it for a second. "Naw. To hell with that. We stick with the original plan. First, we find out what Abednego left in his will because I know he put one together. I know Abednego gave most of his drug money away to charities and stuff but he got some clean money from some films he did and from the restaurant he invested in when he was eighteen, so I know he got some money with that. That's the only reason he didn't have to worry about working is because before he turned to drugs, he used his mind to flip money on the stock market making wise trades and stuff rolling with them white kids when he was younger.

After we find out what he got, then we worry about selling our stuff. The cars can go first cause that's at least twenty stacks between the three of them. Then the electronics and the jewelry can go. We'll sell some of our other stuff on eBay and have a garage sell and as a last resort, we'll hook for the rest."

"What about the condo?"

"What about it?"

"It's paid for right?"

"You have any idea how long it's going to take for us to get rid of that thing in this economy? Besides, where would we stay?"

"We'll figure something out."

"Yeah, 'cause we got to be able to do this and not hip Shadrach to what's going on. Not saying she won't come for them but we got a shot at making this go our way if we stick to the plan."

Natalie exhaled but she continued the walk to the bus stop. Once there, she sat on the bench and looked back at the tent where Elijah was still serving fish and the Street Disciples were still passing out daily devotions. A part of her wanted to let them in on what's going on but another part of her would feel guilty if something were to happen to one of them on the account of helping her out. She prayed to God asking for direction but she hasn't heard a word from Him yet. She didn't want to give up but for every day her prayers went unanswered, she struggled to keep her faith.

CHAPTER TWENTY

RAHLIEM

The Carolina blue casket adorned with flowers sat still as the congregation joined the soloist in her rendition of "The Lord's Prayer." The song brought tears to Rahliem's eyes as he was briefly reminded of the day in which he was baptized.

Pastor had preached the typical funeral sermon about how earth wasn't our home and how everyone had to take an account of how they lived their lives and if they fulfilled their assignments in accordance to the Master's will.

"And we don't know when our time is coming Saints, but it's coming." Rahliem couldn't concentrate on what the pastor was saying. He knew she was encouraging many of the twelve hundred people who had come to pay their respects, as well as the few hundred who were listening via speakers in the fellowship hall of Faith Everlasting Baptist Church, who had been kind enough to lend them their space on such short notice, to get their lives right with God. He had heard the sermon preached many times before, but he'd never thought it would be at a funeral for a guy only a few years younger than him. Even though Rahliem always knew and understood that his earthly place was not his final resting place, he'd always thought he'd stay for a while doing God's work.

"The doors of the church are now opened," Pastor Phelps continued in closing the service, "and I want to give you an opportunity to join our church. I'm not talking about practicing a religion, but joining a relationship with the one who can help you deal with your trials and tribulations. The One who will forgive you for lying on your taxes so you can get an extra few hundred dollars. The One who will still welcome you with open arms even if you are just getting out of bed with your best friends' husband. The One who will go through withdrawal of a drug addiction *with you*, so you can be clean and not have to walk that valley. I'm talking about the One who will accept you if need to come back to God's house after giving the world *another* try. God's house is not a mansion for the holy rollers but a place of healing for the whore and the homosexual, the child molester, the liar, the gossiper, the abuser and the abused, the murderer. God's house, in the name of our Lord and Savior Jesus Christ, is for you.

I know this is normally not how a pastor asks people to join his or her church, but I'm asking you to begin a relationship with Him. There is no way we can call this a home going celebration for Abednego Franklin Green if I didn't do as he would have done and invited you to know our Lord and Savior. If you want to meet him, would you come?"

The funeral directors and the pall bearers moved Abednego's body to the side as a few people began to make their way to the pastor. Rahliem always knew that God was behind Pastor Phelps' uncanny ability to draw people to the Lord. He got up and began to help the pastor with the newly converted Christians who migrated their way to the front. As lay leader and along with Deborah, a member of the welcoming committee, they began to collect the names and addresses, along with explaining how to become saved as each new convert expressed their love for Jesus, the choir sang uplifting church melodies like "I Know the Lord Is Blessing Me" and "Joyful, Joyful."

Shadrach continued to stare at the casket, still having a hard time taking in the fact that his youngest brother, who looked like he was a sleeping angel, was really going before him. Felton looked at the fifteen people who were with the pastor being welcomed into the church and scowled. The Spirit had been nudging and pleading with the man to get up there and Felton just wished that It would leave him alone. This wasn't the first time the Spirit had tried to stir up something within Felton to get him to do His will. He had urged Felton on his wedding day and seven days thereafter, He'd urged him every time he set foot into the clubs and when he went to special parties. He'd try to get him to support Abednego in his last days passing out copies *The Upper Room* but Felton would purposely dodge the corner of New Walkertown Road and Dr. Martin Luther King Jr. Drive just so he wouldn't have to run into the men or Him. In his own way, Felton knew God was calling him but right now, he didn't want to be bothered with Him, he just wanted to mourn his brother in peace.

At the end of the funeral service and under the direction of the funeral director, Rahliem, Donte, Carlton, Calvin, Ezekiel and Oscar rolled the closed casket carrying Abednego's body and walked to the motorcade so that they could drive the body to the final resting place. Kirk Franklin's "Hero" had been blasting in one of the SUV's sitting in the churches' parking lot. Rahliem looked around and was surprised at the number of people who knew the words to the song. It had been a favorite for Abednego and his favorite name for the Lord and Savior. Tears streamed down his face as he thought about some of the people who had come to know Jesus through Abednego's being obedient to the word. As the body was being place in the motorcade, his eyes had made contact with Faith and for a brief moment she smiled. He looked at Donte, who still looked sad and slightly angry. The rest of the men in his ministry group were noticeably solemn and silent, a far cry from the joyous and exciting group of men they had come to be.

CHAPTER TWENTY-ONE

DONTE

It seems we always meet up at funerals." Eve's subtle appearance at Abednego's burial site had thrown Donte for a loop. He was one of the few who had chosen to watch the men shovel dirt on Abednego's casket and watch the burial. He had made peace over their small rivalry years ago and he had been praying to the Lord about Felton's soul and Shadrach's courage as they led their family in seeking the peace that only God could give.

"Where is Eugene?"

"Eugene is with Elicia and Mrs. Edmonds." Donte said as he continued to watch the dirt as it announced its landing on Abednego's burial spot. He didn't even lift his eyes in her direction, not wanting to face her for fear he'd be tempted to give her a piece of his mind. "They had chosen to come to the wake and we agreed that it would be best if Eugene not have to attend the funeral."

"Oh." Eve was shocked as she moved closer to him. She had wanted to reach out to him and touch him, feel his body against hers as they had done years ago. She'd begun to regret kicking him out of his own bed, wishing she could show him what she'd added to the tattoo of her name that was on her breast. "When am I going to get to see Eugene again?"

"When you can tell him what your last name is—by the way, what is it?"

"Lopez. Eve Maria Lopez," Eve responded.

When Donte finally looked Eve in the eyes it appeared that the aura or confusion and discontentment that was between them had fallen. Eve began to look more like the woman he fell in lust with and that memory was about to make Donte take a trip back down memory lane. After closing his eyes and saying a soft prayer, Donte had regained control of his physical and spiritual emotions.

"Hey man, you gonna come get some food?" Donte turned to see Chase pointing towards the reception hall. Donte was surprised that he was able to avoid the strong smell of fried chicken and buttermilk biscuits that wafted in the air. Donte looked at Eve and Chase and noticed the glances they were sharing between them. He'd remembered Abednego telling him how Chase and NuTameka were new converts and were seeking spiritual guidance so that he could stay on the right path in his new walk with Christ.

"I'm going to be okay." Donte said breaking the silence and bringing the attention back to him.

"Okay cool," Chase said as he licked his lips. He was distracted by the inappropriate slit in the cleavage area of Eve's white dress that left little to the imagination. "I'll—uh—tell everyone that you are on the way."

Chase almost stumbled backward as he headed back with the other mourners. Donte felt his stomach growling and he decided that he needed to be among some witnesses—not just to eat but to keep himself from doing or saying something he would regret.

"Just call me okay," Donte said as he pulled out a business card from the card holder that was in his suit jacket. When Eve retrieved the card, a spark grew between them. "We'll work out an arrangement."

Donte wasn't convinced that something could be worked out between him and Eve, but he felt like he had owed it to himself and Eugene to try. As he walked towards the fellowship hall, he resisted the temptation to look back, as he had to pick up his son from his girlfriend's house and he didn't want any reason to keep him from getting there at a reasonable hour.

CHAPTER TWENTY-TWO

SHADRACH

The day after seeing to it that Abednego was properly buried, Shadrach decided to return to the shop. Majority of the funeral expenses had been paid and the account for the Abednego Franklin Green Scholarship Fund had been established. Shadrach wanted his life to return to normal as soon as possible and he knew he couldn't leave the barbershop unattended for long.

Shadrach's shop was located on Patterson Avenue in the North Side Shopping Center not too far from the Food Lion and other franchises and mom and pop shops in the reviving shopping center. It also wasn't too far from a popular middle school and was in walking distance of the notorious housing complex that seemed to make the news every now and then for murder, mayhem or the home of those who committed the Tre-4's most heinous crimes.

The sounds of Mary Mary's self-titled album beat the air with its banging beats and their gospel infused hip hop proclamations of the goodness of the Lord. The strong "Want Ads" loop from The Honey Cones 1970's hit single had everyone singing how they wanted to go heaven. He felt that way every time he stepped into Shadrach's, arguably the most ghetto, spiritual and urban cultured shop in the Tre-4. He loved joking around with the fellas and spreading a word or two while styling and cutting the customer's hair.

Shadrach's was special because the shop was a fulfillment of a dream he's had since he was six years old. It was a positive place for men to hang out and discuss politics. Of course, one would have to be a man to understand the dynamics of what goes on when a man sits in the chair of his favorite barber and can talk smack to everyone and anyone in the shop, and leave with the feeling like he is the king of the world. Women have often bragged about feeling the same way about their beauty salon, but for a man, the barbershop was like a rite of passage into manhood. Finding the right shop and especially the right barber can ensure that a man can survive into the next realm. Most dudes aren't gonna let just anyone cutting their hair.

Shadrach always liked coming to this "slow place" as he jokingly called it. For him, Shadrach's provided him with the opportunity of being around other intelligent black men. He loved being in a place where a man can speak his mind, cause nine times out of ten, he knew he couldn't do that at home, especially if he was married. He also got a chance to work with organizations and put Shadrach's name on projects that benefit the community. And in Winston-Salem that was okay, he didn't have to worry about crime as much as he did in his short stay in Milwaukee, where he'd lived a short while after attending Western Michigan University in Kalamazoo. He was glad that he sat out a year to get his barber license at the local barber school in Winston-Salem before he headed up north to get his bachelor's degree in Business Administration.

He also enjoyed being active in the Black Student Union and becoming a man of the black and old gold. Being from the south, it took a while getting used to the music and way of life there because Shadrach was a southern country boy in two booming industrialized cities. A part of him wished he had moved to Atlanta, but he needed to be in a place where he could stay out of trouble and experience something other than "the south." There were too many single women in Atlanta and he'd never be able to finish sowing his oats.

Shadrach had pulled up to the shop in his pecan colored 1988 Mercury Cougar that he'd just had taken out of the shop yesterday. That pretty penny it cost to get the transmission fixed was enough to motivate him to return to work and to let the boys know he was still in charge.

Shadrach had barely gotten in front of his car when his face was being slammed into his own car. The combination of the exhausting heat and the car running for a good thirty minutes before being shut off did not make for a good combination, causing his skin to burn upon contact. Of all days to get jacked in front of his shop this would be the day he probably should have stayed home to get some rest. He felt a hand reach into his pockets and dig around to find some keys, money, or whatever it was they were looking for. He wanted to fight back, let the guy or guys getting at him know that he wasn't no punk but as soon as the thought hit his mind, he felt something sharp pierce his side. When he went to swing his right arm as a reflex, he realized that was the side the attacker stuck him.

The boy thought he was done and was about to make his great escape when Shadrach grabbed him and flung him against the wall, stunning him. After determining that whatever sharp object he had been attached with had not pierced him deeply, Shadrach lost his mind. He mushed the young man's head in the wall and punched him in stomach. Realizing that he and his attacker were roughly the same size, he dragged the boy into the shop and pushed him down on the smooth black and white tile. Commotion erupted as customers fought to move out the way as two of the barbers made their way to the ruckus.

"What's going on boss?" the older well-built sand colored man with salt and pepper asked Shadrach as he was pushing him behind the counter.

"Get me a belt or rod Na'eem 'cause I'm gonna whoop his butt." Shadrach spit out the tasted of blood and noticed even more discomfort on the left side of his face that made the impact with the car hood.

"And Jesus can watch cause I'm gonna use every verse in Psalms and Proverbs to light little tail up. Spoiled brat."

At forty-five, Na'eem was the oldest barber in the shop. He acted like he was in his twenties and single in spite of the fact that he's been married for twenty years. He treated Shadrach just like he was one of his own two grown children that were in college. Having cut hair for almost twenty years, he had seen more than his share of fights start and sometimes not end on the best of terms in a shop. At that moment, however, his most important job was keeping the man he worked for out of jail for beating child that's not his.

"What you attack Shadrach for?" Davon asked the young man, who was trying to fight him to get at Shadrach. Davon had seen the piece of metal that was in his hands and applied a technique he learned in a martial arts class to get him to let the metal go. "You realize if I let you go Shadrach is gonna wipe the floor with you."

"Whatever man," the young man was bold and cocky, "I'm not going to jail man let me go."

Davon had his hand on one wrist, went behind the boy and quickly locked his arms together and tilted him back in an effort to restrain him. The boy tried to wiggle himself away but found the position he was in discomforting.

"I'm gonna let you go but you got to stop fighting me." Davon said in an effort to encourage the boy to give up his fight.

"Nobody is gonna call the police and Shadrach is not going to whoop your butt, although judging by the blood on his side and the bruise on his face, I ought to let him do a number on him."

The boy tried to get away from him but found that Davon had executed the restraint proficiently and thus he had no choice but to surrender. Besides, he was in the shop and surrounded by people who weren't going to let him get too far. Once the boy stopped fighting, Davon let him go.

"You good?" Na'eem asked Shadrach.

"Yeah."

Shadrach walked up to the young man, grabbed him by his ear. "Come with me."

The boy winced in pain as he was being led to Shadrach's office in the back of the shop. The door was open and Shadrach shoved the boy in the chair by his desk. Davon kept post outside the door and Shadrach got a good look at the boy before he went around the other side of his desk and had a seat. Just by looking at him in the face, the boy couldn't have been older than thirteen or fourteen but was surprisingly built for his age and stature. His face was smooth with light pimples on his forehead. He tried to keep a thin goatee and beard connected with the few hairs that were growing on his cheeks and chin. Each eyebrow had two cuts in it but his most distinguishing feature was the overuse of frankincense and myrrh body oil that he obviously applied to his navy blue shirt and slacks.

"So what's up? What you want?" The boy asked him as if he were in charge of the situation. "I ain't got all day, I got other people I can be jackin' to get my dough, ya' dig?"

"I don't dig, or understand. You don't have all day, yet you picked a time to come up here and messed up mine. And instead of asking me for a job, you figured you'd take what you thought you could of mine."

"You gonna call the police or what?"

"No," Shadrach picked up the phone and handed it to him. "Call your mom."

"I'm not about to call that old—"

"Why not?"

"Ain't like she doing nothing anyway," the boy looked away and was irritated. "She don't recognize your number so it's not like she gonna pick up the phone, if she's home. Look, I was just trying to get some money so my little brother and little sister can get something to eat. It ain't even that serious."

"How old are you?"

"Too young to get a job," the boy gave much attitude, rolling his eyes and slouching in his seat. He started cracking his knuckles and gritting his teeth, almost as if he were plotting on his next move. "What's with the twenty questions?"

Shadrach started to snatch him up again but decided against that. He didn't want to be in jail for child abuse so he kept it moving.

"Why doesn't your mother work to get something for your little brother and sister to eat?"

"She's too busy trying to please that sorry punk that comes over our house every night at ten o'clock when he thinks we are sleep. They make all the noise they want and then she always leaving with him in the morning so she's not handling her business. I am."

Shadrach thought about what the boy was saying for a minute. Davon was still at the door chilling and waiting on further instruction.

"What's your name kid?" Shadrach asked, realizing that the whole time they've been sharing space he never got the kid's name.

"Daniel, but everybody call me D."

Shadrach shook his head. He looked at the kid again and this time, he saw a young man who just wanted some attention. He picked up the phone again and handed it to him, "call your mom."

D exhaled and he reluctantly dialed the digits to get his mom on the line. "Mom, I'm at the barbershop on near the North Side Shopping Center."

The woman on the line could be heard screaming and shouting and saying all kinds of ungodly things to her son.

"No Mom, I'm not a trouble." D didn't even look up at Shadrach or Davon as his mother continued to give him a piece of her mind.

"Well, there wasn't no food to eat and Leon didn't leave no money so I went out and did what I had to do and that's why I'm not home."

Davon took the phone from D, "Hello ma'am, this is Davon Victor at Shadrach's, how are you?" She got to giving Davon a

piece of her mind and he quickly cut her off, "No ma'am. I'm
going to drop your son off with a few things we are going to pick
up from the store. We'll see you in a few."

Davon hung up the phone and told D to get up so he can take
him out of the shop. Shadrach could tell just by the look on his
face that he really wanted to say some other things but perhaps he
was being respectful. Davon can be a trip sometimes, but he was a
hard worker and pretty cool to be around.

After a few minutes, Shadrach left his office and came into the
shop and observed an argument over whether not it is possible to
have a black man for president in this lifetime. Hillary Clinton
had just removed her nomination, paving the way for Barack
Obama to become the first man of color to run for president on
the Democratic ticket. Of course, there are some whom feel like
Barack isn't ready to be president.

"Come on man. I love Barack but he doesn't have any
experience." Reily was arguing with Na'eem. He's the other elder
barber in the shop as well as Shadrach and Felton's uncle. He's
also the pastor of Mary AME Zion Church where Shadrach,
Felton and Abednego were brought up and first introduced to the
Lord.

"Man you out of your mind." Clifford instigated the
argument egging Reily on, "you know good and well the good ole
boy network wasn't going to let a woman run for the White
House. Even if she is Bill Clinton's wife."

"Man, you are tripping. We all know Hillary would make a
better president that Barack. He should wait eight more years or
become Hillary's vice president and get him some experience,
then he'd be able to tell them white boys what to do."

"Man, go somewhere with that." Clifford responded again.
"He aight. He wasn't the best barber in the shop but he keeps the
drama in the shop and challenges everyone to think which makes
him likeable by most. Entertainment, pure entertainment. He's
also only stylist in the shop that can do some perms and coloring
and if it wasn't for him, Shadrach's probably wouldn't be in the
black because it costs more to fix up a woman's head than it did a

man. Another positive was that in most cases he could fix any messed up hairstyle that another barber worked on and make something out of nothing. He was a true hair artist.

At Shadrach's, people had the freedom to speak their peace; all that was required was that there be no cussing, especially in front of the children. That's why men of all ages come to share politics, fuss and fight. A lot of the men wouldn't admit it, but many felt that Shadrach's was the best thing created since the adult entertainment club. Usually while the patrons were getting their haircuts, entertainment was provided by playing a new release or an old favorite. Shadrach hadn't had a customer yet and although he could have been doing inventory, or checking the appointment books to make sure the barbers were on point, Tevin walked in late again.

"Sorry I'm late bossman." The toothpick-slim barber was putting his white jacket over his street clothes. His Sean Jean shirt was barely buttoned and his baggy jean pants were sagging off his behind; a strong pet peeve that on any other day, Shadrach would have addressed. But he didn't feel like calling the kettle black today, that and the fact that Elijah had just walked in for his usually "quick shape up" before a meeting that he was going to have that afternoon. "What did I miss?"

"The world was getting ready to come to an end and you just barely made it." Reily cracked, inciting a few laughs.

"Thanks old man." Tevin responded as he grabbed the next customer and prepped him in his chair. That boy needed to learn the meaning of time management. One would think that by graduating at the top of the class at the barber school and being a few credit hours away from hearing a business degree at Gilbert State University that he'd have it together. He was late to his own graduation ceremony at the barber school. Yet, aside from his flaws, Shadrach hired him because he knew he was one of the best and he had potential to learn everything Shadrach could teach him about running a business if he would just put a little more effort into handling his business. Tevin usually could learn the new hair styles faster and quicker than others. He had the ability to understand what people want, especially if they don't know the lingo and once he got started working he has a tendency to stay busy.

Elijah was in and out in ten minutes. He looked in the mirror Shadrach handed him to see for himself the good job the man just done. "Now don't think that you are going to get out of coming to my church this Sunday."

"Naw, not at all. I'll be in church this Sunday."

"Yeah, I heard that one before. Normally, the family skips the following Sunday after the funeral, but we'd love to see you and Felton there."

"Well I can't speak for Felton, but you know Deborah and I are going to be there."

"That boy's been acting strange. I think you need to keep an eye on him."

At that moment, Shadrach had wished that Elijah had kept his comments about Felton to himself. But the truth was Elijah was only the third person to notice that his brother was a little off. Deborah had mentioned something about calling them last night and Felton picking up the phone, answering "we're busy" and hanging the phone up. And before all the madness with D took place, Na'eem had mentioned something about seeing Felton coming out of somebody else's house at three o'clock in the morning when he had called earlier to check on the shop. Don't ask how Na'eem knew it was Felton, but once Na'eem went deeper into the conversation, he knew something was up and that sooner or later he was going to have to get to the bottom of it.

Elijah followed Shadrach to the front where Dumar was writing receipts and studying for one of his summer school class. Dumar wasn't a barber but a graduating senior at Winston-Salem State University. It was going to be hard seeing him graduate and leave in the fall as Shadrach had become so accustomed to having an office person around and getting to go home early to be with his wife at the end of the day instead of doing paper work all night. Actually gave them a chance to spend some quality time together. Shadrach had seen the bills that were on the corner of the desk and grabbed them so he could follow Elijah out of the shop. He looked around and knew that business would be handled, he trusted his barbers to be on their business, plus, they knew that Na'eem was going to call and tell it if Reily didn't beat him to the punch. Maybe they were right, Shadrach wasn't ready to return just yet. Shadrach grabbed his phone and thought to call Felton to see if they could meet up for lunch or something. Naturally, his call went to straight to voicemail. Figures.

CHAPTER TWENTY-THREE

FELTON

Natalie was sleeping just like a little baby. Felton sat up in the bed and gazed at her beauty. To him, she was just as beautiful as the day they were wed two years ago; she was just as beautiful as the day they met four years ago. He'd given up a lot to be with her, and she's given him more chances that he could have ever imagined. Its times like this that made him wish that he had been more faithful to her in the beginning of their relationship. After giving it some thought, Felton was even *man* enough to say that he wished his first time was with her, and not one of his homeboy's leftovers. He wished she was his one and only instead of being the forty seventh woman he had been intimate with. Natalie should have been number one in everything in his life—except after God.

And there was God, who through the Holy Spirit was calling on Felton to join the church as Shadrach and Abednego had done. Felton was tired of that Man always trying to come for him. Every time he stepped into his car, He was there. When he dancing on stage so he can make some money to not only put some food on his plate, but pay off that Madame Mulah, He was there again. When he wanted to touch his wife and join in union with her in that special way, He was there and as Felton would put it, "blocking" him from what was rightfully his. To put it bluntly Felton was sick of God, and just hoped that the Man would bug one of the other seven billion souls walking this earth and just let him be.

As Felton continued to sit on his side of the bed, he was getting frustrated and angry and he wouldn't admit it publicly, but Felton was also hurt. It's been over three weeks since they made love and to say he was getting restless was an understatement. He'd touch Natalie and she'd almost immediately push his hand to the side. As if his touch would separate her from God. They were married now, so it wasn't as if anything he'd do for her or what he'd want her to do for him would be a sin. He hated the cold showers because all they did was make him feel lonely and miserable. It got so bad that Felton would spend a few hours in the mirror just trying to find out what was it about him that turned his wife off and if he could fix it. The skin on his face was flawless and his bruises had healed nicely, bringing back his baby face features that had women and some men swooning over him. His body was tight—not too bulky like a muscle man but nice and sleek like a basketball player. And everything below the waist was right too and in perfect working order. Even his feet were nice and well groomed.

Felton exhaled and went into the bathroom and stared in the mirror. That's when he thought about the doubts of him and Natalie truly having a future together. Maybe it was because the doctor had told them they couldn't have children. She had problems ovulating and he had a low sperm count so it seemed as if they were destined to be barren. Of course, they'd talk about adopting but Felton wanted *his own* flesh and blood. Wasn't that he wanted to be stingy, but if his grandfather can have six kids and each of his children had at least three children, and both Shadrach and Abednego have paid for abortions before they got right with God, then Felton didn't understand why he couldn't have at least one. It was normal for every man to want at least one of the children he raised to be his own. It's almost like bragging rights in a way. Funny though because when he was younger, he never thought that he of all people would want his own children. Now that the doctor says that they both are infertile, it just made him want them more. Who knows, if he and Natalie made love at the right moment, they might just prove that doctor wrong.

Just when Felton felt the Spirit pegging him and calling him to just listen, Felton turned on the faucet and splashed water to his face. He brushed his teeth and rinsed his mouth out and dried his face. He looked at the man in the mirror and shook his head. He returned to the bedroom and got next to his wife and just cuddled with her. He thought about taking his underwear off so he could get comfortable and just when he was about to reach down and do it, Natalie elbowed him in the chest which prompted Felton to back away and lay on his back.

Forget it, he thought. He looked at the wall and tried to stare into space until he eventually went to sleep.

CHAPTER TWENTY-FOUR

CHASE

What are you doing knocking on my door so late?" Chase complained after he opened the door and let his younger brother in. As he watched the man walk into the living room and prop up on his couch like he was staying for a while, he could feel the steam leave his earlobes like a well-drawn cartoon character. Chase was thankful that he thought to grab the bath towel that was left at the floor after he and NuTameka decided to perform their marital duty. He had wanted to ignore the banging on the door that had woke him up ten minutes ago but when NuTameka got cranky and started cursing him out, Chase relented and answered the call. "Got that crazy woman upstairs cursing me out and—"

"Bro, I'm sorry, I ran into a little problem."

"You always running into a problem." Chase said as he looked at his reflection while he slammed the door shut.

"I killed a man."

Chase felt his heart drop. His legs felt wobbly and he started to perspire. "Yo—yo—you what?!"

"What is all this noise!" NuTameka came out of the room with a bright orange cotton robe barely concealing her natural form. "Paris!"

"Look Tame—" Paris stood up and put his hands up to his chest, pushing away. He remembered their last altercation didn't end pretty after NuTameka hit him in the head with a frying pan.

"I thought I told you not to come around here!" She yelled as she went to jump on him but Chase was restraining her. "You better make this punk get from around here."

"Tameka I'm in trouble, real big trouble and D's back to digging in trashcans searching for food for our siblings again."

Chase scrunched his eyes. He thought about the younger siblings he'd left behind and had remembered giving D a couple hundred dollars just a few days prior. NuTameka calmed down because even though she and Paris had beef ever sense they were in the fourth grade over something that was probably so trivial now, NuTameka always had a soft spot for D.

"He tried to rob the brother of the man I killed a few days ago." Paris said as he dropped his head to the ground. "I was gonna jump in it but he got manhandled when he went into Shadrach's shop."

"You killed Abednego!" NuTameka shouted as she started to run toward him again.

"Stop!" Chase yelled. "Everyone stop and shut up!"

NuTameka pushed Chase away and smacked Paris so hard, he fell back into the couch he was sitting on. NuTameka sat next to him and Chase managed to squeeze between the two of them. Chase processed the last few words that Paris and NuTameka had said and reached over and choked Paris. He remembered all the things that Abednego had begun to teach him about Christ and had thrown it out of the window. "You killed my friend!"

Paris struggled to say something as his eyes struggled to stay open. Chase was squeezing his throat so tight, he could feel his fingers coming together. Paris's air space was being restricted and he was losing the battle to stay awake. NuTameka had managed to pull Chase off of Paris.

"Don't kill him!" She said as she pulled her husband off of his brother. "If I can't kill him, you can't either."

"Why?!" Chase shouted over the tears. "Why did you kill Abednego?"

Paris coughed as he struggled to get up. His lips moved like fish gills, gasping because he was out of water. His labored breathing seemed forced, "it's a long story."

"You woke my wife and I up in the middle of the night, banging on the door like some crazy wild man, get to talking. We got all night."

Paris exhaled and slowly recapped the night starting from where he and another one of Madame Mulah's goons staged a fight to draw Abednego out of his apartment. By the time he got to where he shot Abednego, everyone was crying again.

"I didn't mean to kill him." Paris snuffled. "I just wanted to scare the man and mess with him like I was told to do."

Chase shook his head. He couldn't believe that his own brother was sitting in his living room, confessing to killing a man of God. NuTameka got up and walked to the kitchen. She reached under the cabinet and took out a bottle of whiskey and three glasses. She brought them to the coffee table and poured everyone a drink. "So what are you going to do?"

"What do you mean what am I gonna do?" Paris asked as he lifted up the drink and brought the liquid to his lips, hoping the drink would calm his nerves. "I just want to go to sleep and the pills aren't working."

"I mean when are you gonna confess to murdering that poor man so his family can get some sleep and you can begin paying from your crimes." NuTameka stood up. She hadn't touched her drink but she had decided that she was sitting too close to Paris to want to be around him.

"I'm not going to jail." Paris whimpered.

"You're not staying here!" NuTameka shouted. "I know you didn't come over here to ask Chase if he could let you stay here cause the answer is no—hell no!"

"I think you should leave." Chase said as he got up and opened the door.

Paris looked at him shocked. He hadn't counted on his brother being so cold toward him and he had hoped to make his revelation man-to-man without the hood chick getting involved. Paris got up and left and as he walked out of the door he looked Chase in the eye, a small part of him hoped that Chase would change his mind. When he saw that Chase wasn't budging, Paris shook his head, knowing that he messed up for good.

CHAPTER TWENTY-FIVE

SHADRACH

"So what was your day like honey?" Deborah asked when Shadrach stepped into the door. Shadrach was happy to see the love of his life and watched as she placed her backpack and her rolling suitcase near the door. She was coming in from another day at the school where she dealt with high school students. She was getting in later than usual because the book club she served as the faculty advisor for met and they were going over the latest *Good Girlz* read by ReShonda Tate Billingsley. Though she was feeling working with the group of girls and encouraging them reading age appropriate materials, she wished she had more boys in the group as well.

"Busy day as usual. I'm going to have to talk to Tevin about coming in late all the time. He a good barber but dude needs to learn to be a little more punctual."

"Well, you and Tevin are gonna have to talk that out. If you feel that being on time is important then you may have to express that more clearly. If that means sacrifice…"

"What do you mean *sacrifice*?"

"I mean that you will have to do what you feel is best for the company. Either move his time back an hour or find somebody with as much skills as he has to come in and work for you."

"Naw…I can't fire Tevin over something so petty as coming in late all the time. He's been with me since the beginning, and he's always made up for it in a business stand point."

"If it's petty why are you complaining about it? Come on baby, you can't let you emotions control and take over your feelings. You have to work out what is best for *Shadrach's*. You know I respect Tevin just as much as you do but if his tardiness is a problem then you and I both know you have to consider it. Besides, you are supposed to be looking at this from a *business* standpoint and not a *personal* standpoint sweetie."

She's right! Shadrach thought even though he didn't want to consider firing Tevin, he was his boy; been with him since the beginning and everything. On one hand, business wouldn't hurt too much if he let Tevin come in late. On the other hand, he had to consider the customers, especially the on the customers who took the time to get to *Shadrach's* early just to see him. At the same time, Shadrach needed to learn to be firm with the man. Tevin had to learn to be *on time*. He couldn't keep coming and going at his leisure. He had to treat him like he treated the other guys and he's really setting a poor example for Dumar who's going to college soon. But on the real, Shadrach had just got in and didn't really feel like thinking about work. So he decided to change the subject.

"So what's your day been like?" He asked.

"It was fine. I'll be so glad when these seniors are done researching for their senior projects, but they're in the media center all the time because when they aren't working on their projects, they're typing essays for their college applications and trying to win scholarships."

"That's not bad, at least they are doing something productive."

"That is true. Today, one of the teachers had a substitute and guess where half of class ended up?"

"Man, back in my day, if the teacher *thought* we gave a substitute a hard time, we were in for it."

"It is what it is. I can only do my part to make the system better by encouraging the kids to do their research and to read something other than the school books they carry in their backpacks. The principal is upset that I'm alternating between teen books and adult books but what can I do? Most of the teens don't want to read the school books and some of the books they bring in here, I'd be too scared to bring home and read with you and we're married."

"Oh. It was some authors coming into my shop the other day trying to get some of the men to read and buy books for their ladies."

"How did they do?"

"I think they did aight. I had to give it to the duo, they had an uphill battle pushing that Christian conscious street lit. But once they got that groove and found what worked and didn't, they were good."

"Did you get one of the books?"

"Yeah, I'm a read it first. And then I'll pass it on to you."

"That's cute, I'm a have to give you that one. I never thought you'd read a book before me."

"You underestimate me."

Deborah kissed her husband on the cheek as she walked into the kitchen. Shadrach had a bunch of vegetables on the counter that he was dicing and slicing. "I hope you're making a garden salad for dinner tonight."

"Nope. This is the beginning of a baked fish and vegetable pasta. Already have the fish in the oven."

"Sounds interesting."

Deborah took out a pot and filled it with water. She took three herbal tea bags out of the box and put them in the pot to boil. As the orange tea scent began to overtake the fish that Shadrach took out of the oven, dinner was ready. Shadrach had set the table while Deborah was fixing the plates. Shadrach turned the television on to one of the music stations and the fast, hypnotic salsa inspired jazz beat infused with African instruments from the Africando band played in the background. As luck would have it,

"Betece" featuring Amadou Balake began pumping from the sound system and Shadrach jumped up and started dancing to the rhythm.

"Come on, give me a dance before dinner."

"No," Deborah was trying to insist but she couldn't resist laughing at her husband and joining in. They danced for a minute and by time they returned to the table, their meal it was still hot. They blessed the food and enjoyed their meal. After they ate, Shadrach washed the dishes and Deborah wrapped her arms around his waist.

"Don't you wish we had more time for us?"

"Of course, everyday. But don't worry, one day that will happen for us. You continue teaching them kids and encouraging them to read and get and education. I will continue working at the shop until I get enough money to hire enough barbers so I can work part time and run the business from home. But you do realize that running a business can take a lot of your time?"

"I know."

Shadrach turned around and kissed his wife. Of course, he knew it would be a few years before they could live out their fantasy, but he had faith that God would bless them one day to make their dream come true. One day, he would pray, they would have more time to be together, but right now, they are enjoying what they have now.

***

It's six o'clock in the morning and Deborah and Shadrach were cuddling and kissing in bed. They had begun the morning in the same fashion they had ended the night before and if Felton knew about it, he would truly be envious. They were feeling so good that Deborah didn't want to go to school and work in the media center helping the kids find the books, articles and other resources to help them prepare for their senior projects that they needed to complete before they could graduate. Shadrach was chilling and didn't feel like going to work. He liked his business, but there were days when he wished that money would come to him for once instead of having to get up every morning. Deborah turned around and they kissed and hugged again.

"You know we are going to have to quit doing this," she said sternly yet hugging him tight.

"If you would let me go, I can get up and we won't be doing this." Shadrach responded as he hugged her even tighter. His hand began to wonder again in anticipating of starting some more trouble.

"If you would quit touching me—" She responded with a hint of a smile as she took aim below the belt for an unfair shot.

"If you would quit grabbing me."

They kissed once more but a quick glance at the clock told them that it was past time for them to get out of bed. Deborah got up first and went to the bathroom. Shadrach enjoyed his spot on the bed. He reached under his side of the bed where he kept the remote and turned the television on to see two more young black men get arrested for whatever crime it was that black men seem to be committing. He then turned to the music channel and saw Toni Braxton's video for "He Wasn't Man Enough" and Deborah came out the bathroom shaking like the ladies in the video.

"Oh, see I can do that, too. I wish they would pay me to get on television and sing and shake."

"Naw, I like you the way you are. Plus, some of them girls in those videos got fake hair, fake nails, fake breast—"

"I got real hair, real nails and real breast. I don't need to add a thing."

"I know. That's why you don't have to work on them videos. Besides, women in real life are more attractive than women who aspire to be fake Barbie dolls."

"You need to get out of bed and quit looking at them fake Barbie dolls!"

Shadrach hoped up out the bed and as he went into the bathroom, Deborah smacked him on the behind. He turned around and looked at her and was hypnotized by the way her body moved as she laughed. He turned on the shower and then ran back out to the bedroom and tackled her on the bed. She was still giggling and they kiss again. After playing around for a few minutes, he got up to take a shower.

Once he returned to the bedroom, he got dressed for another day of work and Deborah was downstairs eating cereal and some turkey bacon. She cooked him a few pieces and he poured himself a bowl of cereal. After they ate, he took her to school on his way to work. The two lovebirds were still flirting and fooling around like they were still newlyweds. Shadrach never felt like there was enough time in the world for him to spend with Deborah.

CHAPTER TWENTY-SIX

DONTE

Donte watched Eugene play with the other kids at the park while he and Elicia enjoyed a fish plate from the church down the street. Donte had agreed to meet Eve in a public setting and Elicia wanted to tag along. Elicia was reading the Bible along with a women's study guide.

"I'm glad you are trying to get along with Eve." Elicia said as she closed her book.

"I never said I wouldn't get along with her." Donte clarified. "I just don't want her playing games with my son. Either be a part of his life or leave him alone."

"But you don't want that." Elicia said as she bit into her piece of fish. When Donte looked in her direction, Elicia pointed out Rahliem and a young lady working with some of the younger youth in their church. Donte squinted his eyes, as he thought the young lady standing next to him was his ex-girlfriend, Faith Petree, but she decided that it wasn't her. He noticed Eugene still playing on the monkey bars with some of the other kids. "I know that you want your son to know his mother and for her to take an active part of his life." Elicia had continued after she finished chewing.

"Yes, but I want her to be part of his life because *she* wants to be. I've worked hard to make sure that Eugene neither wanted or needed for anything and I've worked hard to make sure that he's had the best female role models possible."

Elicia smiled. Though she'd never taken on the mother role, she did grow fond of the boy ever since he was left on Donte's doorstep. Between her, her mother and Donte's mother, Eugene wasn't lacking in the mother-figure department. Even with the kids at daycare, Eugene appeared to accept the fact that his mother wasn't around. Out of the corner of his eye, he saw Eve approaching them wearing a bright, orange and yellow sundress and carrying a bucket of Mrs. Wiener's Chicken. Donte smiled as he remembered the popular chicken joint not too far from A&T in Greensboro.

"Hey," Eve said as she paused in her tracks. She looked at Elicia and her plate of food and then down at her own bucket. "I'd brought some food for everyone, I didn't know y'all ate already."

"No, no." Elicia said as she got up and gathered her trashed and dispose of it in a nearby dumpster. "I was eating earlier. Eugene hasn't had anything to eat yet."

"Oh." Eve said as her eyes looked down. She sat across from Donte and she looked in his eyes. "I didn't know you'd have company."

"Elicia's usually with me on outings with Eugene." Donte said as he saw Rahliem and the female he was with playing with Eugene and smiled. He knew his son was in good hands.

"She's been there from the beginning huh?" Eve asked.

"Yeah—she has been there." Donte said, a little disturbed that Eve wouldn't make eye contact. "And there's room for you to be there if you want to be."

Elicia returned to her seat next to Donte, "I'm going to go to the grocery store real quick, would y'all like anything?" Donte looked up at her. He knew she was leaving him so that he and Eve could work out their differences alone as opposed to her being third wheel. Before he could answer, Eugene ran up to her and gave her a hug.

"Hey Ms. Eve, how are you?"

"I'm fine, how are you?"

"I'm good. Just playing around with some of the other kids from church. I wish I could play with them more often."

"And you will," Eve promised as she reached for Eugene's hand. She'd taken a napkin from her purse and wiped Eugene's face clean. Eugene smiled and then ran off. Eve crumpled up the napkin and laid it on the table beside her.

"The two of you need more time." Donte encouraged. "It's going to take more than one or two visits for him to get used to you being a more permanent fixture."

Eve shook her head yes.

"Sup Donte, glad you and Elicia could make it." Rahliem said as he reached over Eve and shook his hand. "And how are you?"

"I'm fine." Eve responded. She shook Rahliem's hand and took in his statue. Even with his black extra-long "Jesus Saves" t-shirt, his bulky muscular frame still stood out and had her in a trance. The tattoos that went from his wrists to his forearms seemed to meet and blend in with some of her unique designs that shined in the sun's light. "I didn't know you were into body art."

"Old passion of mine from prison," Rahliem addressed as he released her hand. "You must be Eve."

"I am."

"I can see so much of you in Eugene."

"Thanks."

"Well, I won't keep the two of you. I'm going to go back with Faith and make sure these other kids stay in line. It was nice meeting you and when you get the chance, come by Grace United off of Butler and Waughtown—we'd love to have you."

"Okay, I will."

Rahliem walked off and Donte noticed Eve's eyes following him. But he was more interested in Faith...surely Rahliem didn't mean the same Faith that had walked out on him because they both almost gave into their fleshly desire to unite their bodies as one when they were dating? Donte tried to remember if he'd ever told Rahliem about Faith or if he'd introduced her to him in some kind of way. At the moment, his mind was drawing a blank because he couldn't remember a time when Rahliem and Faith would have been at NC Tech at the same time for him to introduce them or mention that she was his girlfriend. Faith had graduated with a degree from accounting at A&T and he'd graduated with a degree in business management from NC Tech. She'd gone on to become a CPA with one of the big five accounting firms in the city while he started a career as a brand manager for Miriam and Mary, an international faith-based fashion firm that was started by Elicia's best friend and former Miss Gilbert State University, Mary Braxton-Tatum.

"He's as hood as they come." Eve said breaking Donte's focus on his ex and in perfect timing as Elicia had come back with a plastic bag containing paper plates and other utensils.

"Call Eugene over here so he can eat," Elicia suggested as she'd taken her seat next to Donte. "We can leave y'all to spend time together and Donte and I will go to the recreation center." Donte looked at Elicia as if she were crazy. Elicia grabbed Donte's hand and tried to pull him up but he wouldn't budge. Once Eugene came to the table and sat next to Eve, Donte reluctantly, stood up and began to depart from the table. As the distance between them and Eve and Eugene grew, Elicia spoke up. "You have to let her earn your trust."

"What you mean by that?"

"You have to loosen up a little bit. You are so uptight with her and that's reflecting in how Eugene interacts with her."

Donte gave Elicia the side-eye. "How do you know?"

"My minor was psychology, remember." Elicia smiled. Donte had forgotten. They'd spent so much time together in school going over business-related homework assignments and then the bulk of their junior year planning for her own Miss Gilbert State University campaign, he did forget she was a psychology minor. Probably didn't help that she earned quite a few of her credits while in high school, taking the advanced placement courses. "I want you to do the godly thing and allow her the space and time to be a mother. Give her the same second chance that God gave you."

Donte smiled. Sooner or later, he knew someone was going to pull that card. Rahliem had been encouraging him to do more public meetings and arranging private sleepovers and things of that nature for Eve and Eugene. It appeared that everyone wanted mother and son to be reunited except him—at least he felt he had been made to feel that way. "I've struggled with that." Donte admitted as he turned back to see Eugene taking a bite out of the chicken Eve had brought. "Ever since she broke into my house and caused that commotion at Olive Garden, it's been on and poppin' with her ever since."

"I know. But my spirit feels good about this. I feel like we can work this out."

Donte nodded his head. He felt good that Elicia was neither intimidated or discouraging of the efforts Eve was making to get to know her son. As they entered the recreation center, Donte went to the window and watched as Eugene and Eve shared a laugh before Eve rubbed her fingers through his hair. Donte felt a slight tinge before a calm wave ran across him.

"That looks like Faith." Elicia said as she noticed the woman standing in the crowd of children.

"I said the same thing." Donte responded quickly. "I didn't notice her until after Eve arrived."

"Looks like she's leaving." Elicia said disappointed. "I wanted to go introduce myself. Usually when Rahliem has the kids, he typically has them by himself. I was surprise he had a female escort since he had the boys. The girls go to the park on a different day."

"Yeah."

"Well, if it was Faith, we'll catch her again. She's lost quite a bit of weight. Maybe we'll find out what she's been up to."

Donte wasn't sure how he felt about that. Between watching Eve and Eugene eat and the possibility of Faith being back in the picture, old feelings were beginning to take shape in his heart. He began to question whether he had completely closed the door on

Faith before he and Elicia moved forward to rekindle their flame —and he was beginning to question the effect on his friendship with Rahliem if in fact Rahliem were dating his ex. As soon as the negative energy began to take a shape in his brain, Donte dismissed it, decided to deal with the matter if it should arise again later. First priority was to make sure that Eugene enjoyed his meeting with his mother and from the looks of things, everything was going to be just fine.

CHAPTER TWENTY-SEVEN

RAHLIEM

Rahliem stepped into the conference room at the offices of Tinsley, Phelps and Gitus for the reading of Abednego's will. He was surprised to see so many people sitting around the table. He knew of Abednego's legal and former illegal business dealings but he didn't think they would be this complex or involve this many people.

Rahliem recognized Eric Warren, one of the earlier members of Street Disciples sitting at the head of the table. He was happy that his boy completed law school and was even more amazed that Abednego had retained his services. To either side sat Shadrach and Felton along with their wives. The owners of Halo, an upscale Ethiopian-themed vegetarian restaurant also surrounded the table along with other members of the Street Disciples Ministry. The shocker was seeing the legendary Madame Mulah in the flesh. The woman was as fine as Rahliem had always thought her to be. She stood out with her spiked auburn red hair and a huge princess cut pendant choker. The business blouse was unbecoming of a witch or someone who believed in or practiced voodoo. She glared at him and her eyes were following him as if she were hunting down an animal in the woods. All that were missing was a rifle and a stethoscope.

Rahliem immediately caught an open seat next to Pastor Phelps. "It's a lot of people," Rahliem confided his thoughts and Pastor Phelps confirmed by nodding her head. "I got to give Abednego his props, he was organized and handled his business."

"I welcome you to Tinsley, Phelps and Gitus. For those of you who may not know me, I'm Attorney Eric Warren. While my general practice is in family law, I have been retained and qualified to be the executor of Abednego Franklin Green's last will and trust.

On a personal note, I met Abednego while I was a student at Gilbert State University. He had been handing out fliers for a new chapter of The Street Disciples Ministry in Greensboro. I had just rededicated my life to the Lord after helping a former friend of mine run for Miss Gilbert State University."

Rahliem had heard about that election. Donte was helping Elicia run as well and even though neither lady won, Donte redeemed himself as Chief of Staff as well as being a charter member of the Greensboro Chapter of For Father's Only, a nonprofit organization dedicated to helping single fathers learn parenting skills and utilize resources in the community to help them talk care of services and be able to work with the women they've fathered their kids with.

Eric read from the will that according to him had been prepared almost four months prior to Abednego's murder. A lot of the legal terms Rahliem didn't understand and he'd almost wished he hadn't been in trouble in his youth and had gone to college. However, due to being a convicted felon, attending a four year university and getting accepted into law school would present a challenge, but weren't completely unattainable for him.

"I, Abednego Franklin Green, residing in Winston-Salem, North Carolina, being of sound mind and spirit declare this instrument to be my last will and testament," to say that everyone straightened up and paid close attention was an understatement. It almost seemed as if the room shifted. After saying that his will revoked any previous wills Eric continued, "To my brothers, Shadrach Felix Green and Meshach Felton Green, I give an equal share of my interest in Halo, my savings accounts at Mechanics & Farmers and Bank of America and as noted, have been named the beneficiaries of my life insurance policy and are collectively credited with making a $25,000 donation to the church."

Shadrach and Felton nodded to each other and a tear escaped Pastor Phelp's eyes. Grace United desperately needed money to replace the fellowship hall and to make other repairs done to the church.

"To Madame Mulah, the money you have let me 'borrow' has been kept in a variety of interest-bearing accounts that are co-signed by Rahliem Victor. I request that Rahliem transfer all funds to you including ninety percent of the interest earned on said accounts with the remaining ten percent going to The Street Disciples Ministry Scholarship Fund. I also, for your troubles, transfer ownership of my Wachovia Money Market account and my ING investment accounts to you."

Everyone noticed the shocked look on Madame Mulah's face. At that moment, Rahliem remembered going to the bank with Abednego at various times and signing some papers for different bank accounts, but he never asked what they were for. When the church received anonymous donations amounting to almost $50,000, Rahliem had assumed that Abednego was behind it. In their talks about their past, Abednego had revealed his dealings with Madame Mulah and their torrid past but Rahliem assumed or had been led to be assured that he had no further dealings with her. Natalie got up as did Deborah and walked over to where Madame Mulah was sitting. She bent down to Madame Mulah left ear and not so discreetly asked, "I guess that means the debt is paid in full right?"

Rahliem didn't know what that meant but his spirit had raised enough discernment to encourage him to pay attention. Madame Mulah all of a sudden didn't look too comfortable. Madame Mulah mumbled, "yes, paid in full." Natalie stood up and fixed her blouse and walked out with Deborah hot on her trail.

Shadrach leaned across the table and asked Felton, "what is Natalie talking about?"

"I'll explain later," Felton asked, looking down to conceal the frown that had appeared on his face.

Rahliem had wondered whether or not Madame Mulah had anything to do the damage being done to the fellowship hall and the fact that Felton and Natalie were dumped in the church as Adam and Eve in the Garden of Eden. Natalie had left the office briefly and returned to her seat. Eric had called for Rahliem to join them at her end of the table.

"These are the forms releasing full control of the interest-bearing accounts and the Wachovia Money Market and ING investment accounts to Madame Mulah. She will get these accounts immediately since these are listed to pay the debts to her."

Eric passed the forms over to Rahliem so he could read over them. He glanced at the figures totaling just shy under a million dollars and quickly signed his name where instructed. He wanted nothing to do with that money and saw no reason to delay or contest following the directive that Abednego had left in place.

"Thank you," Madame Mulah replied and smiled for the first time since being in the office. "You're a pretty boy, you know that Rahliem."

Rahliem blushed. He hadn't expected the cougar to say anything about his physical appearance. "Thank you."

"Well, maybe after all this hoopla dies down over Abednego's death and all of his business taken care of and what have you, we can go out for a dinner or two."

"I'm already taken, but I appreciate the offer."

And just like that the smile was gone from Madame Mulah's face. For a brief second, Rahliem wondered whether or not he should be concerned about rejecting Madame Mulah's advances. But as soon as the fake notion of fear set in, Rahliem rejected it, remember that God was with Him and that as long as he was walking with Him, no weapon formed against him would prosper.

CHAPTER TWENTY-EIGHT

FELTON

"Yo, what was that about back there?" Felton questioned the moment they stepped foot into their home. "Acting all gangstress and—"

"Boy please," Natalie cut him off. "I was just putting that southern fried voodoo practicing witch in her place. Just letting that heifer know that not only is she not getting another dime of *our* money, but that she better not mess with us again."

"And what are we going to do if she decides she wants to test you on that threat?"

"I'm going to give her a good ole fashion butt whooping."

Felton shook his head and put his hand up. He couldn't believe that Natalie turned into Mrs. Gangsta Chick all of a sudden. This new, hardcore demeanor was more of raunchy female rapper Lil' Kim's personality than the virtuous woman that he married. "I guess Jesus gave you a new set of balls huh?"

Natalie was livid. He couldn't believe that her soul mate had the audacity to use Jesus' name in vain. "What is that supposed to mean?"

She almost immediately felt guilty for using that line of questioning. When she had gotten saved, Natalie promised that she would work on her "foul language" but Felton and this situation were getting the best of her. "I put that chick in check so she could back up off of us. Give us room to breathe."

"What are you doing, listening to Toni Braxton for advice? Please, what you really did was set that chick off and I hope she don't come to our house like she Cleo or some sh—"

Before Felton could complete his thought there was a knock at the door. He exhaled loudly and went to go answer it. He had thought to look at the peephole but found it useless because they had been arguing so loud that whoever it was on the other side probably heard them anyway. "Speak of the devil."

"No, speak of the witch. Isn't that what your wife just called me?" Madame Mulah walked in and made herself at home. She took a seat on the sofa and propped her feet on the coffee table. "Go ahead, pretend that I'm not even here."

"How dare you come into my house?" Natalie was rushing at her but Felton grabbed her by the wrist and restrained her. "Let go of me!"

"Oh, no bother, I won't stay long." Madame Mulah got up as fast as she had sat down. "I didn't think that Abednego was going to pull that stunt from the grave."

"Well—you got your money so you really don't have no need to communicate with us."

"See that my dear is where you are wrong." Madame Mulah interrupted. "I have witnesses that I need to make sure don't try to do anything, how should I say this—um, drastic. Like go to the police and say they saw a video of who shot Abednego."

"Even if we wanted to go to the police, which I do," Natalie continued, "we couldn't go because we don't have the video."

"That's right, which is where I come in."

"No, this is where you leave. Touch us and the police will automatically assume you did it."

Natalie walked closer to Madame Mulah. "I'm sure everyone heard our little conversation. Curious minds want to know what it was we were talking about what debt we owe that would be paid in full."

"Abednego didn't—"

"You lie!" Natalie shouted. "Abednego left you almost a million dollars, plus with what we already paid you is more than enough to cover the amount he borrowed from you with interest."

"Be that as it may, I still need something from you." Madame Mulah insisted in a calm voice.

"You don't need nothing from us."

"I had hoped we could settle this the diplomatic way."

"We did, you got your money, now you can get the hell out!" Natalie showed her to the door. "To the left to the left," she commanded as she imitated pop songstress Beyonce point to the door.

"Uh—you a feisty one." Madame Mulah made her way out the door. "Oh, don't think you've seen the last of me."

"Get out!" Natalie slammed the door and barely missed her where the good Lord split her. She and Felton stared each other down. "I refuse to let that woman have me in fear in my house."

"I didn't say that—you know what? Why don't I sleep on the couch, you go to *our* room and we talk about this in the morning?"

"So what, am I on punishment now?"

Felton ignored Natalie as he went into the room and grabbed his pillows and the blanket that was at the foot of the bed. He stormed into the room past Natalie, who at this point was growing furious and propped himself on the sofa, put his feet on the table, turned the television on and even had the nerve to slide his hand inside his pants.

"So you're not going to come to bed with me?"

Felton turned to her and made eye contact, "When's the last time we've *really* been to bed?"

Before Felton could think to turn his head good, Natalie had slapped the taste out of his mouth. He sat up quick and turned around to find that Natalie had made it to their bedroom, slammed the door and locked it. Felton banged on the door.

"I told you about putting your hands on me!" Felton yelled as he kicked the door so hard, he knocked it off the bottom hinge.

"See, now I got to buy a new door because you want to act like Wonder Woman."

The thought had crossed Felton's mind to kick down the rest of the door but he thought better of it. He walked away from the door and had almost made it to the living room when he was hit with a blunt object in the back of the head. He turned around and reached up to feel the spot that opened up. He looked at the blood on his hand, the picture frame that had their wedding picture in it was cracked on the floor and his wife, heaving at the door. They stared each other down. A part of Felton wanted to do her in, but he knew that wasn't the manly thing to do. He looked at the blood on his hand and started to shake his finger out her. He could feel his blood pressure rising and his anger starting to over take him. He bit his bottom lip to keep from going ballistic.

"I'm out." He said through gritted teeth.

"Sounds like a good idea to me."

Felton grabbed the pillow, blanket and his car keys and walked out of the door.

CHAPTER TWENTY-NINE

SHADRACH

To say that Shadrach was ticked off at the loud banging on his door early in the morning was an understatement. If it been up to him, he'd continue minding his own business, but Deborah pushed and prodded him to get out the bed and see what the emergency was. He grabbed the bath towel that had been discarded on the floor and wrapped it around his nude waist. Upon opening the door, Felton didn't waste any time walking in and having a seat on the couch.

"What's going on Felton?"

"I just need to get away from the house man. Natalie is getting on my nerves." Felton through down the pillow and blanket and grabbed the remote and turned on the television.

"And you decided to come here?"

"Why, is that a problem?"

Shadrach could feel his anger building. "Bro, it's three o' clock in the morning. You couldn't find no place to go but here?"

"You act like there's a twenty four hour hotel in this city. Look man, I don't want no drama, I just want to rest my head and ease my mind. And I don't have no place else to go so I'm here."

Shadrach shook his head. "You couldn't call?"

It's not like Shadrach would have picked up the phone anyway, but still, at least the thought would have counted.

"Bruh, I didn't mean to interrupt y'all or anything, I can leave if my being here is going to inconvenience you."

"Don't bother man," Shadrach had brought back a pillow and a blanket from the linen closet. "We'll talk tomorrow after I get off from work."

***

Shadrach was surprised to see that Davon and Tevin have opened shop. No arguing and only one customer was waiting to be served. *Something's not right here. Maybe Na'eem is hiding somewhere or they are trying to play a practical joke on him,* he thought.

"Aight, all right—who's hiding where? What's broke? Who got a free haircut or who's trying to quit?"

"Why you got to think something wrong?" Tevin asks with a sly grin.

"For one, you're early, which is a first. To see you and Davon opening shop and y'all not have words about who was late or whatever. This is just a first that's all."

"Well, I don't know why you expect me on time. You know I'm black and I'm on colored people time."

"Well Tevin, it would be nice if you can be on EST, Eastern Standard Time because that is what I operate on."

Shadrach took the customer waiting in the chair and as soon as he got him seated, Jaron and his son, Kente come in the stop. Kente was six now and in kindergarten. Jaron and Kente were Shadrach's first customers when he opened up shop. He had literally just put the open sign on the door and they come walking in. Kente was begging for something, he didn't remember what it was it seemed like the boy always wanted something. At the time, Shadrach was happy that he didn't have any children yet. He knew of Jaron because he was his peer advisor at Gilbert. They had been connected through the school's entrepreneurship mentoring program at the time Shadrach was consulting with another small business owner before he started Shadrach's. In truth, it seemed like Jaron was advising him. Being a father at fifteen, getting married at seventeen and going to school full time. Shadrach found it hard to believe that Jaron had been handling his business at such a young age, he didn't think he could do it all if the shoe were on the other foot. Jaron took off his hat and his little Afro could use some trimming; as for his son, his fade could use a touch up. He knew right away that Davon would be cutting their hair. Shadrach looked at the clock and remembered then that Dumar wasn't scheduled to come in until eleven today. He had forgotten that it was Thursday and that he worked a half day before he checked in at Halo for the business meeting. Messing around with Felton had thrown him for a loop for the rest of the day.

Davon finished the customer he was with and he brought Kente to the seat. Kente hopped up and he was trying to talk about Barack Obama being the first black president. Shadrach couldn't help but listen and adore him while he spoke. He was such an intelligent young man. Anjanette and Jaron got him started on the right path right away. That's the one thing he liked about them the most. Most of the time, Kente came in and picked up a magazine usually without being told. Every now and then Kente would ask for some candy but it appeared that Jaron succeeded getting him off of asking for candy every time he comes to the shop.

"He's a smart young man." The customer in Shadrach's chair commented.

"Yeah I know. He's got a good set of parents."

"Yeah. I can tell, I can tell. Is that young man sitting next to him his brother?"

"No, that's his father."

"He's doing a good job."

Shadrach continued to cut his customer's hair while they continued to listen in on the conversation.

"Daddy, when do I get to meet the man who called us last night?" Kente asked, trying to get his father's attention.

"Kente! I told you not to put my business out on the street like that!"

"I'm sorry."

"He's talking about my father." Jaron says while he covers Kente's ears.

"That hurts." Kente says.

"Sorry." Jaron says and he moves to Davon's side and talks to him.

Kente was trying to listen to what Jaron was saying while Davon was cutting his hair. Davon was almost finished and Jaron tells him he'll finish when Kente goes to read. Kente's haircut was shaped up and looking nice. Tevin wrote a tab for Kente and Jaron since he didn't have a customer. Na'eem came in and set up shop on the other side of Tevin. Kente got up and Jaron gave him two quarters so he could get some candy out. Jaron sat in the chair and Davon started to cut his hair like Kente.

"Nineteen years pass and now he wants in my life. I'm practically a grown man now and I got my own wife and two children and I'm getting ready to open my business."

"Have you talked to him?" Davon asked.

"I'm not going to waste my time trying to speak to him. He cheated on my mom when she was pregnant with me. Then he went to jail for robbery. All that time he spent in jail, he ain't bother to write me a letter, send me a cards or acknowledge my existence. I don't even know if I got any brothers and sisters by this man. No wait, I got two brothers, neither one of them I know him from Adam. I don't know what he wants from me?"

"Well, we've been in the news lately with the For Father's Only projects we have implemented throughout the county. Maybe he wants to meet you and tell you how good of a job we've done with the program. He probably wants to meet Kente and Latrice; or meet your wife."

"I don't want to meet him."

"Maybe he got in contact with one of your brothers and could be trying to hook y'all up."

"Well, I'll be willing to meet with my brothers, but I don't want to meet with him yet. There are still some things I need to sit down and think about. You know he hurt my mom leaving her to raise me by herself with no help. I'm not bitter though, Mr. Tyler did a good job playing the father role."

"Yeah, and Kenyan was a good brother."

"I don't mean to be rude," the man in Shadrach's chair said as he got up from getting his hair cut, "but why don't you want to give this man a chance? I see that he hurt you, and I'm not saying that you have to forgive him right away, but being in jail all that time can change a man. Some men get colder, but all men think about what they miss and maybe he's just trying to make up for the wrong he's done to you."

"Yeah, but you can't undo nineteen years of wrong in a phone call. I don't want to be bothered with him right now and as he did things on his time, I should do it on mine."

"I still think you should give him a chance, even if it is not today. Take the man's number or address and write him when you are ready, something. Regardless of the wrong he's done to you, he is still your father, biologically. Give him that much respect."

"I haven't changed my number yet, I think that is respect."

"Well. I'm not going to tell you how to live your life, but you can't live your life holding grudges. I'm not trying to excuse the man because he's wrong to begin with; I am trying to get you to put your differences aside and be the bigger man and give the man a call."

"Aight."

Shadrach watched as his customer paid for his haircut and Tevin took his money. He brought Shadrach a tip, and the customer was redirected to put in the tip jar in the front. Discussions like that seem to happen every day, that's why no matter how bad Shadrach may think about staying at home, he always find a way to drag myself out of bed to come to work. Of course, Shadrach thought Jaron should reconsider not wanting to see his father, regardless what the situation was, but he was going to keep his opinion to himself until asked. Eventually, Davon got done cutting Jaron's hair. He got Kente and Dumar came in just in time to take care of Jaron and Kente's ticket. Shadrach looked at them two, and he couldn't help but think about how similar they appeared in looks and how they didn't seem to notice their close resemblance.

"You see what I see?" Na'eem asked.

"What you talking about?"

"Jaron and Dumar look so much alike from the side and I never noticed that before. Look at how their face is shaped. Yeah..." Kente waves bye to everyone and they respond in kind, "Kente notices it too. You see how he kept looking back at Dumar like that. I can see their daddy right through them."

"Now what makes you suggest that Dumar and Jaron might be related, let alone have the same father?"

"I'm a father, and when you have kids or when you have a family for that matter, you learn to see what traits are dominant that you pass down, and that were given to you. I'm telling you for a fact that those two are brothers. If not, they very close first cousins. Trust me. How about this, the next time they come in, why don't you look at Jaron and look at Dumar very closely and you will see what I see."

"Okay."

"You young, you don't see it now; but study Dumar and when you see Jaron tomorrow for that For Father's Only function you go to next week you will see exactly what I'm talking about."

***

"How come you are just telling me about Madame Mulah and her connection to Abednego?" Shadrach had finally cornered Felton and got him to talk about what happened a few weeks ago.

"Man, we wasn't trying to get you and Deborah into no mess. She had us tied up, literally."

Shadrach was understandably heated. Not only did this witch arrange to have Abednego killed, she brutally beat his brother and sister-in-law and walked away with almost a million dollars. That money could have went to the scholarship fund or to help grow the restaurant they were now partners in. Or, it could have been given back to the police since technically it was "drug money." After finding out the truth, Shadrach had more questions than he had answers.

Felton for his part felt relieved in being able to confide with Shadrach but now he had a new set of issues. One, he'd have to keep an eye on Shadrach just to make sure that the man didn't do nothing crazy. Two, he'd have to make sure Madame Mulah's goons didn't come to the barbershop or the restaurant trying to tear the place up. Three, he'd have to hear Shadrach continue to nag about how he needed to get his soul right with Jesus and do things His way and all of that. And finally, he wouldn't get no sleep trying to keep an eye on Shadrach and Natalie at the same time. This wasn't going to be easy.

"So we can't go to the police and say she had Abednego murdered?"

"No. We'd have to get our hands on the tape first and she has her mansion heavily guarded. Goons everywhere."

"And just how do you propose we do that? Go door to door like we're Jehovah's Witnesses."

"We'll find a way," Felton tried to convince his brother. He almost regretted telling him about everything that went down, but he knew that the truth would come out and it was just better for Shadrach to hear it from him.

"But until we do, we watch our backs and keep our noses clean. That means keeping Natalie from turning into Wonder Woman and reminding Deborah that she's not Nancy Drew."

Shadrach shook his head. He couldn't wait until Madame Mulah was out of his hair and behind bars where she belonged.

CHAPTER THIRTY

RAHLIEM

As Carlton delivered his poem about the road to redemption at lightning speed, almost rivaling the speed at which Twista spits his verses, Rahliem was amazed and satisfied at how well the crowd was keeping up with him. With as many heads moving and bounce up and down, Rahliem almost thought he was at a rap concert—something he hadn't been to since the nineties. And at that moment when he could see people getting into his verses, he was proud of the complete transformation that had overtaken Carlton. Just a year ago, he was released from prison after spending almost fourteen years behind bars for a murder Calvin committed and finally, he was beginning the process of living his dream.

He didn't get to enroll in divinity school as he would have hoped, but he did begin work with the Street Disciples Ministry and even helped with some administrative and leadership tasks. Rahliem couldn't have asked for a better second-in-command. Carlton spent a lot of time speaking to young black and Hispanic boys at detention centers across the state of North Carolina and he's also passing out daily devotions on the corner of New Walkertown Road and Dr. Martin Luther King, Jr. Drive every day.

"Yo' man, you were hot." Calvin said to his older brother when he came to their table. Calvin almost didn't go to the bookstore for their poetry and jazz night. Calvin had complained of not really being a jazz fan and almost every time he went to a poetry joint, he got the feeling that he was on the set of the movie *Love Jones*. Even though "Inspiration and the Lord Above" was tonight's theme, Calvin felt anything but inspired. The poetry wasn't bad but the mood wasn't vibing with him at all. Rahliem had to agree that there was something missing in the atmosphere, but there was a good chance that Carlton may have put it there.

"Thanks man," Carlton said as he took his seat and sipped on his elixir. The frankincense and myrrh was strong and lingering everywhere he walked. Rahliem could see the heads turn as he walked past the other patrons in the room.

"I told you not to put so much of that stuff on man." Calvin said as he watched Carlton take out a small bottle and reapply the lotion to his hands. Rahliem shared their allergy to colognes was one of the many things they all had in common. "These chicks are looking at you funny and stuff."

"Man stop hating, the ladies love Carlton."

"Man, I thought you were going to be a born again virgin?"

"I am," Carlton said as he retrieved a number that had been passed to him by a fine sista sporting a sandy brown Afro and wearing a skin-tight orange and green print dress. Rahliem and Calvin looked at her feet and notice that she wore sandals that had a big orange flower across her feet that matched the one on the right side of her hair. Her skin was radiant and gave off the appearance of having been exposed to gloss to give it a finishing touch. Calvin quickly snatched the paper from Carlton and peeped her number, email and her Facebook page. Before he could fold it, Carlton snatched it back. "But just because I've chosen to be celibate doesn't mean that I can't look at women or find them attractive."

"Well, as long as you not trying to hem them up in the locker room bumping and grinding on them and stuff, I guess that's all good."

"Sounds like somebody is still jealous."

"Whatever you fake Fresh Prince looking—" Calvin stopped mid-sentence as he caught on to what he was getting ready to say. Rahliem was surprised too because he remembered Calvin telling him that the guy he killed so long ago once called Carlton that. Truthfully, it had always been a running joke about how Carlton looked like Will Smith and Calvin looked like DJ Jazzy Jeff, except he was a few shades lighter than him. They used to call each other that all the time when they picked on each other and cracked jokes. When the Crips were stomping on Carlton and beating the hell out of Calvin from his desire to get revenge on them because they killed their older sister a few years prior, they stole their jokes and used them against them. "My bad man."

"I'm not offended." Carlton took another sip of his drink and stuffed the number back into his shirt pocket. For somebody who claimed he was going to be celibate, he was doing a good job showing off what thirteen years of pumping irons in prison could do. The white t-shirt was doing a horrible job at concealing the decidedly masculine features underneath the shirt. And the sleeves of his unbuttoned shirt outlined the guns that hung off his shoulder. Not that Calvin was a slouch either because their father and grandfathers on both of their parents' sides were into maintaining that physical appearance. Their younger brother, Casey had them both beat as he was an athlete, having wrestled for six years and now making it as a professional football player overseas.

The lights dimmed and the room was near dark as Rahliem heard a familiar voice sing a few bars of Jazmine Sullivan's "In Love With Another Man."

"Is that who I think it is?" Calvin sat up straight and strained to see the woman as she continued singing the song that could have been the theme song to his divorce that was finalized six weeks ago. He looked down at his left hand and the imprint that used to be where his wedding band rested at and made its home was gone. "I wouldn't have come if I knew she was going to be singing here." He knew Maria's voice anywhere. Once the light began to get brighter, everyone could see his ex-wife clearly. She wore a neon pink T-shirt that hugged and accentuated all of those curves—curves that used to belong to him exclusively. As she hit the bridge of the song, it appeared that their eyes made contact. Then she looked away and that's when they saw him, the man responsible for breaking their marriage up. It had been a minute since either of them had run into Bilal and Calvin had swore if he ever saw him again, the side that Garfield met was gonna come out. He still was trying to figure out what it was they drugged him with when Maria left him that night. Carlton grabbed his arm before Calvin could get out of his seat good enough.

"Jesus wouldn't like that." Carlton said as if he could read my mind. "He's not worth it."

"Naw man, when I punch him on the left side, I'm gonna make sure I get a good shot at his right side too."

"We're supposed to be Christians, Calvin. I thought you said you forgave him."

"I didn't forget that I was going to whoop his ass though." Carlton started pulling Calvin away while he kept his eyes on Bilal. For his part Bilal looked hurt and sad and if Rahliem didn't know any better, he'd thought that Maria was singing that song to him. Calvin didn't resist Carlton only because they had agreed that once he got out of jail that they wouldn't fight no more, play fight or otherwise. "Come on man, let me go. I said I wasn't going to hit him."

"I know you're not. I'm about to take you home."

Darn! Rahliem was beginning to wish he had driven instead but since Carlton had the car, and they were trying to save gas money, he had to deal with the extra company. He started to suggest that he'd drive Calvin's car so they could have some extra time but Calvin didn't look to be in the mood to talk to. As Rahliem was getting into the passenger side of Carlton's Ford Focus, he could see Maria making a quick exit to her car.

"You need to let that woman go man," Carlton bolted out of the parking space and away from the bookstore. Rahliem braced himself as Carlton continued to fly as if he were a NASCAR driver.

"Yeah you're right." Calvin looked out of the window, never taking his eyes off of Maria. "I need to get laid."

"What?" Rahliem almost choked on his words.

"I never said I was celibate." Calvin got it out quickly, "Maria and I still had sex until the week of our divorce. We were still married and I still had my needs."

"Wait a minute," Carlton interjected, "I thought after you felt guilty about almost hooking up with Kima and swore off sex?"

Calvin had talked about Kima to Rahliem privately after it happened. They had met a dinner date and were tempted to fornicate until Calvin remembered that he was still married to Maria and simmered down. Rahliem had spent the afternoon in prayer of his healing and rebuilding his relationship with God after he decided to move forward with his split from Maria.

"I felt guilty because Kima wasn't my wife and I still was married to Maria, in spite of the fact that I knew that she and Bilal were out there going further than I did with Kima. Then a week later when Maria and I said we'd talk to about the possibility of reconciling our marriage so it wouldn't end in sin our bodies spoke more than our lips did."

"Y'all were supposed to be working things out." Rahliem was disappointed that Calvin had not been forthcoming about his twisted and conflicting relationship with Maria during their sessions. He began to question whether he had reached the man or not.

"I did work out."

"Calvin stop taking things in the literal sense," Carlton was clearly frustrated.

"I can't judge you because you and Maria will have to answer for your relationship once you stand before God again." Rahliem stated trying to ease the tension. "I just hope you have thought about the repercussions of your actions."

"I have and once I find another woman, preferably one I can call my wife, I can get Maria off my mind. Y'all have no idea. I still dream about the children we had and wanted to have. I wake up and it's frozen on her side of the bed. For ten years I had someone to lie down next to and just talk to. Someone who I can share my growing pains with without being ashamed of who I was and who I'm trying to be."

Carlton started to interject something but decided to end the conversation by not responding. Rahliem didn't continue the conversation either. They listened to a few hip-hop inspired gospel songs on the radio. Calvin's mind went back to Maria and wondering whether or not Bilal were going to have any fun after leaving the bookstore. Rahliem's phone buzzed with a text message from Faith.

How was the show? Faith had asked.

It was alright. I'm almost home now ... going to read some passages out of the Bible and go to sleep. Rahliem had replied.

Say a prayer for me.

Don't I always.

At that moment, Rahliem was happy to have someone he could trust and talk to. He could also relate to Calvin's desire to continue having a sexual relationship. As his relationship with Faith grew beyond being platonic, he's thought about being intimate with Faith a couple of times. But he also knew that the flesh was weak and he had to hold out in order not to disappoint God or himself and to continue to set a good example for the men in the ministry.

CHAPTER THIRTY-ONE

SHADRACH

Shadrach woke up and turned on the television in the room to see what the weather was going to be like since it had been raining for the past few days. This Saturday was the day he agreed to volunteer at For Father's Only, a local organization for teenage fathers that Davon helped founded and still took an active part in. On the news station where Shadrach and Deborah had left the channel on last night, the first thing he saw was a blonde hair, blue-eyed chick talking about how another black man has been accused of raping women all over the city.

"I don't want to hear this negativity first thing in the morning." He was disgusted because this chick had already started the day off on the wrong foot. He changed the channel to a community access channel to see a guy he went to school with named Jamon Howard talk about what was going on in the community.

"Today, we have some good events going on in the community. First off, I need to commend some young teenage fathers in the area; they are really doing their thing. For Father's Only, the nonprofit organization created to help young men in their new role as fathers is having a forum today at the Winston Lake YMCA on 901 Waterworks Road, about a couple of blocks past the New Walkertown Road intersection. They have arranged for men ages thirteen to twenty-five to look for jobs, find daycare services, participate in fatherhood forums and that's not all. Women and teenage mothers are welcomed to participate in the events as well. There will be several fraternities as well as civic and faith-based organizations in attendance as well as members so if you got time, from noon until seven, come check these guys out. On to other things…"

"Now this is what *I* want to listen to." He says to himself as he makes an exit to the bathroom. After he takes care of business, Shadrach contemplates what he's going to wear. He finally decides on a black pair of slacks with a tan shirt with a black, gold and tan tie to match. He's looking forward to working with these young men. It's been about three months since he's seen any of them, and he wonders how much they've grown and the children too. Just everything about this program is good. He knew a good number of his frat brothers as well as the Grace United Methodist family were behind the event and looked forward to being in fellowship with positive black men doing something to uplift and encourage the young men in the community. He wished that Deborah could be here too, but she's on a trip to Washington D. C. for her entrepreneur's convention.

Shadrach looked in the mirror as he adjusted his tie and he thought about how he should have been a teenage father. No older than D when he got the first girl pregnant and he shook his head at the two other abortions he'd quietly bribed and begged the young women to have so he could further pursue his studies and continue the façade of being an upstanding and bright young man. He knew that if he had ever admitted to his parents that not once, but three times he had fathered children out of wedlock, his parents would've been devastated. He felt even worse when he thought about how he coerced Abednego into talking the girl he knocked at up sixteen to get an abortion too, especially since Abednego had gotten a taste of the streets and he'd been fighting unsuccessfully to pull Abednego out of them. The kids would be between the ages of four and nine.

When Davon had extended the invitation to work with For Father's Only, Shadrach finally felt like the Lord had forgiven him because he was able to encourage the other men to handle the responsibility that he did not. Deborah had forgiven him for robbing her of the opportunity to be a stepmother as did Felton and Abednego for not being the man he falsely had portrayed himself to be and for pushing Abednego not to handle his responsibilities as well. Sometimes, Shadrach would reflect on whether or not if Abednego's girlfriend at the time had went through with pregnancy, if the child could have influence Abednego to get his life together earlier and leave the streets alone.

But enough with the lamenting, Shadrach was sure God had forgiven him by now and he knew he had finally forgiven himself. As he looked at the clock, eleven o' clock came around so fast that the next thing he knew, he was at the center already. "Radio" from Musiq's forthcoming CD, *On My Radio* was a different sound for the smooth neosoul singer, but a welcomed tune that reminded Shadrach of his college days that swiftly passed of studying, fellowshipping and being in tune with his radio. Shadrach arrived at the Y and sees a guy he has never met before standing at the door, shaking the people's hands and showing everyone where to go and things. He gets out the car and when he gets to him, he tells him where the volunteers are to go.

"I don't think we've met before, are you one of the fathers?"

"No, Ezekiel Hall. I'm one of the volunteers and graduated with Donte from Gilbert State a few years ago."

"Okay, I guess I will be seeing you later then."

Shadrach shook his hand and went inside the building, where he could see Kente running around with the other little kids. Davon, Jaron and their friend Hosea are standing by the room where the forum is going to be held.

"What's up gentlemen?" Shadrach greeted as Hosea turns in his direction.

"Aw, what's up man." Davon says as he shakes his hand.

Jaron and Hosea greet him as well, and they began to discuss how they wanted the forum to be run. Shadrach and Hosea were going to moderate the forum, in which they will be talking about job placement and educational opportunities for the young men.

"Is Rheysean going to be here? I know he's out promoting his new album and everything. I tried to get in touch with his agent but he never could come to the phone." Jaron was asking.

"Last I heard Rheysean is going to be here, along with Laren Lawson. At least that is what my wife said." Hosea said. Rheysean was a popular rapper with songs on top of the secular charts. Laren was a bestselling street lit writer who had recently given his life to God and started using his talents to write inspirational works. Not only were they the celebrity appearance at For Father's Only, they were the sons of the late Lewis "Big L" Lawson, a notorious gangster who had reportedly had an affair with Madame Mulah fifteen years ago and whom Abednego had aspired to be like in his drug dealing days.

"So how is Kei doing?" Shadrach asked. He had known of Davon's side aspirations to be a music producer and that she was one of the artists he'd been working with when he wasn't cutting hair.

"She's good, Davon's giving her a hard time about this album." Hosea said.

"Now you know I'm a perfectionist. I like my lyrics sung right and I'm like that with everything I do." Davon said.

Shadrach was the least bit surprised, Davon had a reputation for trying to be Mr. Perfect at the shop. Shadrach looked at his watch and noticed that it was time to start the forum. He looked in the room and admired the set up. He and Hosea took their seats at the head of the room and while they were talking, he notice that a lot of young men were coming into the room. While some gave off the appearance that they could pass for nineteen or twenty, others looked like they could barely be thirteen. He saw quite a few of them bringing their toddlers and babies to the forum, but Ezekiel was telling them were the daycare was so they could attend the forum. He noticed one of the guys, looked about sixteen, had three children with him; two boys and a girl. With the girl being the oldest, they looked about two, one and a baby.

Then he realized it was D, the guy that tried to rob and punk him at the shop.

"Daniel Abriel Jackson, but everyone calls him D. He's fifteen, very straight forward and smart; but he's hardheaded and he gives us a hard time."

"When did he start showing up?" Shadrach inquired.

"About two months ago. He thinks he's the man because he got three kids. I don't know what to say man, I feel sorry for him sometimes because I know he must be tired trying to care for three children. He's not a bad person, just a little arrogant sometimes and you know how I feel about arrogant folks. Not to mention he's also raising his younger brothers and sisters despite having two older brothers who barely chip in and help."

Shadrach could feel where Hosea was coming from. The forum was about to start and the room was filled to capacity. There were some instrumental playing in the background and Hosea gets ready to do the icebreaker. He was to start the topics while Shadrach provided insightful input and led into the next topics. The hour they spent talking seemed to only take up about fifteen minutes.

"I'd like to thank everyone for coming to the For Father's Only Forum. Today, our main topic will center on this question: What does it take for a man to be a father to his child? We chose this topic for this month because there have been a lot of debate on whether or not we as black men are doing enough to be fathers to our children, and since most of us are young fathers ourselves, I personally think that we are the best ones to answer that question."

D was the first one to speak, and Shadrach agreed with what he said. He talked about men running way from their responsibilities and how the first thing men needed to do was accept them. He had everything going until he brought the women into the picture. His comment was that women should not be so quick to critique men when they don't meet their expectations.

"So what are you saying? That every time child support isn't paid, we are suppose to accept that and be okay?" one of the women in the audience said.

"No, what I'm saying that we shouldn't always be so quick to jump on what the man is doing wrong. Men need to take responsibility and then follow up on that responsibility. You can't just say 'I have a son' or 'I have a daughter'; you have to be there to provide and take care of the child. And regardless how you feel about the mother, follow up with her and see how she's doing because after all, you helped her make that baby." D defended himself.

"But sometimes, you don't have it that easy, you can't find a job to take care of the baby. And then if you do have one, you have to work enough so that your child can be taken care of. Sometimes, I feel like I can't do everything I need to do and I'm always sacrificing something." A young man in the crowd says.

"That's when you have to learn time management. But that is what you sacrifice when you have a child. The mother sacrifices her social life among other things. The guy must sacrifice something too." The woman from before made her point.

"And that is where accepting responsibility comes in. The father has to accept responsibility for helping make the baby because he was there when it happened; in turn the mother must not put her personal opinions of the father in front of his responsibility to that child. As where men sometimes don't take responsibility; women are prone to bring problems into the relationship, trying to push the problems into the raising the baby itself."

"Hold up! Explain where the woman is at fault! Let's face it, men are known to neglect their responsibilities more than women; and men have it easier to do so."

"I'm not saying men aren't neglecting their responsibilities, I'm saying that when it comes to raising the child, personal opinions and problems with your relationship should be put aside to put the child first."

"I have to agree with that." Hosea jumped in before it got out of hand. "Whenever a child is brought into the world both parents personal problems with each other should be put aside. The both of you have to be able to work together to provide for the child and do for the child. Most importantly, the man and the woman in the relationship have to learn to get along. Part of that learning to get a long is not putting stereotypes in the relationship. Not assuming that the next time the woman gets pregnant that it will be by another man; or assuming that all young men run away from fatherhood. Men and women are not perfect, so in no way can you expect both parties to be perfect in raising the child."

The forum had gone on for another hour with different takes on the main discussion of what does it take for a man to be a father to his child. As the forum got underway, Shadrach gained a new level of respect for D, he liked how he thought, and how he defended his positions so well. How he didn't always take it personal that people disagreed with him. Even the attacks on his parenting ability by one of the girls he still kept charm and sportsmanship. When the forum had ended, he made it a point to talk this young man.

D had gone to the daycare to pick up his three children. His oldest was just turned two, which means he got this girl pregnant when he was twelve. Man! Anyway, his next child was fourteen months and the youngest was five months.

"You need help with them?" Shadrach extended an olive branch.

"Naw, man. But thanks for the offer. Keyanna's mother is here so she'll be with her."

"You did a good job with your defending your positions on the forum."

"Thanks man. It's kind of hard being a gentleman sometimes when Nachelle is trying to air our personal business for the public. Sometimes I just want to say 'look chick shut up,' but I ain't trying to get kicked out of the forum."

"Well, sometimes you can't help what people say because forums are usually open for discussion. Maybe you should avoid looking at her when answering the questions and if you have to look at her, do it without making any facial expressions."

"Aight, thanks Shadrach."

Nachelle came so they could try to talk about their problems in a civilized manner.

Keyanna went to her mom, and asked where Derrick and Raymond's mothers were. Shadrach pulled himself away from their drama for a moment to look at the other fathers who were at the event. About thirty showed up overall. He was still amazed at how many teenage fathers existed in the Tre-4 area but proud of them handling their business just the same. Majority of the men here are under twenty, some are going to Bethune or Truth Technical Colleges in the area. Jamon Howard was seen by the exit door with his two sons, one of them is about thirteen or fourteen. Shadrach had wanted to make his way over there to speak to him before he left but D had come back with a small business card in hand.

"Shadrach. If you have any job openings at your barbershop, can you let me know? This job I got at Wendy's ain't paying enough and I need another job so I can try to pay child support for my three children. If you can do that, I'd really appreciate it."

"I can't promise you anything, but if anything opens up, I will call you and let you know."

He shakes my hand and he goes with Nachelle and his children to another room. Shadrach headed toward the exit to see if he can catch Jamon before he leaves but he was too late. He figured he had his number and that he could call him later on when he got home today, and maybe see if he have an opening at Shadrach's or see what he can do to help D out. Even though they started out on the wrong foot, D seemed like the type of brother worth saving and he was going to see to it that he gave it his best shot.

CHAPTER THIRTY-TWO

DONTE

Donte watched as Eugene packed his bags to spend the night with Eve.

"Daddy, can I take this with me?" Eugene held up a miniature teal blue, purple, gold and white basketball that represented the New Orleans Hornets that had Chris Paul's signature stamped around the logo.

"I thought you weren't going to play with that ball anymore, that you were going to wait until Chris Paul came back to town and have him sign it?" Donte asked as he refolded the shirts and pants that Eugene stuffed in the bag.

"I am. I just want to show Ms. Eve how to play basketball."

Donte shook his head.

"Daddy, do you hate Ms. Eve?" Eugene asked as he passed the ball to Donte, knowing he wasn't supposed to play basketball in the room.

Donte decided to demonstrate his skills dribbling the ball, doing crossovers before doing a layup on the rim that was on the back of Eugene's door. Then he stopped when he seen Eugene sitting on his bed at awe, but with a slight disappointment on his face. Donte sat on the bed next to his suitcase and put the basketball on top of it. "No, I don't hate Ms. Eve."

Donte knew that Eugene interpreted the rough tone in his voice to indicate that he was fibbing. He noticed pieces of Eve in Eugene's eyes and lips as well as saw the ears and nose and skin tone that came from him. "When you're old enough to understand the whole story of how your mother and I met, I'll tell you. But what you need to know and understand know is that I don't hate Ms. Eve. I'm working hard not to hate anybody because you can't hate anyone and love Jesus at the same time, you understand?"

Eugene looked away from Donte and murmured a "yes." Donte reached over and gently lifted Eugene's head up and turned it toward him. "I love you with my whole heart and soul and I wouldn't let anything bad happen to you—I hope I've shown you that for now. Ms. Eve and I have a lot of disagreements we need to sort through, which is why we are not together as man and wife as some of your friends were fortunate enough to have. No matter how many disagreements we have, I will always have a level of respect for her because she helped me with one of my greatest creations," he paused when Eugene smiled, "that would be you. So I can't hate her because if it weren't for her, you wouldn't be here. I'm glad you got to meet your mother because I know and understand how hurt you were last Mother's Day when you didn't have a mother to give your card to."

"Will you and Eve make me a brother or a sister? I would like to have one."

Donte felt his heart sink. He had no idea that this was what his son was hinting at. Sure, he'd over heard some of his son's prayers for a sibling but Eugene had never asked him before. "If it's the Lord's will, anything is possible." Donte answered with the safest answer he could think of at the moment. He wasn't going to outright say "no" because while he was certain that God's will for him included marrying Elicia eventually, he couldn't rule out the possibility of succumbing to the flesh and getting any woman, including Eve, pregnant.

"Okay, I'll keep praying." Eugene said as he stuffed a shirt in his bag. "Maybe you and Elicia can have a baby and you and Eve can have a baby, and I'll have two siblings."

Donte chuckled to himself. "Naw, man. You have no idea what you are asking. You trying to get me in trouble."

Eugene chuckled and laughed too. "Nun-uh."

"Let's finish packing so you can be ready for when Ms. Eve picks you up." Donte took out the shirt that Eugene stuffed in the bag and folded it correctly. After putting the last of Eugene's clothes as well as his bathroom supplies in the bag, they heard the door ring. Eugene ran out of the room and went to open the door. Normally, Donte would've scolded him about running in the house but he decided to let this one ride. He knew he would be wrong if he stopped Eugene from being excited about seeing his mother. He'd promised himself, as well as his family and friends, that he would not impose his personal feelings about Eve on his son because regardless of how he felt about Eve, he wanted Eugene to respect his mother, no matter what. Donte zipped up the bag and carried it over his shoulder as he went into the living room to face Eve.

Eve wore a tight fitting t-shirt that had the BabyPhat logo in the center of it as well as some hip hugging Applebottom jeans with some off brand black boots. *Don't pass judgment*, Donte reminded himself as he walked toward them. He took the bag off his shoulder and passed it to Eugene.

"I see he's happy to see me." Eve said as she reached in and hugged Donte and he obliged. The scent of her perfumed lingered in the air. He noticed it was different than the one she normally wore and if he didn't know better, he could've sworn it matched the fragrance Elicia had on when they met in the park. He tried to place it off but in the back of his mind, he wasn't feeling it one bit.

"Yeah, he's been talking about what he wants to do when the two of you hang out." Donte said keeping it cordial.

"Maybe the three of us can do something together sometime —that is if Elicia doesn't mind." Eve tossed out there as she gazed seductively at Donte. Donte looked away and shook his head. His mind and spirit confirmed what he had begun to suspect a minute ago.

"That's up for discussion." Donte said as he bent down and gave Eugene a hug. "For now, I don't want to keep Eugene from spending time with you so I'm going to let you guys go." He looked Eugene in the eye. "I want you to be good for mommy. Don't ask her twenty million questions and you only got five dollars and once that's gone, that's all you have, alright?"

"Yes Daddy." Eugene wrapped his arms around Donte's neck and Donte returned the hug. When Eugene let go, he stood up and watched the two of the walk out of the apartment. He was hoping that Eve wouldn't plant seeds in Eugene's mind about the possibility of them getting back together intimately, but Donte decided that he'd address his suspicion only when he had enough evidence to do so.

CHAPTER THIRTY-THREE

FELTON

Felton was about to step out of the house to go work out when Natasha walked in. It had been a good four months since he had seen his now visibly pregnant sister-in-law. In the face, Natasha reminded Felton of the pictures he saw of how Natalie looked at eighteen and she was a banger then. These days, she looked a shadow of herself as the new baby weight made her fill out in places Felton didn't know she had.

"Hey Big Bro, long time no see."

"Same for you," He was tempted to be angry that Natasha didn't show up at Abednego's funeral but he quickly dismissed the thought and hugged Natasha. "Natalie is at work and I'm on my way to work myself."

"I need your help." Natasha got straight to the point. She held onto her stomach as she lowered herself onto the couch. "I'm in a fix and I need to get out of it."

"Did you talk to Natalie?" Felton inquired because he knew that they had had a falling out when Natalie tried to introduce the word of God into her sister's life and her sister didn't want to hear it. When Felton tried to get Natalie to see that not everyone believed in *her* God and should just leave it alone, that was the beginning of the problems they started having in their house.

"You know that chick is still mad at me because I didn't tell her who the father of my eldest son was and I won't tell her who the father of this one is. Oh by the way, I'm sorry about Abednego. I don't do funerals but I did visit the gravesite at the Evergreen Cemetery every weekend and I bring Montell, too."

Felton just nodded his head. He knew that Abednego and Natasha had a past as Natasha was a prostitute and Abednego would sometimes pay for her services when he wanted her to work with the guys who were in his own set of flicks. They actually had done a movie together, according to one of Felton's friends who had seen the video. Felton knew the only reason his little brother was making flicks was because he didn't like Donte and felt he could cut into the man's business. Of course, when Felton started dating Natalie, he knew nothing of Natasha and Abednego's relationship, but since Abednego was cool with it and had sworn he'd left her alone, Felton and Natalie continued to let their relationship blossom.

"Where's Montell?" Felton was concerned about his five-year-old nephew. He personally thought that the boy should have been in school but his birthday fell in September and thus he had to wait another year. He and Natalie tried to talk Natasha into at least putting the boy in pre-school and even offered to pay for it but Natasha would hear nothing of it and his loving mother-in-law, who had been missing in action for a minute as well, backed Natasha in her decision.

"He's playing with some kids down the street. The kids down there looked perfectly harmless and I figured we could talk first."

Felton exhaled and refused to hide his frustration. Most times, Natasha didn't have the sense that God gave her. Felton put his fingers to his temples and slowly massaged them while quietly inhaling and exhaling. "Well you have a seat while I go get my nephew." He said as he opened the door.

"But I wasn't done—"

Felton walked out before he could hear what excuse Natasha could come up with this time to bring trouble to their footsteps. He knew that Natasha was coming for something or coming with something and that sooner or later he'd get an answer for it. He found Montell playing alone on the sidewalk and he shook his head. He could see why Abednego had just had his way with Natasha and moved on to the next chick—the girl was a complete ditz. "Hey lil' man."

"Uncle Felton." The boy excitedly jumped up and wrapped his arms around Felton's neck. His clothes looked a little dirty, but that didn't bother Felton as he was always happy to see his nephew. "I'm going to be a big brother soon. Just like you and Uncle Shadrach."

Felton thought he was going to break down then but he held it together.

"Uncle Felton, what's wrong?" Montell asked as he walked hand in hand with his uncle to the condo.

"I miss Abednego."

"Where did he go?"

"Heaven."

"When do we get to go?"

Felton was uncomfortable answering that question. Shadrach and Deborah were sure without a doubt that they were going to heaven. Natalie was sure that she was going too. Apparently, Natasha at least knew about it and gave Montell a jumpstart on believing that *heaven* was the place to be. It seemed that Felton was the only one *not* going.

Great, now He's using the boy to get at me. Felton thought upon entering his home. He saw Natasha stretched out on the couch, half asleep from watching cartoons.

"She sleeps all the time," Montell asserted, "got any towels or blankets to cover her up in? I need to make sure my little brother is warm."

"Hold on," Felton went to get a blanket when he heard the door open. He didn't even have to check who it was cause Montell welcomed Natalie in with open arms. He was adorable and seemed to only serve as a reminder that he would never be the man he wanted to be. Felton came in with a blanket and Montell thanked him while taking it and quickly covering up his mother.

"We see who's gonna be the man of the house." She smiled at her nephew as she walked toward Felton and kissed him on the lips.

"That we do."

Felton and Natalie continued to watch as Montell covered his mother up and then turned the television on to Nickelodeon.

"She's due any day now."

"Natasha thinks she's slick. She knew that if she brought Montell that I wouldn't kick her out."

"What is going on?"

Natalie looked at Felton and exhaled. "The same thing that happened when she had Montell, she needs a place to stay and decided to bum off of us until the baby is due." The hurt and pain of the incident returned to Natalie as if it happened yesterday. "She played me, had me believing that she was going to let me adopt Montell, give me an opportunity to turn my life around and then she got with some dope pusher and decided that *I* wasn't good enough to be the mother to the son that *she* didn't want."

Felton had remembered Natalie telling him the story all too well and every now and then when the subject of their infertility came up it was still a sore spot.

"So what are we going to do with Natasha?"

"Let's wait until she has the baby and we find out who she's running from because I have no doubt in my mind that she's running from somebody. Then we figure out how we are going to take care of Montell and her newborn." Natalie looked over to Montell who was lying at his mother's feet as he struggled to watch the television show. "Montell, you want to go get something to eat?"

"Yeah. That sounds great. Thanks Auntie Natalie."

And with that, Felton and Natalie took Montell by the hand and walked with him to the car so that he could enjoy a kid's meal at one of his favorite restaurants.

CHAPTER THIRTY-FOUR

RAHLIEM

Rahliem was happy to be back on the corner of Martin Luther King, Jr. Boulevard and New Walkertown Road. The six young black men wearing black baseball caps that said Jesus Saves, long black T-Shirts, baggy but not sagging jeans and various brands of sneakers stepped out of the white, silver and maroon van. Each man had their maroon backpacks filled with copies of *The Upper Room*, and a couple of books in their hands ready to pass out. Each of the young men who followed Rahliem out of the van had a mission and method to spread the word of God in the hood.

Just the way things needed to be, Rahliem thought as he gave a copy of *The Upper Room* to an elderly couple who had walked to the van. In the week before Abednego passed, some of the guys thought it would be a good idea to sing one of the popular gospel songs and they immediately drew comparisons to Jagged Edge.

With the clean cuts, sharp clothes and swagger, they attracted attention from the crowd. The people were just as happy to see them again so they flocked to them from the nearby shopping center. The men could have given them an impromptu concert in the middle of the street. After the last man stepped out and pulled the door shut, the driver of the van drove off cautiously trying to find a parking space near the barbershop at the top of the hill. For Rahliem and the rest of the Street Disciples, this stop on this popular hill in East Winston was their home.

Another Saturday after the masses had been paid and people were at this busy shopping center trying to catch fish dinners, the hip hop inspired gear, African American Art and the sweet smelling soap from the make shift car shop greeted customers as they made their way up the hill to the shopping center. Also at the popular intersection were a group of young men in the Nation of Islam that were the same age as Rahliem's twenty-something Street Disciples. Dressed in all black from the bow ties to the tailored suites and spit shined black shoes, the young Nation continued to sell their *Final Call* to the masses. They had many supporters just as the older homeless man who was hawking copies of *The Winston Salem Journal.*

Rahliem watched his best friend, Vincent X give the young men instructions as they traveled as far as the eye could see on New Walkertown Road.

"As-Salamu Alaykum Rahliem. You got to go further and deeper." Vincent taunted him.

"Wa Alaykum As-Salam, and that is true, my friend." Rahliem answered the challenge. "That is what Jesus called us to do."

"Are you trying to start with me this morning?" Vincent had already shown his impatience. Rahliem preferred to keep the peace because this was the first Saturday that they've really been out in full force since Abednego was killed and he didn't want to start the day by getting into an argument with his best friend. Religious differences aside, Rahliem still cared for Vincent as if he were Davon.

"Naw man, I come in peace as I'm sure you do."

Some of the students from Winston-Salem State University made the one mile journey on foot to get their news, taste the food and get away from campus. Vincent recognized a few of the college and alumni men wearing the black and old gold where out in their letters picking up trash for the Adopt-A-Highway program. He gripped them and let them on their way.

"It's good to see my brothers out here." Vincent told Rahliem as he rejoined them on the corner. "We always come out to make sure the street named after our brother is clean."

"That's a good thing," Rahliem replied as he remembered Vincent telling him not long ago that he had pledged the fraternity while at State. Rahliem would have been at State during that time as well if he had not been at the infamous Butler Juvenile Correctional Facility for aggravated assault and attempted murder. But all things that don't feel good can work out for good as that is the place he met the Holy Spirit and began the walk that led him to this place.

"How is Vanessa?"

"She's good." Vincent went along with Rahliem's change of subject. "I almost wish my sister had gotten with you instead of the man she's with now. But thank God she's not with Craig no more."

Rahliem remembered the middle of the night rescue in which he went with Vincent to pick up Vanessa and her son so they could leave an abusive relationship. At first it seemed that sparks would fly between Vanessa and Rahliem but after a few dates that proved to not be the case. "I'm sure the Harpers would have been pleased to have someone else in their never ending fight to convert you back to Christianity and rejoining the Baptist church."

"But you go to a Methodist church."

"But I'm a servant to all, thank you Jesus."

Out of the corner of his eye, he saw Calvin approach them.

"Everything cool over here?" Calvin questioned when he switched his backpack for Rahliem's. He was trying to give Rahliem an out to go to the truck in case he needed one.

"Everything's fine man, go on back to your spot." Vincent tried to send him away. Calvin shot him a look but Rahliem shook his head and nonverbally sent the man away.

"Man, you shouldn't be so mean to Calvin. You know that boy loves to fight and Martin is not going to be there to break it up between you all the time," Rahliem warned Vincent. Rahliem knew that Martin was Calvin's best friend and Vincent's line brother.

"Nobody is worried about Calvin out here. Number one, I know that Carlton will keep him in check and besides, after that blow up a few months ago, we both promised Martin we'd keep a healthy distance from one another."

Rahliem shook his head to that as he thanked Celtius for bringing him a bag filled with copies of *The Upper Room*. He continued giving out copies to the students and accepting donations for the church and the scholarship fund. One of the men sporting a mohawk and wearing skinny jeans was trying to get Celtius' attention.

"I'm still abstaining," Celtius assured Rahliem. They had had a talk a few nights before about Celtius' urges to unify with a man coming back. Rahliem felt for the man because he believed that Celtius was committed to leaving that lifestyle behind but he also knew that the man was tempted every step of the way. Tonex' coming out was not making things any easier for Celtius as his friends in that lifestyle continued to try to convince him that he could have his cake and eat it, too.

"Do what you can do," Rahliem encouraged him.

"As always." Celtius left him reciting Psalms 91. That was one of the last things Abednego and Rahliem had worked on Celtius with. Now, weeks later, he had the psalms down by memory.

Mya came a few moments after him. The long flowing braids he sported weeks ago had now been replaced by a bald head and a goatee. Tired of the criticism over his girlish looks, Mya decided to promote his more masculine features.

"Them boys still coming for Celtius aren't they."

"Mya, I've told you. Celtius can handle himself just like you need to handle that tongue." Rahliem felt like he was a broken record trying to get through to Mya. He wasn't annoyed, but just frustrated that after all these years Mya still found a way to judge Celtius.

"Man, I can't help it, I call it like I see it. Skinny jeans?" Mya replied frustrated, "You see how feminine that makes these dudes look now, skinny jeans. I don't see how dudes can breathe."

Rahliem had caught the subtle jab and before he could chastise him Mya continued, "but I give him props though for holding out and continuing to encourage the young people to abstain from sex. He's doing a better job at that than me."

"What do you mean by that?"

"I've been married for almost a year," Mya. I would be encouraging other married couples to do the opposite." Mya had surprised everyone by marrying the daughter of one of the city councilmen last year. And with that marriage came a change in his outward appearance. They had seen Faith getting out of her car and walking to the intersection.

"Let me let you go so you can talk that lady over there to walk down the aisle with you."

"It will happen in God's timing my friend."

Away from the business attire that Faith was accustomed to wearing, she was now seen sporting a black hoodie, baggy jeans set off with tinted shades that gave a throwback to the nineties looks befitting R&B girl groups SWV or Xscape. She walked over to where Rahliem was and gave him a kiss and a hug.

"Surprise!" She said as she took some of the daily devotionals out of his hand and started passing them out.

"Surprise yourself," Rahliem replied. "I wasn't expecting to see you here."

"You know I had to come out and support your ministry. I've heard you speak, I know you can sing, now I get a chance to see you work."

"That's what's up. I'll have to return the favor."

"So how did you become a street disciple?"

"We take our name from the Book of Matthew 28:19 which states *'Go therefore and make disciples of all nations, baptizing them in the name of the Father and of the Son and of the Holy Spirit.'* The streets connect so many people in the world and we are supposed to be spreading the gospel to those who travel in it. We wear what some would call hood gear because more people are receptive to getting the word from someone they can relate to. If you look at this neighborhood, we are in an area where the rich meet the poor. The poor and the lower class citizens live within two miles of this point and all of your social services for the community are also within two miles of this point."

"Interesting concept. How does one become a street disciple?"

"We started with seven guys whose past resembled the seven deadly sins. It's a big thing with the Catholic church yet a concept most in the world can identify with. The guy you see with the glasses and the little boy passing out devotionals is Donte Speaks, the former porno star who's given his life to the Lord. We used to have to keep an eye on him because his secular videos are still popular and the ladies still flock to him like he's a superstar. Celtius has slimmed down some since he's become a member and Abednego used to have a thing for flashy cars, big jewelry and cash. On the top of the top of the hill you'll find the Rice brothers. Carlton always got by on his pretty boy looks and hardly ever has had to work for anything… even in jail for the murder Calvin committed he still was lazy… except when it came to working out. Calvin's anger issues far supersede mine. That's part of the reason he's a murder and a fighter. Back when he was twelve, he killed the boy who killed their older sister. Carlton shot at the man's dead body when the police arrived and made it appear as if he had done it. Mya, the bald headed one down the corner has a nasty jealous streak and can use his words to tear a man down to where he is less than he is."

"So what would that make you?"

"Pride can be a dangerous thing. Before I got saved I used to believe I was the best thing next to God."

"I would have never picked that up from you."

Rahliem and Faith continued to talk and pass out the daily devotions.

"We've never had a woman passing out the devotions." Rahliem hadn't even seen Donte making his way to the medium. "Faith?"

"Donte, how have you been?" Faith quickly embraced Donte and observed him.

"I didn't know y'all knew each other," Rahliem interjected. His mind was spinning because he had just got done telling Faith about the different guys in the ministry that were present and she seemed unfazed by it all. He noticed that Donte wasn't drawing a larger crowd of ladies who were more interested in him autographing their bootleg versions of his old videos from his former life.

That used to be a problem because the women were known to cause traffic jams from the men who wanted their phone numbers and the women who wanted them to go home and put some clothes on. Even still Donte made things easier by remembering to wear the sun glasses that they had to make another trip to the mall so they could avoid any unwanted incidents.

"We dated before," Faith said. She glanced at Donte but quickly looked away. Rahliem caught that but decided to wait until later.

"Yeah, but we cool now. I've been busy with Eugene so no ladies for me." Donte said as he quickly grabbed his son to keep him from going in the street. "As you can see he likes to get into everything and go everywhere."

"Dad, I want to go across the street." Donte looked across the street to see what or who has his little reflection's attention.

"Well, I'll catch up with ya'll later. Good to see you again." Donte addressed Faith.

Rahliem watched Faith watch Donte and Eugene walk away. He got back into passing out devotions to the different drivers as they drove past the intersection. He didn't know what to think about the fact that he was dating his friend's ex. His mind started spinning, wondering how long they dated and what they may or may not have done together. He tried to remember whether or not Donte had mentioned dating Faith in their conversations but he couldn't recall. Rahliem just resolved to take up the issue another time.

"I'm sorry," Faith said as she walked with him. "I didn't realize you and Donte knew each other."

"They say it's a small world," Rahliem tried to joke. Inside, he had a lot of questions he needed to ask Faith and Donte, too. He wondered who else knew that he was dating Donte's ex. He hadn't seen Eziekel, Neal, Malachi or any of the other guys from Gilbert State so there was no way they could have told him. He knew that Elicia didn't know that he was dating Faith because Rahliem had always strived to keep his personal life private so that his worship of God could be seen, not his stature as a church celebrity. He was sure that Pastor Phelps didn't know but he also knew that if she did, she wouldn't have said anything that would've brought any controversy.

"What's troubling you?" Rahliem knew he was losing his edge as Vincent snuck up on him again.

"Nothing to talk about now. Just thinking about something someone else said."

Rahliem watched as Vincent stepped back jokingly as if he were offended. "Nah, I'm messing with you. I got to get ready to get out of here, let some of these young guys handle the ministry. You be careful out here old man."

"You the one that's old," Rahliem chuckled, briefly excited that Vincent had managed to take his mind off of the thought of Faith and Donte being intimate. Calvin and Mya were approaching and Rahliem nonverbally assured them that everything was cool. He looked at Donte and noticed that he turned his head when he looked his way—he also noticed the distance was greater. Rahliem shook it off as his mind trying to play tricks on him and that Satan was trying to make a situation bigger than what it should be. But he knew he would need to clear the air with Donte as his feelings for Faith were getting deeper by the day and he didn't want to lose his friend over his love for a woman his friend used to talk to.

CHAPTER THIRTY-FIVE

SHADRACH

Once Shadrach arrived home the first thing he did was call Jamon. He hadn't talked to him in a long time. Seeing him with his ten-year-old son reminded him of how wild they used to be when they were young. He missed those days; giving their parents hell and keeping them up late at night. They never got into gangs or messed around with drugs or anything like that, just the two of them being bad and terrible. Both being blessed with pretty boy features, they had their share of women too; and that was how they got caught. When one of the girls they had been passing around like a game of hot potato came back and said she was pregnant, they knew right away that life would not be the same for one of them. The woman in question knew of Shadrach's history of sending women to the clinic so she waited to tell him after she told Jamon's parents first and waited until his parents were home to tell him. They had worked at Jay's Restaurant as waiters and gave Jay hell every chance they could, too. It was fun and worth it. But once the baby came and looked more and more like Jamon, Shadrach saw less and less of him. Of course he would give him money from time to time because he knew that it was hard for him; and he would fill him in on the chicks and things like that. They both ended up turning in their player's card before they even had it.

"Shadrach?"

"Yeah, Jamon, what you been up to?"

"Nothing much, nothing at all. I'm helping Jamari out with his math, I feel like I'm in school. And Kembal reading *Scorpions* by Walter Dean Myers."

"I remember when we read that book, when it first came out."

"Yah, Walter Dean Myers was no joke. Made a young black man want to read and get lost in a book. How is the barbershop treating you?"

"It's doing lovely man. It's hard work at times but man it is worth it. It is worth it. How you like working on public television? I know you like the control of things."

"My show is doing so well; that and my radio spot on KDNV. I put a lot of money into it but I can't complain because unlike some of the folks you see and hear me doing shows with, I can actually pay my bills because I have a good set of sponsors. For Father's Only is going to be my next special, as soon as I can get the financing for it. I wish they had something like this when I was their age."

"I know, it would have helped you out a lot. Raising babies is expensive and everything."

"You ain't telling me nothing I don't know. Just watching some of them dudes pushing strollers and trying to through game to some of them girls reminded me of them days we was sharing them girls and stuff."

Shadrach couldn't help but laugh cause part of it was true. Some dudes had the kind of bond where they could anything together and for Shadrach, that bond was with Jamon. But in a way, Shadrach didnn't miss them days and was glad that they both grew out of it because doing something like that today would cost them their friendship.

"I'm happy for the program though." Jamon said continuing the conversation. "I'm glad it's out there because it shows that black men are responsible and that we are fathers. I saw you talking with D, you thinking about hiring him or something?"

"Yeah, I'm a give the guy a chance. I'm not going to lie; he caught my attention with his intelligence. Besides, Dumar going to school and I can't depend on him that much on the weekdays. Maybe D will work out."

"That's good. I'm going to wait until the Entrepreneur Fair to try to sponsor somebody to work with me. By then I will be able to afford to hire him. So you think you can fit me and the boys in on Saturday for some cuts?"

"You know you don't have to ask, just walk in."

"I understand you running a business, no special treatment."

"I treat you any different than I do anybody else."

"Yeah. I love to stay and talk, but Kembal got me looking up words in the dictionary, and I done ran across a math problem I can't solve."

"Aight man, I'll let you go."

Shadrach hung up the phone and figured Jamon was probably scrambling to find them words in the dictionary and helping Jamari solve them math problems. Just thinking about it brought memories of the abortions again, but he shook them away.

***

Shadrach got up early to open shop, arriving at 5:00 a.m., which was unusual for him because he normally got there at six and open at seven. He inspected the books to see what was happening with the finances. He was impressed because Dumar had done such a wonderful job keeping everything straight and recording everything like he taught him. Before he knew it, seven o'clock gets here and the first customers are a little early. He looked at the schedule on the lounge area of the shop, and noticed that Davon doesn't come in until nine thirty. That doesn't seem right but that was okay because D was coming in at eight and he could at least teach him how to sign customers in, collect money and answer the phone. It's an easy job. Ironically,

Shadrach's first customer of the day was none other than Jay himself, the man who gave him his first "easy" job.

"I see my child has come a long way." He said when took his seat on the chair.

"Yes I have. And when was the last time I seen you in my shop?"

"About a month ago."

"I can tell."

"Well Shadrach you know how it is. My business is expanding and I am getting ready to hang it up and let my son take over. I never had to worry about getting a haircut because I always wear a hat on my head when I cook."

As Shadrach began cutting his head, he remembered those silly little sailor's hats Jay used to try to make Jamon and him wear. They hated those things because they thought they looked silly and gay and the thought of any female seeing them in the hats would degrade their masculinity. Nevertheless, they wore the damn things to keep their jobs, and from keeping Tasha, the chick they were messing with from going to the welfare lines.

"I see why you made Jamon and I wear those hats."

"I knew you would. I know that the two of you hated those things, but the point was not to make you look silly, but to make you realize that businessmen and women have to dress up. Back in the day when I grew up, I went to a private school because my parents could afford it and we used to always wear uniforms. Just like you have to wear your barber's coat to keep from getting hair all over your clothes; we had to wear uniforms to identify us as students and you had to wear those hats to identify you as my employees."

"If you like uniforms so much, why didn't you make us wear one then? Why the hats?"

"I am a unique individual just like everyone else. You see, a lot of restaurants and other places like that want their workers to dress alike and things like that, and that is fine. I just wanted you to wear my hats. I had to make you wear the hats because when you work in the restaurant business, you are expected to cover your hair. Besides, nobody wanted to see those lopsided high top fades you had going on."

"I remember them fades. We used to go to Eric because he was the only one that knew how to do them the way they were supposed to be done."

"So you understand my point, well obviously you did because I see how you let your barbers come and go as they please. And some of the things they wear… I don't know what to tell you."

"I make sure that they got their coat on."

Shadrach thought it was at that moment that he knew what Jay was trying to say, and he agreed with him. That in today's world, everyone has gotten to be so liberal about what they wear, that sometimes they forget the order and the pride people once had in wearing uniforms. The pride in wearing a uniform was not in the reason why someone was wearing them or how to wear them; it was the fact that folks wanted to wear them. As he was getting done cutting Jay's hair, D came in. Shadrach was patient as he showed D how to write up the sales ticket and told him how much he was accountable for in the drawer. Jay was laughing at Shadrach because he didn't necessarily have a register. He had a little tan safe that had to be locked up. When the safe was open, one could see the color coded containers for each coins and dividers for each of the bills.

"I see you are trying to change the way we collect money." Jay pointed to Shadrach's set up.

"It works for me."

"That is what matters. You don't want your customers asking you for dollar bills all the time so you make it look like you don't have any. Plus, it is hard for someone to just reach and take the dollar bills. I like that myself."

Shadrach watched Jay walk out of the door and finished showing D how to do his job. He took the next person and began cutting their hair. D had taken out his CD player and was playing the new album by Carl Thomas. He had it up so loud that everyone could hear him at the other end of the booth. At first, Shadrach didn't say anything about it until the phone rang about three times and he didn't answer it. Then Shadrach yelled for him to pick up the phone and he answered it.

Davon and Clifford walked in and they start to pick up some customers. Shadrach could see that Clifford and D didn't get along from the minute Clifford walked in. Shadrach was hoping that D could avoid another fight in his shop. Clifford took the booth next to Shadrach and he had some man about my age in the chair.

"You hired that nigga?" Clifford questioned as he set up his tools to be sanitized before he began to work on his client's hair.

Shadrach turned his clippers off and did not bother to hide his discontent for Clifford's lack of respect for his shop, "what have I told you about using that word in this establishment?"

"I know what you told me," Clifford rebutted, "I'm telling you that you hired a nigga."

"Word? And what makes him a 'nigga' to you?"

"He ain't about sh—" Clifford almost used the profane word but saw the stern looks from the various customers and fellow barbers in the shop and thought better of it. "No, you'll see what I'm talking about. He's lazy as hell man. He got three kids by three different girls and he don't do sh—not a damn thing to support them. All I do is see him trying to spit some game at some female every time I turn around. See, look, he's doing it now."

Shadrach looked at the front desk to see that D was spitting game to a fine young lady who he though he saw earlier come in with her man. The guy in Shadrach's chair made one of those sighs; the one that says 'when I see this punk out in the street, I'm a whoop his butt!' Shadrach quickly diffused the situation by calling D and warning him about fraternizing with the customers. Shadrach sent the customer to the front and as Tevin walked in late as usual. Shadrach told Tevin to mark up the man's ticket while he talked to D. Shadrach wanted to talk with him too, but he had to deal with D first.

"So what's up?" D asked casually as if he were talking to his friend instead of his boss.

"I don't know man you tell me. I'm paying you to do a job and it looks like you in your own world partying and bull jiving."

"You messing up a Biggie song, you got that on one of these CD's somewhere?"

"I'm serious man! Look, I'm trying to help you and I want to help you, but you got to do things right around here. I can't have you not answering my phones and trying to talk to every sexy lady that comes in the door. Some of these woman are married you know."

"She didn't have no ring on."

"But her husband did." Shadrach began wondering if hiring D and giving him a chance to work in the shop was a good idea. Then he remembered the conversation and the reflections he had with Jay earlier and realized that some of the seeds he'd sown in his youth were harvesting in his garden. He also began to understand why Jay had so much patience with him in spite of having multiple reasons to fire him. "Look, the point is that you are on the clock, and most importantly, you are the first person my customers see when they walk in here. You need to look and act professional and quit goofing off all the time. Do we understand each other?"

"Aight," D looked away from him put his head down.

"Tell Tevin I need to speak to him when you go back to the front."

Great, just great, Shadrach thought as he could see his whole day getting ruined because he had to tell two of his employees how to do their jobs; especially one that has been around for a long time. Shadrach watched as Tevin walked as if he had all day to be about his business.

"Yo' what's up?"

"Sit down."

Tevin followed Shadrach's lead and took a seat at his desk. Shadrach couldn't help but admire the haircut Tevin had given himself. He's amazingly talented, but that could not excuse Tevin for coming in late all the time.

"Hey, if it is about me getting here late all the time, I'm working on it."

"Tevin I don't want to hear that. You know how I feel about excuses. I can't adjust a set of rules for you and have one for everyone else."

"Ah man, you trying to tell me I got to set all my clocks to *Shadrach's* time? I got this job and another one that I am working."

"Maybe you need to start coming to this job on time and the other one a little early. I never complain about you being late in front of the other barbers but you not being fair to everyone else."

"Aight."

"I don't want to have to have this discussion again."

"I said aight."

They walk out of the office and pick up two more customers and start cutting hair. Davon looked at Tevin and started chuckling.

"Shut up faggot!" Shadrach heard Tevin mumble under his breath. Davon had put his clippers down as he had no problems getting at Tevin for clowning his sexuality but Shadrach shook his head no and nonverbally encouraged him to continue cutting his client's hair. Tevin looked back at Shadrach and knew that between being late and that last comment, he didn't have any more chances to screw up. In all honesty, Shadrach had given him more chances than he gave anyone else, but Tevin got to learn to follow rules just like everyone else. That's why the business was called *Shadrach's* and not *Tevin's*.

CHAPTER THIRTY-SIX

FELTON

"Waahhhhhh!"

The birth of a new baby boy was a joyous occasion in many cultures. He carried the family name and will be the one to inherit land. A baby boy's birth was different than a baby girl's birth. A baby boy completes the family legacy; he was a mother's gift and a father's pride and joy. And the world loves its baby boys so much that they lie to them and tell them the world was theirs, instead of the Lord's, thus setting them on a path to destruction before they were able to seek the One who can create a clear path. The world encourages our baby boys to be whores and plunder the world while expecting our baby girls to be innocent and pure for their wedding day. Baby boys could go to jail for murder and folks will mortgage their houses, sell their cars, work an extra job or three, perform some sick, twisted favors... anything will be done to keep our sons out of prison. Anything. But girls who mess up...they are stoned with evil words, pushed to the side and made to feel inferior to men. Instead of encouraging and uplifting them, they are downgraded to the hookers that bring pride and joy to a pimp instead of a pride and joy to the families they belong to.

Natasha had just given birth hours ago and Natalie was sitting at her bedside. Their mother had refused to be at her bedside so once again, Natalie was biting more roles than she could chew.

She thought about the last time she was at the hospital and the cruel trick Natasha had played on her and Felton and that was part of the reason he'd chosen not to be in the room. After giving birth this time around, Natalie was stunned when she heard Natasha respond to the nurse who requested to know the name of the child she was to put on the birth certificate, her mouth dropped so low, it could of made a *thud* sound as it hit the floor. When the nurse left the room and Natalie was confident that they wouldn't be interrupted for a while, she decided to confront her sister.

"You can't name your baby Christian?" Natalie said as she had Montell sitting in her lap. It has been a rare moment for Natasha to actually have her first born in her presence. Montell's father had to go out of town for a business trip and after months of Natasha begging to keep Montell, at the last minute, Montell's father granted her wish.

"And why not?" Natasha tried to sit up but she had just given birth three hours ago. The razor-sharp glare didn't go unnoticed by her older sister, who returned one of her own. She placed Montell on the floor so he can play with some toys that were brought for his baby brother. "How dare you look at me like that when you are just as big of a whore as I am?! I had the best teacher in you!"

"If I weren't saved and you weren't in stitches I'd slap the taste out of your mouth!" Natalie returned to her seat. She didn't remember getting up but she did remember she was two seconds from smacking the hell out of her sister. "And I still say you can't name that baby Christian?"

"Oh yes I can and I will," Natasha continues as the nurse comes in with the paperwork to fill out for the baby's birth certificate. "I don't have to be saved to be able to say Christian and since I like the name so much and I think Jesus is the kind of man I want my baby to be like then damnit, that's what I'm going to do."

"But Tasha, you aren't a Christian?"

"And you are so holier than thou that if that is what it takes to be a Christian then I don't want to be one. I'll explain it to God when that time comes. But in the meantime, I believe that this little boy will get it right and be better than either of us were and break the generational curse for all of us."

"And what about your baby's father? What does he have to say about all this?"

"I'm not worried about what Paris got to say," Natasha had blurted out and immediately regretted that she did. She had no intention of telling her sister that the man who tortured and molested her months before was her baby's father but now that it was out in the open, she'd have to deal with it. "He's so busy chasing behind that old witch that he wouldn't give two flips about his son."

Natalie was beyond flabbergasted. Just when she thought she could get rid of that witch and her demons, here comes her sister bringing them to her footsteps. "Paris is the baby's father?" Natalie couldn't believe her ears. She sat down and tried to catch her breath. As she looked at the baby being brought back by the nurse and placed in Natasha's arms, she tried not to hate it for the sins of its father. Natalie took out a piece of bubble gum and started chewing the flavor out of it to calm her nerves. The gum she was chewing was making an annoying smacking sound that was giving Natasha a headache. The watermelon fragrance was filling the tight space between the two.

"You would do that knowing that I can't have a piece."

"If I were still a smoker I'd have about two cigarettes in my mouth right now. Consider this progress." Natalie continued to exhale as she let her mind absorb everything that has happened thus far. "But don't you think it's just wrong naming your baby Christian when you aren't one and will probably never be one, according to you?"

"Nope. Who better to name my baby after? Who better to guide my baby? See you don't understand, I'm giving my baby to the One who I know can love it far more than I can and can take care of it better than I can. I may not have much longer on this earth but if I have to leave my baby is in good hands." Natasha looked down where the father's name was and identified him as Meshach Felton Green. Natalie looked at her sister and started to snatch the birth certificate from her and tear it apart. But Natasha picked it up and dropped it on the opposite side of the bed. "Look, I know I promised to give you Montell and I reneged on the deal, but Christian, he's yours. As long as Felton comes down here and claims paternity, I can get the hell out of dodge and away from Paris and the two of you can have the baby you've always wanted."

"Get out of dodge? Where are you going?"

"I don't know and I don't care, but I know that you and Felton will figure something out. Consider this paying me back for giving you custody of my son."

Natalie cut her eyes at her sister in frustration, "you are sick, you are so sick." She quickly apologized to Jesus for being insensitive to her sister and got up and left the hospital. She dreaded the thought of what Felton would have to say once he found out what Natasha did.

***

"She did what!" Felton had taken it just how Natalie thought he would. "I'm not signing that birth certificate. She can forget that."

"But look, if you put your name on the certificate, the baby will be ours legally and Natasha is willing to give up her parental rights to us. It will be our baby." Natalie couldn't believe she was going along and pitching the idea to her husband. Maybe Christian will be what they need to save their marriage and for Natalie, a way to bring her husband to Christ. She was close to desperate and willing to try anything at this point.

"So all I got to do is sign my name on the certificate and the baby is mine? No questions asked, no blood tests and your sister is going to sign over the baby to us." Felton's heart had softened a little. As he thought about it, maybe this would be the way they could save their marriage. Going to the therapist hadn't been as effective as they hoped but at least they were getting their problems out in the open.

"That and we got to find a way to get her out of Winston-Salem immediately before Paris and Madame Mulah finds her and tries to sell the baby on the black market."

"I knew we were never going to get away from her." Felton shook his head and grabbed his keys and headed toward the door. He looked back at Natalie who was still standing in place. "Let's go before I change my mind or worse yet, she changes hers. We'll plot more when we get to the hospital."

Natalie smiled on the inside and follows her husband out of the door. She knew her sister had been up to something but for once, maybe some good would come of this.

CHAPTER THIRTY-SEVEN

RAHLIEM

Rahliem had just gotten done hanging up his choir robe when he seen Donte and Eugene walking past the room leaving the church. The choir had just got done singing a soul stirring version of Patti LaBelle's "You Are My Friend/What a Friend We Have in Jesus/Amen" melody as Pastor Phelps dismissed them for the benediction. Rahliem was disappointed that Faith had missed their church service this week and suspected that it had something to do with their conversations about her and Donte's relationship at school. And while he was concerned about Faith, he was equally concerned about his friendship with Donte. They had grown close over the past few years and he felt he betrayed Donte's trust by dating his ex. He didn't know about the relationship but still—he couldn't shake that thought from his mind and he felt that he owed it to himself and Donte to make things right between them.

"Donte, come here real quick." Rahliem called out. He hated the idea of addressing the issue in church where the congregation could speculate and exaggerate what they've heard but he didn't want the issue to linger around any longer. He had tried to call Donte a few times but he was either always busy or playing phone tag. Being able to talk to the man face to face, Rahliem had helped he could see how sincere he was and be able to deal with the situation man to man.

"Alright, let me hand Eugene over to Elicia and I'll be there in a minute." Donte responded. Rahliem went to the desk next to the piano that the choir used to practice. Before he could grab what he was looking for Celtius and Calvin stopped in. Rahliem was really hoping that Celtius hadn't relapsed because he really wanted to handle the situation with Donte, but decided to hear him out anyway.

"Ay, boss, we don't have a meeting this week do we?" Calvin asked. Rahliem breathed a sigh of relief because they did meet in the choir room and seeing him in here, they probably had thought that Rahliem had called an emergency meeting and didn't get to announce it in church.

"No, I'm just going to talk with Donte and another worshipper and then be out. We'll handle Street Disciple stuff on Wednesday unless something has come up."

"Aight then, just checking."

A few minutes after the hallway cleared up, Donte emerged and closed the door.

"How have you been man?"

"I'm cool, keeping up with Eugene and getting it together. I may go to another election party they got for Barack Obama on Gilbert State's campus—I haven't been to one in awhile."

"That's cool. I wanted to talk to you about Faith. I mean," Rahliem decided to cut right to it. Normally, he'd have the words to say what he wanted to say but for some reason he couldn't do it now. "I didn't know y'all two had a relationship."

"Yeah man, after I got saved, she was the first girl I dated. And we both had issues. She was about forty or fifty pounds heavier than she is now and I was still dealing with everyone wanting to know when my next video was coming out. People still ask me that."

"What can you say, you're a star." Donte chuckled and Rahliem was happy to see a smile on the man's face. He felt he could relax a little and that this might not be as bad as he thought it would be. "I just wanted to make sure things were straight between us because I do care a lot about Faith and I see this going a lot further than just a few dates here and there, but I also value our friendship and I don't want to feel like I'm caught in the middle."

"You not caught. If anything, we ended everything abruptly and took months to try to reconcile things ourselves. I got so heavily involved in Elicia's campaign and she was on internships and practicing to take the CPA exam we just lost touch. But it's cool. Plus, I've rekindled things with Elicia and I can't let that grow if I'm holding on to Faith."

Rahliem shook his head. He thought about the years between when Faith and Donte were together and when he started dating Faith and figured enough time had passed and that everything should've been on the up and up. Plus, Donte and Elicia's relationship was growing and he knew Donte was more interested in getting serious with that.

"That's what's up." The two shook hands. Rahliem had wanted to ask some other questions but felt it was best to let things be as they were.

"Donte, are you in here?" Elicia asked as she knocked on the door.

"Yeah, I'll be out in a minute." He yelled out. "I can't believe she and I got back together but she's really taken a liking to Eugene and he likes her a lot too."

"So when's the wedding?"

"I should be asking you that?"

"Naw, Faith and I have a ways to go. You and Elicia been back together almost since y'all graduated and were high school sweethearts too."

"Yeah. I just want to make sure it's in God's timing and that I am the man that God would have me to be. I can't be perfect but I can make sure I give it my best shot."

"You know what I tell people," Rahliem said as he grabbed his briefcase so he and Donte could head out of the door. "Just because I sin and make mistakes doesn't make me any less of a Christian...that is my way of showing you where I need help in my walk and in prayer and that is what you should be doing for me."

"Can I get an amen to that?"

"I'm glad I had a chance to talk to you about it man. I didn't want it to eat me up and then have both you and Faith mad at me."

"We're straight. Just give her some time if she hasn't reached out to you yet." Donte opened the door and Eugene tried to jump on his father so he could carry him. "No, you got to walk."

"I don't want to." Eugene pouted and stuck out his lip.

"Eugene, don't show out in this church, or I'm gonna have to show out on you."

Eugene looked at his father sideways and walked ahead of him. Rahliem saw Donte grab Elicia's hand as they headed out of the church. He was confident that everything had been solved and he'd be able to move forward in building something with Faith. In his dreams, he saw the two of them walking down the aisle in the near future and she being the first lady of the church he dreamed of building. He felt good knowing that there were no objections being made to his desire to move forward with Faith and continue down the path they had started.

CHAPTER THIRTY-EIGHT

FELTON

Don't ask me to do this ever again," Natalie said as she helped her sister into her car and Christian into the car seat provided for him. Natasha just rolled her eyes as she remembered all the times she's helped her big sis out of a bind without flipping her wig.

"I am so out of here so you won't have to worry about that." Natasha said as she started singing along with the Ashanti song on the radio.

"So what time do I fly out of here tonight? I know you got my plane tickets."

"You fly out of here by twelve noon."

"Dang, Natalie!"

"Look chick," Natalie was past frustrated with her sister. "You decided yesterday that you wanted to fly out of Greensboro. You know you are not supposed to be on no airplane anyway as you cannot handle heights. Now I couldn't buy your airplane ticket at the airport so I had one of Felton's clients arrange for this Arabian guy to fly you on his private plane."

Getting Felton to go along with the plan had been much harder than Natalie had anticipated. After signing the birth certificate, Natasha turned over all parental rights to both Natalie and Felton. Then after that, Natalie had to talk Felton into talking to some of his "well to do" clients who would be willing to provide Natasha a safe haven in exchange for Felton to commit to certain future performances.

Natasha thought her sister was crazy. Even though September 11th has past, the wounds had not healed and there was no way in hell she would be caught with in the air or anywhere else next to an Arabian or a Middle Eastern person or whatever the correct terminology was to be used to describe them people.

"I'm not getting on that plane!"

"Oh yes you are," Natalie was furious and was regretting going through all the lengths she did to guarantee her ungrateful sister's safety.

"I done went through too much to make too much preparation for you to make off like Joseph and Mary for you to go around and mess this up for me. You will get on this plane and you will not say nothing else to me about it!" Natalie snapped as her sister rolled her eyes.

"Don't think just cause you gave birth you can't get corrected cause I can and will beat you if you mess this up for me." And she got firmer and grabbed her sister by her collar.

"Now I'm in this to save your life and the life of *my* son and I'm going to do that one way or another and you are going to go with the damn flow! If you can't do that speak now and I can just turn you in to Social Services where your other son would be if it weren't for that good man who helped you get pregnant! Do you want that?"

Natasha was silent, partly because her sister had never manhandled her like that before.

"Anything else you want to say!" Natalie continued to say. "Good now shut up and get with the program! We don't have much time and I got to get home at a decent hour so I can spend time with Christian and work with Felton to repair our marriage! Come on!"

Natalie and Natasha sped away from the hospital with little Christian in tow. Natalie's radical driving almost caused her to hit a man that was walking across the street. He flicked her off and while she thought to do the same, she just remembered the un-Christ like tongue lashing she just gave her sister.

"I'm sorry for coming at you like that but you need to be more appreciative of what folks are doing for you instead of running off at the mouth all the time."

Natalie felt good when she repented and equally as well when Natasha didn't respond and they stayed quiet for the rest of their ride to the airport.

***

After dropping Natasha off, Natalie returned home so that she could help Felton put Christian to sleep. When she stepped into the door, she was surprised to see all the baby stuff on the table. She walked to what used to be the spare bedroom and seen office desk and equipment outside and watched as Shadrach and Felton put the finishing touches on Christian's new crib. She was shocked because she knew getting Shadrach and Felton together to complete any task was like trying to mix oil and water and expecting them to peacefully coexist. Shadrach lifted the guardrail up and down while Felton was put up one of the mobile toy units that hung over the face of the crib. Natalie was speechless.

"This looks nice." She was happy that she could relax after a stressful day with her sister.

"Anything to make sure my nephew is safe and loved and in a good environment." Shadrach said as he gave Natalie a hug. "Knucklehead finally agreed to get the crib that our parents had in the storage. All three of us had slept in this crib and we came out fine. Don't see why Christian can't sleep in the crib either."

At hearing his name, Christian turned his head, opened his eyes and went back to sleep. Upon seeing the crib being completed, Natalie recognized it from the pictures of Felton when he was a baby. Felton hated those pictures because his parents had his biblical name along with Mickey Mouse, Goofy and Donald Duck stickers all over the wall. Natalie loved the pictures because she dreamed that one day she wouldn't be barren and that she and Felton would finally be granted their dream of having a child of their own. As she looked at the crib, Christian was ready to try it out and she put him in it so he could continue sleeping.

CHAPTER THIRTY-NINE

SHADRACH

Since Shadrach and Tevin's little talk, Tevin had managed to make it on time, even early on some occasions.

He'll be alright; I have faith in him. He does try at least. Shadrach thought. He should have known when he hired him that the boy didn't have any professional experience; he's probably used to flipping burgers or bagging groceries or something like that. Shadrach wasn't downgrading those jobs because his first job was waiting tables for Jay at a local restaurant, he just didn't believe that every teenager should be subjected to doing working as a cashier or bagger as their first job. *I don't know, maybe I am beginning to think more like Jay every day. That's bad because I remember the days when Jamon and I swore we were not going to be like Jay.* Shadrach thought to himself. He never hated the man but he didn't expect some man in his mid forties to early fifties to be some hard head's role model? That's like all the boys swearing up and down that they weren't going to like their father's when they got to that age. Reflecting on where most of the guys his age are act today, Shadrach found that they act talk and sound more and more like him each day. Figures.

As another Saturday approached, Shadrach felt good about Dumar being in attendance to help run the office. The first assignment he was going to give him would be to go over all the tickets Re wrote so that the books don't get messed up. Going over the books and having the barber that wrote the ticket along with M.C. or Re was important to making sure that the barbers got the correct amount of pay at the end of each day. Na'eem was also here too which was all good because Shadrach could step away from some of the clients and concentrate more on the office work. Usually when Na'eem was there, Shadrach stepped to the side and let the elder man run the shop and keep the "law of the land." Saturdays were a favorite day for many at the shop because they lead to Sundays and Mondays, which were the customary days off, even though Shadrach usually came in on Monday to handle administrative issues and for certain clients who needed him, he'd cut hair on an appointment basis.

Re was at the counter while Dumar and Shadrach were in the back doing some accounting work. Chancy, Dumar's uncle stopped by to assist and provide that extra set of eyes to make sure that the shop stayed healthy as the fiscal year was coming to an end and the shop needed to get ready to pay taxes and do all that legal stuff that needed to be done at this time of the month.

In the background, the song by Wyclef and Mary J. Blige about calling 911 brought along old feelings and memories for Shadrach. He could feel that song, and he remembered when he first heard it a couple of years ago when he was on his way home from the shop. He and a lady he was seeing at the time were arguing over something petty. But the song didn't remind him of her; it reminded him of all of the drama and bull one goes through with the person they love. Reminded him of the woman who managed to make her way to the private bathroom in his office. Theresa Baker, his first love; or at least he thought they were in love. That girl put him through some drama, and he probably did the same for her now that he was thinking back on it. He concluded that they both were trying to love each other but the relationship just didn't work out.

"Oh, what's up Shadrach?"

Shadrach got up and left the office and could see the smirk on Chancy's face, as if he was trying to insinuate something. She'd seen him before she could make it to the bathroom.

"Hey Theresa, how are you doing?"

He wanted to be careful how he hugged her; partly because in the past when either of them weren't seeing anybody, the two of them usually spent the night together off of one embrace. Shadrach kept his distance from her, and he could tell that she felt that he was being cold and distant, but didn't want to come off that way.

"I'm fine, I'm fine." She said with a hint of disappointment in her voice. Shadrach almost felt sorry for her, but he like the way things are going between he and Deborah and he was not going to ruin it for anyone.

"So who did you come in here with?" Shadrach asked, trying to be formal in my place of business.

"Him, over there."

Shadrach snuck a peep outside the corridor and he could see that the brother sitting in Davon's chair was not her type. She usually wasn't too fond of heavyset brothers.

"He's your brother?" Shadrach questioned.

"Oh stop it! He's my business associate and we have a presentation on Monday. We have been working on this proposal to buy Lewman's Travel Agency for three weeks now. It seems that every time we come up with a good one, they always want to up the price or do something sheisty. I'm only putting up with them because we are trying to get into the African travel market and with them on our team; we can give Markell's a run for their money. And you know Stanley don't play fair."

Shadrach knew that. Theresa had a successful career at G. A. Morgan Travels and her and Stanley always seems to be in the middle of some big problem, especially after she broke up her engagement to him.

"So what you want me to do about it?"

"I want you to try and find out what Stan's plans are and give me a little side info so I can make their proposal look bad."

"Now you know I can't do that. I've never gotten between any argument or whatever the two of you been having."

"It ain't never been a problem hooking up with me before." She said as she brought her hand closer to Shadrach's crouch. She was right—there was a time when he wanted her so bad, he ambushed Stanley when he was getting out of his car on the way home, just so he could make him late for his date with her and for her to spend the night with him. When she started to capture him in her hand, Shadrach gently moved her hand away from him.

"I'm married now, and you know I would have to tell her if we got too close." Shadrach felt tempted to take Theresa back to his office and let her tame that beast for old times' sake, but when he saw Dumar glancing in his direction, he knew that others were watching too and he wanted to continue to set a positive example.

"Ah man," she purred softly and seductively, trying to convince him to change his mind, "I know we are not on this 'I have to tell my female trip again'."

"No, we're on the 'I have a wife trip' and I love her very much." Shadrach backed off, putting more distance between him and his old flame, "Why don't you get yo' boy over there to try to hook up with a connection if you're not going to wait until you are married?" Shadrach knew that last line stung her. He wasn't trying to take a subtle jab at her but from the daggers he felt coming from her eyes, it sure did feel like it.

"Because that fat boy is always talking about 'play by the rules.' If I were doing things his way, G. A. Morgan wouldn't have a foot to stand on." Then she closed the space between her and Shadrach and whispered in his ear, "besides, being with him doesn't even feel right."

Shadrach just looked at her and shook her head. He took that to mean that God was convicting her for her fornication but that she was ignoring it. He actually felt sorry for the guy because Theresa was dogging him like he wasn't even human but he knew that there was an ulterior motive involved if she were having sex with him. She must have done or said something, and whatever it was, he was blackmailing her for it. Even though Shadrach was no longer with Theresa, he still knew her like the back of his hand. But neither one of them were good for each other.

Shadrach was happy to see the dude leave from Davon's chair, and as he was leaving she walked up and grabbed his hand.

"For a minute there, I thought the ring was gonna slide off your finger and end up in your back pocket." Chancy had confided. Shadrach was so unfocused that he didn't even notice that Chancy had approached him.

"Nah," Shadrach shook his head and spoke confidently, "I love Deborah too much for that."

"You cool man. You fought her off and you didn't give into the temptation bruh—you did real good."

Shadrach smiled because everything Chancy said was cool. He looked at the time and seen Na'eem handling a younger, rowdy customer at the front. He grabbed his bag and decided that he was going to take the rest of the day off—he'd let Na'eem run the shop for the rest of the day.

***

Shadrach was glad to take the rest of the day off, especially with all that drama Theresa put him through earlier in the day. He decided that he'd have to have a *long* talk with Deborah to not only keep the honesty in their marriage, but so that she could continue to trust him. She knew about the flings and the many wild nights of passion that they shared and they had successfully worked through an earlier temptation before. This time should not have been any different. The phone rang and Deborah's number appeared on the screen.

"So you were going to stay home from work and not call me?"""

"Not until three or four or so. Don't you have a class you need to be going to?"

"No, I don't have class until eleven. Then I got a one to two twenty-five and I'm done. Are you going to invite me over or should I just enter at my own risk?"

"You can come over, but I'm not responsible if you are late to class, or if you don't make it to class."

"Oh, you're not going to be responsible, I'll be gone by ten. I just want to have breakfast with you that's all."

"We can have breakfast."

"So I'll see you at in an hour or so. Bye baby."

"Bye baby."

Shadrach turned on the television to see reruns of *The Cosby Show*.

Man, that was the show back in the day. Shadrach thought to himself as he remembered the episode.

In the back of his mind, he knew he was going to need to tell her about the episode with Theresa that played out earlier. He knew she would be a little upset but he also knew that both she and God would be pleased that he successfully passed one of Satan's many tests.

CHAPTER FORTY

RAHLIEM

Rahliem was nervous about being around the fine, toffee colored woman that was sitting in the front seat next to him in her black, 2007 Nissan Maxima. He stared into her coffee-colored eyes and was mesmerized by the way her eyes seemed to smile at her. She grabbed his hand and interlocked it with hers as they laid it on the arm rest. Rahliem looked down at her French acrylic nails then looked at that smile. He was imagining something so beautiful that was missing on that bare finger and he knew that if everything had gone as planned, that finger wouldn't be bare for much longer. Rahliem's eyes followed her lips—he betted that her lips tasted as good as the cinnamon air freshener in her car.

"Are you sure this is not too much for Jay's Restaurant?" Faith asked as she turned off the ignition. She'd gotten self-conscious at seeing the casually dressed patrons leaving the restaurant.

"Trust me, this is perfect." Rahliem said as there was a light tap on the driver's window. Mya smiled, showing all of his pearly white teeth. Faith exhaled and unlocked the door so that Mya could open it and help her out—Rahliem had remembered that Mya worked at the restaurant part time and he was sure that for what he had planned, that he would agree to help out. Rahliem watched as Faith gracefully stepped out of the car in her cream-colored Vera Wang evening dress. It was the perfect dress this moment. Rahliem had intended on getting out of the car after her, but instead he watched those glide gracefully on the ivory white steps and the matching Jimmy Choos pumps pound the slates as they made a rhythmic clapping sound. Rahliem got out of the car and closed the door.

Faith turned back around. "Come on Rahliem...we don't have all day."

He smiled as he saw her reach into her clutch and press the LOCK button on her remote and Rahliem lightly jogged to catch up to the woman that was moving her hands franticly to hurry him along. Normally, Rahliem hated dressing up outside of church, but he was thankful that Davon had helped him pick out a collarless shirt that complimented the tan suit he was wearing so that he didn't have to wear a tie.

Mya had opened the door for them as they entered into the back of the restaurant for a private dinner party. Rahliem hadn't wanted to be put on the spot and he wanted the moment to be just about them two. They followed Mya into a private room which had a small table big enough to sit two people. Some of the candles seemed to brighten up when the two of them entered into the room. He saw how Faith's eyes lit up and he smiled to her as he helped her into her seat.

"Baby, everything is gonna be alright." Rahliem assured her.

"I can't believe you pulled this off." Faith said, "I've never had a man who went through all this trouble just to have a private dinner with me."

Rahliem was nervous. This wasn't just a private dinner—this was a night that could change the rest of their lives. After he cleared the air with Donte and was confident that his dating Faith would not jeopardize their friendship, he revealed his plans to Pastor Phelps about asking Faith to be his wife. They talked about having a very short engagement due to his leadership in the church and to keep parishioners from speculating about their "pre-marital activities." Just the day before, Rahliem and Davon went ring-shopping so Rahliem could present her with the best rock he could afford. After being pleased with the selection, he'd arrange to have Mya help him plan an intimate affair so that he could pop the question.

He smiled as Mya came back and walked them through their order. Rahliem ordered the strawberry chicken salad as an appetizer, parmesan chicken with mixed vegetables for the entre served with the house wine. In the background, the jazz version of "I Need You" by Mary Mary flowed softly through the speakers.

"I didn't even know they had Mary Mary in jazz," Faith commented on the song in the background.

"I think this might be a local artist's CD, either way, the song sounds good."

Rahliem could feel himself perspiring in his suit. He was beyond nervous as he looked at Faith as she continued to talk about her accounting work and her looking to do some work with the new Women in the Spirit chapter that had just been formed at WSSU. Hearing her talk about the group confirmed for him that Faith was the woman that God had picked out and designed just for him. When he talked about the Street Disciples ministry and shared some of the tales involving Mya and how rugged he was when he joined to where he was at this moment in time, he could tell that Faith could relate.

Their meals were brought out and Rahliem and Faith continued to eat as they talked about everything from Jesus to her plans for an accounting firm that specialized in working with small businesses to the latest books they had read. As they finished their meals, Mya had approached them and offered to refill their drinks and made recommendations for their desert. Rahliem discreetly placed his hand in his suit jacket to make sure the ring was still there. Feeling it, he pulled it out and got one knee.

"Faith—we've come to know each other over the last two years and I've never felt as close to any woman as I've felt toward you. I feel that you are the woman God has selected and designed just for me and I think we can spend the rest of our lives building the accounting firm and working on our ministries together. Will you marry me?"

Rahliem was nervous as he opened the box to reveal a small princess cut diamond that he'd been saving for the past four months to get. He had hoped she'd like the ring because they'd never gone ring shopping and she'd never hinted at the type of ring she wanted.

"Yes—yes I will marry you." Faith smiled as she allowed Rahliem to slip the ring from his box and place it on her finger. Rahliem got off his knee and gave Faith a hug and he held onto her tightly not wanting to let go. They heard clapping in the background and saw that Mya and a few members of the kitchen staff were applauding the acceptance of his proposal. A tear of joy slipped from Rahliem's eye as they sat down to enjoy the slices of chocolate marble cheesecake that Mya had recommended. Rahliem looked into Faith's eyes and saw her look at the ring with pride and he knew he'd made the right decision.

CHAPTER FORTY-ONE

CHASE

Y ou're not going to leave me in here alone are you?" Paris
looked at Chase as he pulled up to the Winston-Salem
Police Department. Finding a parking space near the
precinct had been difficult with the location being downtown.

"No man," Chase promised him. "I told you that if you did
the right thing, I'd stand beside you and my bringing you here is a
manifestation of that promise."

Chase watched as his brother smiled, then quickly exhaled as
he opened the door to the car for what may be the last time in his
natural life. Just as Paris was about to step out of the car, he
closed the door. When Chase looked into Paris' eyes, he saw a
look he never thought he'd be able to identify his brother by—
fear. "You know she can have me killed in here right?" Paris
suggested, almost as if he were delaying the inevitable. "Madame
Mulah got powers ya'know."

"And I believe in the Lord and Savior Jesus Christ and that
His power is greater than any witch or demon—maybe if you
repent of your sins, Madame Mulah will lose whatever power she
has over you." Chase opened the door and urged Paris to do the
same. "You will need to accept Him as your Lord and Savior. No
matter what you did, you need to own up to your sins and ask
Him for forgiveness. Until you seek retribution with the master
and learn to forgive yourself, you will never know or have peace."

Paris closed the door and waited on Chase to walk around to
the other side. A small stream of tears fell from his eyes as he
looked around and realized that it could very well be the last time

that he would see the outside of the free world again. "What do I tell my son when he grows up?"

Chase thought about their inability to find Natasha so that Paris could do the right thing and take responsibility for the son he'd left out in the world. He had no idea where Natasha or the baby was and that weighed on his heart deeply. Chase promised him that he'd put aside some money for the boy if they ever found him. "You tell him the truth. That's all you can do is tell him the truth and trust and pray that wherever he is, that he's being raised to love and know Jesus Christ." In their short conversation, they'd reach the front of the building and had stepped inside. "In the meantime, you get to know Jesus Christ. I promise you that once you get to know Him, give Him a chance, he'll not only protect you in here and on the other side, He'll show you His full power and He'll make all of this right in no time. It'll happen faster than you think."

Chase followed Paris into the double doors and through the metal detector where they walked to the officer sitting at the first desk. "I'm Paris Jackson." He spoke through trembling lips. Paris looked back at Chase with a tear in his eye and he grinned slightly seeing Chase shake his head in affirmation. "And I'm here to confess to the murder of Abednego Green."

CHAPTER FORTY-TWO

DONTE & SHADRACH

Donte couldn't believe that he'd heard the news correctly—another young black man who lived not too far from where Abednego resided turned himself into the police station earlier that day to confess to his murder. His spirit immediately moved him to pray for that man's soul and as he looked on at Shadrach, he could tell that the man was shaken up. Donte knew that the man had stopped cutting Eugene's hair for a reason, but he didn't know that this was the news he'd received until that moment.

Donte watched as Shadrach had taken a seat in the empty chair next to where his son was sitting. A few of the barbers had consoled him as he listened to the recap of the night Abednego was gruesomely murdered in his apartment complex. A few tears fell from his eyes as he thought about how hungry and how passionate Abednego was for people to know God.

"It's okay Mr. Shadrach sir." Donte saw Eugene hop out of his seat and hug on Shadrach's leg. "It's okay."

Donte walked to where his son was and was surprised that Shadrach had picked him up and placed him on his lap. Shadrach had wiped his tears from his face and smiled at Eugene. "Yes, I'm going to be fine."

Donte took Eugene from his lap and Tevin had offered to finish cutting Eugene's hair. Tevin picked up the clippers that Shadrach was using and he went to finish the job. Shadrach was actually almost done but it wasn't nothing Tevin couldn't finish. Donte looked on as Shadrach slowly got up and headed toward his office.

CHAPTER FORTY-THREE

FELTON

F elton finally agreed to accompany Natalie to church after missing service for several weeks. The admission that one of his co-worker's brothers was the murder was too much for him to bare and he couldn't stand the thought of faking it for Christ because he knew that if he had saw Chase, he'd kill him or die trying. When Natasha confirmed that the same Paris Jackson that had murdered his brother was also the father of the baby they were raising now—his heart wanted to shatter into a thousand pieces.

Yet, every time Felton looked at Christian, he grinned. He was happy to have the boy and Montell into his life full time. He and Natalie had tried, without success to have children for years and now, they had two boys that were constant factors in their lives; who brought them joy and peace. Natalie would read to them from the children's Bible every night and then return to her side of the bed and he would go to his. Even with the joy of children, Felton longed for the love to return between he and his wife.

So after dodging Shadrach's numerous calls and invitations and after getting sick of seeing Natalie come home with a warm smile on her face but embrace him with coldness, he'd given in. He was still mad at Chase for being Paris' brother, but he decided to bear it and grin because he wanted to set a good example for Montell. Montell seemed to enjoy going to church and he always was sharing his stories about Bible school and what the other children were doing in the youth groups that he'd taken a liking to participating in.

Felton was surprised to notice that the members of Grace United seemed as welcoming as they had when they clothed him from being dumped in the fellowship hall. Truth was, the members of this church were always this welcoming to Felton and other visitors who were not members, but Felton dreaded the thought of going to church so much, he hadn't paid it much attention.

"Uncle Felton," Montell asked as he prodded him with a red hymnal that was in the seat. "We're on whatever page 'I Need Thee' is on."

Felton cautiously took the book from his hands as if he were handling a hot potato and began to flip to the back of the book. Upon hearing one of the parishioners mumble the page number, he found the hymn in time to lip synch the words with the rest of the congregation. He could hear Montell trying to sing the song and he lowered the book so that he could read and point the words to him. Natalie smiled—first smile she'd given him in weeks as she watched Felton keep up with the words by finger as Montell sang his heart out.

After singing the hymn, Felton noticed an older lady walking to the front of the church to read the acknowledgments. He stared at the frail woman who reminded him of the deaconess who'd stolen his innocence and had her way with him. As the woman spoke, Felton could hear the deaconess' words ringing over and over again. His molester confused him—praising his bedroom prowess and his endowment in one breath while demeaning him and demonizing him the next.

Felton watched as the woman left the podium and walked back to her seat, which was a couple of rows behind him. As she walked by, he thought he heard her call him a "demon." Felton shook it off and tried to pay attention to the prayer requests and the praise reports—but he couldn't hear beyond the parishioners in front of him as he heard someone say the word "demon" again. He turned his head in that direction and the deaconess' voice began to follow and torment him—*demon*. Felton looked at Natalie who'd started looking at him funny. He flashed a quick smile in hopes to avert her attention but his face betrayed his emotions, baring them all for Natalie to see.

Demon—that deaconess—that "Christian" woman who was supposedly called by God to help minister the word to his people had him a *demon*. As he watched a few members of the congregations walk to the altar to have a few minutes with the Lord, he realized that the moment she called him a demon, that name set off a chain of events in which Felton would begin to act opposite in the ways his parents had raised him. Being called a demon had hurt his feelings and crushed his spirit. The hurt was very deep. After the molestation was discovered and denied, Felton remembered crying randomly for no apparent reason. He remembered the moments when he used to get angry and do things to hurt himself and others intentionally. Felton used to bash his head against things when he got frustrated. He would fast one day and gorge on meals the next. He had this imbalance because he did not know that his spirit was still hurting. Felton knew he wasn't a demon, yet he didn't know at the time that he was supposed to rebuke that comment either.

Felton blinked his eyes and when he opened them, he could've sworn he saw scales falling off his eyelids and he noticed that the lights in the church appeared to be brighter. He'd been so caught up in his memories of every act that he'd done with that deaconess that he missed the choir singing the latest Trin-I-Tee song. Instead, he found himself frustrated at the fact that he had tried his best to apologize to the woman for hurting her feelings, once again overlooking the hurt and pain he was feeling.

Pastor Phelps was speaking on the root of all evil and Felton understood at that moment that being called a demon and not rebuking that false calling had been the root of many relationships with some people whom he had no business being with. After no longer being able to please the deaconess sexually, Felton decided to explore his sexuality. Felton wanted to feel good because those people were taking care of him physically; made him feel like a man. He didn't understand that those people were not only created for him, nor did belong to him. The women with whom he lustfully shared his temple with didn't care about him, but Felton was so in hatred with himself that he couldn't see that. Felton continued to get in and out of different women's beds at will...but somewhere around the fifth or the sixth time he began to feel a piece of him disappear. It was subtle at first but the pieces seem to get larger and larger, like chipping away a rock. There were days when he thought he saw boulders falling. What little bit of him he had left he was losing control of and Felton felt that he needed those people to make him the man he needed to be. As he lost more and more and more of himself, he cleaved deeper and deeper into them.

As Pastor Phelps continued her sermon on finding the roots of problems and plucking them to solve them, Felton had a vision. He was driving home from Hunks & Honies after work one night and it was raining. He felt his car constantly slip and slide off the road. The car was going too fast to come to a stop and being unable to control the steering on the car, he'd ran into a ditch. As he looked in the sky, he'd seen what appeared to be angels and demons fighting in the clouds. He was sure he was going to die because the winds were getting worse and he felt sore all over his body. Felton was not ready to die and it was at that moment and time that he realized that Heaven and Hell existed and he knew beyond a shadow of a doubt that with the way he'd lived his life and renounced Jesus, he was going to regret that decision.

He felt the demons taunting him, promising him that he could recite one Bible verse, they'd give him another chance to live and make things right with the Lord. Problem was, Felton couldn't remember a single Bible verse, not even a simple verse such as "Jesus Wept," despite listening to the explanation a few times before in *Barbershop 2*. He couldn't remember any of the gospel songs he heard in church in spite of the fact that he sang along with the songs he heard on the radio that were Christ-centered.

He didn't remember how to pray—all Felton knew how to do was make promises and how to break them. Felton needed to reach the Lord and he didn't feel or know that he had an intercessor who could reach him on his behalf.

"Is there someone in the crowd who'd like to know Jesus as their personal Lord and Savior. The doors to the church are now open."

Surprisingly to himself and to Natalie, Felton found himself standing up and walking to the middle of the aisle. He thought about the dancing and the freak shows he'd participated in just a couple of hours ago and he almost turned around to run out of the church but he felt his feet continuing to walk forward, waiting to be embraced into Jesus' loving arms. Felton knew he was so deep in sin and he felt that he had no chance of being able to be a real Christian. Besides, when he had the opportunity to get saved once before, he'd already told the Spirit no before, he almost couldn't believe that He was giving him another chance now.

As Felton hugged Pastor Phelps and listened to the thunderous applause from the congregation, he felt drops of water on his forehead. As he looked around the applause seemed continuous not just from the church family but from heaven. When he looked at the cross it was like he could see different angels hugging and protecting him. It was official, Felton had done what he never thought was possible—he'd gotten saved. He was starting his new journey fresh and if he had died in the next few seconds, he was completely assured that regardless of how many verses he could quote, the number of songs he could sing or what he did in the church, he was going out a Christian.

CHAPTER FORTY-FOUR

CHASE & FELTON

Holding Christian Abednego Green was one of the greatest joys Chase had ever experienced in his life. In his arms the baby boy laughed, slept, cried and whined. Chase could've swore that the boy knew he was family—that he was his uncle. If he didn't, he sure was doing a good job of pretending as if he did.

"It's my turn to hold him." D said as he reached out for his nephew. Chase carefully put the boy in his arms, even though D had a few children of his own.

Felton and Natalie were sitting on the couch. The fact that they'd allowed Chase and D to visit with their nephew was scandalous to some but only the Godly thing to do. Since Felton had been saved, he had decided to work on his ability to forgive and reaching out to Chase was a huge test of that forgiveness. Chase had admired Felton's new get-up, the new school Karl Kani outfit with the cross and some eclectic design on the left side of his dark, navy blue jeans and a open blue, silver and white pinstriped button-up with the same cross design on the left pocket and covering the back of his shirt. It reminded him of the big gothic cross tattoo 2Pac had on his back with Exodus 18:31 on his back. Definitely a step up from the revealing or barely-there shirts and slacks he'd been accustomed to seeing Felton wear. Natalie was equally eclectic in brown knee high boots and she had Nelly's

Apple Bottom jeans painted over the curves on her waist. The Afro-centric shirt showing prominent black women over the continent of Africa was a little out of touch with cool weather, but the black turtle neck she was wearing more than made up for her fashion faux pau.

Felton was pulling out a Blackberry, turning on the phone and commanded, "Shadrach." Felton had left the room while Chase and D were entertaining their nephew. He noticed how happy the boy was in their arms and knew that in order for his nephew to continue being happy, he was going to have to work on his tolerance because if it had been up to Felton, Christian they would never see. It wasn't even about the child support Chase had offered or the apology letter that Shadrach was going on and on about. Felton walked to the mailbox and sure enough, along with the bills and some junk mail was a letter from the brother missing in this equation.

"Chase!" Felton called once he'd enter the house.

"He's with you?" Shadrach questioned over the phone.

"Yes, they are visiting with Christian." Felton had explained how he found out that Paris was Christian's father the night before and how he and Natalie had come to the conclusion that it would only be right for Chase and his family to see the boy and perhaps the nephew could be the bridge over the sea of hurt and healing that both families needed.

Chase had put the sleeping boy in the crib and escaped the nursery. Natalie had turned on the mp3 player dock that was at the head of the crib and played some calm and soothing relaxation music from Paul Collier. He knew that would keep Christian quiet for a while and soothe him while he slept.

CHAPTER FORTY-FIVE

DONTE

Donte headed to his office at the apartment complex he managed that so he could handle the tenants' issues and be ready to collect rent at the first of the month. He also needed to find a new receptionist. He had been reviewing resumes and doing applications; even tried out a few temp agencies but he had yet to be successful at finding the person he needed. The last good office personnel the complex had was a young lady who had graduated from school last fall.

Donte walked into his office to begin processing some leasing applications and he hadn't had two sips from his virgin Kahlua flavored coffee when he heard the bell ringing at the front. He was trying to remember what tenant may have had an issue with their apartment when he saw Eve and another lady walking in having a seat at the receptionist desk. Neither one of them were tenants of his, so he knew this visit was a social one. Both ladies looked like they had just come from church with their outlandish hats, black blouses and skirts with matching stockings and some plain pumps that looked like they came from Payless.

His spirit was discerning but he chose to stay alert. *Stay calm,* he encouraged himself as he didn't want to get too excited.

"Good morning!" Donte said as he stood up to shake their hands. "What brings you by this morning? Are you interested in an apartment?"

"Actually, I am." Eve surprised him. "Where are my manners, Evelyn, this is Donte, Donte this is my younger sister Evelyn." Eve said as she smiled like an old white lady who had just taken her dentures out.

"I've seen some of your videos—you look nice." Evelyn smiled seductively. Eve had given her a sharp glare and Evelyn dropped her head. Donte nodded his head and reached in the file cabinet under the desk to pull out an application. Truthfully, managing the properties had become a handful and having Eve in one of the buildings was sure to add to the mix. But he was fortunate that he was able to put that business degree he got at NC Tech to good use after all. Most employers weren't interested in hiring a former adult video star and the owner of the complex was the only employer willing to look past the videos—it helped that she thought he was attractive but Donte never put himself in position to compromise all that he'd built beyond the videos. Evelyn stepped out of the office and Donte figured that she was going to look around—leaving the two of them to talk.

"I just realized how close the apartments are from your own condo." Eve paused and looked up from the paperwork she filled out. "Just think, Eugene will be able to walk to and from our places once he gets old enough."

"That sounds like a good idea." Donte admitted. He figured that Eugene would benefit from having his mother and his father nearby—if having them under the same household wouldn't work, being within walking distance was the next best thing.

"I got the job at the mental health agency that I applied for." Eve had made small talk. "I won't start for another week or so— but I met the young lady I will be working with and I'm excited."

Donte was happy to hear the progress that Eve was making in her life. He'd wish that she'd give the Lord another try, but he trusted that the Lord wouldn't rapture the saints out of here without the mother of his son being in that number. He realized that as far as her salvation was concerned, he would have to try another approach. "That's good."

Donte was happy that Eve seemed to be getting her life together and he took her getting the apartment close to where he lived as a good sign. He was starting to trust her more with Eugene and his reserve had decreased significantly since she'd taken a genuine interest in having Eugene as a part of her life.

"I know that we have a lot of things to work out and work through," Eve started. "I'm just doing the best I can to make this work."

"I understand." Donte confessed. "At the end of the day, we have a son and I want nothing more than for him to have both of us and seeing us work together as a team. He deserves at least that —especially since I came from a two-parent household and he sees my parents together often."

"I know. And maybe I can go to church with you guys sometimes—I still need to find God for myself, but it seems that Eugene genuinely enjoys going and I want to support him in that."

Donte smiled when he took the papers from her. He knew that once Eve stepped foot in the church, her life was going to be changed and that there was nothing she would be able to do about it.

CHAPTER FORTY-SIX

FELTON

Are you going to wake up?" Felton whispered in Natalie's ear.

As they were lying next to each other in their king-sized bed, her side of the bed was warm and her body next to his brought him a level of comfort he hadn't felt in a long time. Felton rubbed his hand down the length of her slender arm and she nudged him away from her gently. Felton knew not to cuddle against her. Last time Felton did that, she tried her best to push his body off the bed with her feet.

Natalie mumbled. Felton looked at the clock and saw that it was 3:57 and the alarm clock had been going off for the past twelve minutes. For the first time in a long time, Felton and Natalie had joined as one body in the way a man and his wife should and even though he'd only had about two hours of sleep, he wanted to reunite with her again before she had to go to work-reliving their wedding night all over again.

Felton exhaled and continued to breathe slowly as if he were still catching his breath from running a marathon. He smiled, feeling good knowing that Natalie wanted and needed him again and that he was still her man. The buzzer rang loud again and Natalie jumped out of bed and ran to their bathroom. Felton heard the water pounding the shower walls and soon the smell of the Nubian Heritage's Lavender & Wildflowers body wash infiltrated the air and brought a sense of calm and peace. The fragrance was one of her favorites and one of his, too. Felton lifted his body off the bed and he decided that he was going to make sure that she was okay. He decided to forgo the boxer briefs that were crumbled up on the side of the bed. Although he didn't have work to do on this day, thought he'd join her in the shower and perhaps catch up on their love making. Felton had figured that maybe an intimate session with the water falling down their backs would continue to soothe their tensions and offer a sense of relaxation that only a doctor could order.

Felton opened the door, glad not to find it locked because that meant she may have been more welcoming, maybe even anxious to see him. Felton let himself in, determined to fulfill his mission. Felton opened the Tempered glass shower door and stepped inside. Natalie looked up at him and smiled. Felton returned the smile as he reached for her to pull her into his chest for an embrace. As they hugged, Felton enjoyed the warm water and the steam. The lavender calmed his nerves and the wildflowers grew stronger. When they let go, the look in each other's eyes were enough to ignite both their passions and encourage more consummation of their marriage.

THE LAST CHAPTER

One Year Later
RAHLIEM

"**A**re you sure you wanna do this?" Rahliem heard Donte ask as they got ready to walk to the altar. The night before Donte and Davon surprised Rahliem with a small bachelor's party at Dave & Buster's in Concord. They made arrangements with the managers to have the adult gaming center closed to the public so that they could have a lust-free, alcohol-free, entertaining night with the fellas—one that they were sure that Faith, Pastor Phelps and others would've approved. They still managed to keep him up until about four that morning with a late-night barbeque at one of his cousin's house and a late-night viewing of a heavy weight boxing match.

"Yes I'm sure." Rahliem spoke confidently as he and Donte took their places and began walking to the altar. Rahliem glanced down, looking at the sky-blue collarless shirt that Faith had chosen for him. As he walked past a mirror, he did a quick glance to make sure that his facial hair was on point, his lips weren't chapped and he licked an index finger and made sure that his eyebrows and goatee were straight. Rahliem knew he didn't have one strand of loose hair on his face or neck. He was confident that he was ready for his close up.

"I'm glad that y'all are ready," Pastor Phelps said as she met with Rahliem and Donte in the hallway before they made it into the sanctuary. She knew about the bachelor's party and she eyed both of them carefully to make sure Rahliem was mentally sound to participate in the ceremony. She had agreed to perform the wedding ceremony in front of a small audience on a short notice because she knew that with Rahliem having a leadership in the church, a long engagement between he and Faith would not be beneficial for him or the congregation.

"I'm ready." Rahliem assured in, a barely audible baritone. "I can't wait for Faith to be my wife."

"In a few minutes, she will be." Pastor Phelps smiled as she led the young men into the sanctuary. After a few minutes, the flower girl and the ring bearer had made it down the aisle, followed by groomsmen, Davon and members of the Street Disciples ministry. Some of Faith's friends from A&T and Gilbert State University were her bridesmaids. They were led by Shadrach and Deborah dancing down the aisle, doing the cupid shuffle to Kirk Franklin's "Looking for You." Elicia was chosen as the Maid of Honor.

As Rahliem stood at the altar waiting on Faith to walk down the aisle, J. Moss' hit song "I Want to Give You More" came on, the members of the church's the dance ministry did a silent-interpretation of the song. Rahliem had selected the song because it reflected not only how he felt about Faith, but how he felt about God.

When Faith and her father were about to enter the sanctuary, the music switched to "Pretty Wings" by Maxwell. Just as Maxwell made his first appearance in seven years, Faith realized this would be her first appearance as Mrs. Rahliem Daniel Victor.

Rahliem's face beamed with pride knowing that the woman walking down the aisle was hand-picked by God to be with him. His missing rib was returning to him to be made whole in the body of God. He knew that in the next few minutes, he was about to begin the rest of his life with the woman who would join him as part of his ministry.

Pastor Phelps began the ceremony and no one objected to their union. Pastor continued to talk about the union of a man and his wife was comparable to Jesus' union with his church. For Rahliem, everything moved fast, the rings exchanged hands and they were saying "I do" while reciting vows that would spiritually bind them as husband and wife.

Rahliem looked into Faith's eyes and he noticed a tear drop in her eyes. Then he saw her smile and relieved of the tears of joy as he knew she was just as happy as he was. It wasn't too long when he was able to kiss his bride.

"By the power vested in me by God and the State of North Carolina, it gives me great honor and esteemed pleasure to introduce to you Mr. & Mrs. Rahliem Daniel Victor."

The kiss that sparked between them made one of the lit candles flicker brightly. Then, as in a traditional African ceremony, they held hands and jumped over the broom that was before them—heading face first into the life and ministry God had in store for them.

Before your leave, check out one of Isaiah David Paul's tales.

Chapter One

Early Sunday Morning, November 7, 2010
Grace United Methodist Church—Before Service
Winston-Salem, North Carolina

"Heavenly Father—please don't send me to hell for sleeping with my ex-wife…again." Calvin repented as he backed his car into his favorite spot on the other end of the church property. Only two parking spaces separated him from the brand new trash can and recycling bins the church got after the parking lot had just been paved the week before. The traditional markings were the same.

Calvin cut off the ignition and looked down at his platinum wedding band. The divorce was final a year ago and he still wore it as if he said "I do" yesterday. He twisted the ring on his finger with his thumb. *It's because you haven't let her go,* the voice inside him spoke. Calvin could decipher the Spirit's conviction almost instantly. And it was right, Calvin found it hard to let Maria go, even after she cheated on him and he caught her in a series of lies about her infidelity that led to their divorce.

"Naw, I haven't let her go," Calvin confessed. Calvin agreed to meet with Maria two days ago. He took her up on an offer to get out of town and go sightseeing. In their short trip down I-40, Calvin and Maria experienced a level of intimacy they'd never shared during the five years they were married. In Durham, they'd spent time shopping, eating, and sightseeing. A few more miles down the road in Raleigh caught them spending some quality time with one another. Raleigh proved to be a good escape from their life in Winston.

Upon returning from their short trip, Calvin and Maria pretended they were back in their younger days. They hastily made a return to the marriage bed that legally, and in God's eyes, no longer existed.

"God, sometimes when Maria and I get together, I get confused because we stood before You and said we would stay together, and remain faithful to one another until death do us part. But the State of North Carolina parted us because *she* didn't want to be married no more; *she* wanted to be with another man."

Calvin's mind turned to thoughts of Maria's smooth bronze-colored skin that felt like cool Jell-O butterscotch pudding. An irony at times, her touch was as cold as an icebox. "Now I'm the other man; I'm playing the role of the man I despised."

Calvin was about to step out of the car. He grabbed his Bible and his small backpack that contained copies of the current issues of *The Upper Room* that his ministry group, the Street Disciples distributed and sold. He opened the tattered and worn Bible to pull out a note on some verses he needed clarification on and his eyes were glued to the verse, *blessed is the man who endures temptation; for when he has been approved, he will receive the crown of life which the Lord has promised to those who love Him.*

The twelfth verse in the first chapter of James was right and Calvin sat up, feeling like a fool. "God, I trust and pray one day I will have the strength not to go on like this," he prayed as he made his way out of the car. He reached in his pocket and locked the door using the keyless remote and headed toward the door of the lobby.

God, You said in Your word that if I repented with my whole heart that my sins would be forgiven. I trust You to do that and to give me the strength to resist the temptation the next time it arises. Calvin thought of these words as he stepped through the doors. Immediately he'd heard compliments on his dark gray Sean Jean suit, which was highlighted with a bright, neon blue button up that he managed to acquire on the trip to Raleigh. The matching black Stacy Adams dress shoes was a comfortable choice, and he was glad he'd chosen them. He shook hands and hugged the other parishioners, as he made his way to a small room two doors down from the sanctuary. There, he removed his suit jacket, revealing dark gray suspenders and a blue and gray diamond tie that completed the look he was going for. Calvin was surprised to see the television on, but decided he'd catch a few minutes of a Dr. Bobby Jones interview with an up and coming gospel act before Sunday school was to start. His spirit was at ease.

"All right gentlemen, we're going to talk about repentance." Calvin heard his older brother, Carlton command the attention of the others whom were in the room. He stared at his lighter-reflection and smiled at the fact that they nearly had the same taste in suits…save for Carlton's was black and he wore green where Calvin had blue.

Calvin knew that once Carlton got started, God was going to reveal a message specifically for him. He pulled out a highlighter from his pants pocket, traced the verse. He was anxious to receive the Word.

Chapter Two

Sunday Afternoon, November 7, 2010
Central YMCA – Street Disciples Ministry Outreach
Winston-Salem, North Carolina

"To God be the glory," Carlton said as he and other members of the Street Disciples Ministry Group were finishing their reps on the various workout machines in the weight room at the Y.

Calvin looked at his older brother in his black South Pole hoodie and matching cargo sweat pants, a sharp contrast from his attire that could've easily made him a model in the JCPenny's catalog. As other members of the group were sporting workout attire, it was painfully obvious that the dress code was casual, and that Calvin had forgotten they would be going to the gym to minister the city's lost souls.

Calvin stood out in his heavy black work shoes, black and green swimming trunks and lime green and white Sean Jean polo. Unlike the Stacy Adams he had on before, the SAFETRAX slip resistance shoes would be uncomfortable for walking long periods of time.

"Bro, I tried to call you last night, where were you?" Carlton questioned as he took a seat next to Calvin at the bench press.

"Some place I shouldn't have been." Calvin knew that his lack of ability to put together something more presentable would start something with his brother sooner or later, and now was just as good a time as any.

Carlton stepped to Calvin, took a couple of sniffs and chuckled. "You and Maria get married again?"

"Shut up," Calvin mumbled back.

"I wish I could marry my ex-wife every time the temptation hit."

Calvin scowled and he was tempted to forget that he and the man sitting next to him had the same parents.

"Cartlon, be nice."

Calvin turned around to see Rahliem Victor, leader of the ministry walk toward him. Even with the towel over his shoulder, the netted tank top only concealed some of the tattoos that were on his arms from an earlier prison stint. The massive artwork spanned from the top of his neck, down the length of both arms, and covered his torso and back. His wedding band sparkled. Calvin looked down at his own left hand and found that he still had his ring on.

"Everyone falls short of the glory of God from time to time," Rahliem reminded everyone as he sat down to work on the exercise bike.

Calvin nodded his head as he saw Donte and his son, Eugene take a seat near the back. Calvin remembered when Eugene used to cling to his father and wished that he had a son that would do that. He could hear Eugene counting the reps his father was doing.

"The important thing is for us to repent and get back on track," Rahliem encouraged as he picked up his pace.

"It's difficult," Calvin spoke up. He wasn't about to let the lay leader of his church and his older brother gang up on him. "But I'm determined to see a better future...the one God designed for me. That is the only way I get through the next hour sometimes."

"I face the same problem," D had stated.

Daniel Abriel Jackson aka "D" was a young teenage father, having three children by the age of seventeen. D found God and joined Grace United Methodist Church after witnessing the work being done in his older brother, Chase. D became active with the

Street Disciples Ministry, working to spread the word of God to other teenagers at his school and the For Father's Only ministry which the group had become affiliated with.

"Let me guess," Carlton was on a roll, "you still sleeping with Nachelle?"

"I don't understand," D complained as he stopped cycling, "there's a reason why we didn't have any more children after we had my first child. We fight like cats and dogs," D complained.

"That's usually how it starts," Calvin mumbled.

"So you admit it?" Carlton badgered.

"Get you an ex-wife and see how well you do," Calvin challenged.

"Look," Rahliem was being the rational one again. He slowed his pace as he faced Calvin. "I can't sit here and condone what you and D are doing. As long as there is no ring on the finger and no commitment to God, or if that commitment is broken, then sleeping with your ex-wife, ex-girlfriend or whomever, is a sin."

Calvin looked down at the ring he was still wearing.

"That doesn't count Calvin, and there is no commitment behind that," Rahliem picked up the speed.

It was as if Rahliem had read his mind.

"Have you ever had pre-marital sex?" D directed toward Rahliem.

The room almost was quiet. Nosy Nancys and busy bodies wanted to hear if the great man of God would confess to this sin. For some, it would be the juiciest piece of gossip they'd get to spread all year. Rahliem had amassed status as the favorite guest speaker and respected religious leader. Could he have been as perfect as the Word he professed to following?

"Yes, I've had premarital sex. I did some things before I went to jail and fell short after my stint." Rahliem admitted—no shame or guilt in his voice. "But I'm not proud of it. I wish my first time was with my wife and I wish that prison turned out differently. But it happened, I repented and now I'm only seeking that level of comfort with my wife."

Calvin felt a sense of conviction he'd never felt before. It wasn't that he took joy in lusting and living a fantasy every time he and Maria connected. "I know why I sleep with Maria."

"Why?" Carlton interrogated and pressed for more information.

"Comfort," Calvin confessed. Didn't take much to break him. "Maria and I were married for five years and been dating since I was sixteen. I know her body as well as I know my own. I trust her in the bedroom and I'm comfortable with her. After all, in the eyes of God, we are still married."

"No you're not," Rahliem wanted to snap. Calvin could see Rahliem trying to contain his temper. "You are not married. Once the judge declared you divorced and you rightfully filed for divorce because she committed adultery…in God's eyes you are no longer married. But the fact that you are sleeping with her even though she's with the man that she committed adultery with, is what makes you wrong. In God's eyes, you're sleeping with her, and Bilal's sleeping with her, makes you both sinners. You are just as much of an adulterer as he is…and as I was."

"I sleep with Nachelle for comfort too," D admitted. "We argue so much about everything. The kids, my other baby mamas, child support, my hours at my job. Make up sex seems to be the only way we know how to make up. And we'd be cool for a while until she starts tripping."

"Naw, you sleep with her because the other two baby's mamas cut you off," Carlton answered honestly. D had his head down, which also confirmed that what was said was the truth.

"Carlton, that was not nice and you can't go tit for tat with these dudes like we used to do when we were in the pen," Rahliem admonished him. "We are here not only for a physical work out but a spiritual one too. I bared my soul not to brag about my sins, but to show you and others who were listening how transparent our ministry is. We are not a holier than thou association, we are a group of men, God's men, who have fallen short, and have come back to work and encourage others to do the same."

"That's why I'm here," D testified. "I've fallen and gotten back up many times with no judgment from anyone. I can still come to Rahliem or Donte or Celtius or even you two knuckleheads and read the word. And, I've been broken but I'm healed here too," D testified.

"Hey brothers," they were interrupted by a slender young man with a baby face.

"Robert, what's going on?" Rahliem got up and gave him a hug.

"I'm hanging in there. Sorry I'm late," the soft-spoken man responded. Robert looked at all of the men in the room and smiled.

"No, you're okay. We're working out our bodies and our problems."

"Good, I'm done backsliding and I'm looking to be with like-minded individuals who are willing to help me stick with my goals."

Robert stopped talking. Everyone noticed the black and Asian mixed man he was looking at as he was walking with another, taller, light skinned guy.

"Aurice," Rahliem addressed the light skinned guy.

"Trouble," Aurice cracked back as he looked down at the shorter man. Rahliem shook his head.

"Aye, this is my roommate Cedric. Cedric, this is the infamous Rahliem Victor. He's the leader of the Street Disciple Ministry I was telling you about."

Rahliem introduced Calvin, Carlton, D, Donte and Eugene. The men shook hands and began working out in close proximity.

"I didn't know you knew Aurice," Robert was noticeably uncomfortable when he and Cedric shared glances.

"Aurice and I went to school together. He was trying to get me on the straight and narrow in back then, but I had too many anger management issues. Right now, he's working with teens with behavior issues and he's active in his church. I know Pastor Goodwill, he's a good man."

"Well, I'm going to catch you later," Robert gathered his stuff quickly and walked away. Carlton scrunched his lips and was as confused as Calvin was.

"Rah, what was that all about?" Carlton looked between Robert and Cedric and still couldn't figure it out.

"Everyone has things they must leave behind and I trust Robert is doing what he must," Rahliem advised.

Calvin shook his head, "I need to have the same kind of will power that Robert has."

"You will be tested again and every test will build up the power you need to resist the temptation that will come in many forms. The question is, are you willing to receive that power?"

Calvin shook his head yes. It wasn't like he and Maria had sex often but when they did, he couldn't get enough. He wanted to reconcile but knew that wasn't the best option.

Until Calvin could figure something out, he was going to have to find a way to resist Maria's temptation.

About the Author

Over the years, Isaiah David Paul has written in a variety of genres and became a writing partner and ghostwriter for a few award-winning and best-selling authors. With his string of successes and renewed faith in God, Isaiah David Paul has finally decided to follow his calling to write under his own name. He has a business management degree from North Carolina Agricultural & Technical State University, a Masters of Entrepreneurship from Western Carolina University and a MAT-Elementary Education from the University of North Carolina at Greensboro. He is the author of over fifty titles under various pseudonyms and has contributed to the publication of nearly two hundred books. He lives a private life with his family in the Southeast United States.

Follow Isaiah David Paul on Social Media:

Official Website	IsaiahDavidPaul.com
Instagram	@IsaiahDavidPaul
TikTok	@IsaiahDavidPaul
Blue Sky	@IsaiahDavidPaul
Facebook	@IsaiahDavidPaul
Linktree	@IsaiahDavidPaul
X/Twitter	@IsaiahDavidPaul